John McDowell Leavitt

The American Cardinal

John McDowell Leavitt

The American Cardinal

ISBN/EAN: 9783337065447

Printed in Europe, USA, Canada, Australia, Japan

Cover: Foto ©Andreas Hilbeck / pixelio.de

More available books at **www.hansebooks.com**

THE

AMERICAN CARDINAL.

A NOVEL.

———

NEW YORK.

DODD & MEAD, No. 762 BROADWAY.

1871

CONTENTS.

CHAPTER VII.

PAGE

CHAPTER VIII.

CHAPTER IX.

CHAPTER X.

CHAPTER XI.

CHAPTER XII.

CHAPTER XIII.

CHAPTER XIV.

CHAPTER XV.

CHAPTER XVI.

CHAPTER XVII.

CHAPTER XVIII.

CHAPTER XIX.

CHAPTER XX.

CHAPTER XXI.

CHAPTER XXII.

CHAPTER XXIII.

CHAPTER XXIV.

CHAPTER XXV.

CHAPTER XXXIV.

CHAPTER XXXV.

CHAPTER XXXVI.

CHAPTER XXXVII.

CHAPTER XXXVIII.

CHAPTER XXXIX.

CHAPTER XL.

AMERICAN CARDINAL.

CHAPTER I.

A SUNSET MEETING.

THE sun was just disappearing as two young men stood on the bank of a stream rippling beneath a hill, which was darkened by trees, and crowned with a village. Day's last glory was pouring itself in a flood of gold through a thin cloud, and mirroring its splendors in the tranquil waters. The white cottages behind the wood shone brightly, and each cheap window dazzled in a flame gorgeous as if it looked from a palace. Above, could be seen through the foliage, the stone turrets of a collegiate building, and towering from its centre a lofty spire, whose cross, as it caught the upward rays of the sinking sun, gleamed like fire. The youth had plainly the air and attire of students, and were engaged in the most earnest conversation. They appeared of nearly equal age—the full whisker of the one, and the dark moustache of the other, giving decided tokens that each had attained his manhood. At the moment our story commences, Edward Ellingwood was the speaker. He was of middle height, with broad shoulders, and muscular but finely shaped limbs. If his full blue eye when unexcited, impressed you simply with the benevolence lurking in its depths, any suspicion of weakness was corrected by the firm jaw, and the compressed lips, disclosing, when opened, teeth unusually regular and splendid. Just as you conclude that the chiseled nose is too beautiful for manliness, your eye fixes itself on a noble forehead, shaded with dark curls, but indicating thought, and command. Hand, foot, tone, manner, expression, denote descent from some distinguished, and cultivated family, living, as you soon decide, in a northern State. The tall, slender, graceful form of his companion —the dark eye, the full mouth, the musical voice, the peculiar intonation, the languor, habitual, but now excited into suppressed but fiery earnestness, just as clearly afford proof of high Southern blood. The two young gentlemen, although so different in both education, and temperament, were yet linked together in a true friendship resulting from mutual and instinctive esteem, and admiration. Through four years of Freshman verdancy, Sophomoric wildness, Junior aspiration, and Senior dignity, in frolic, study, and recitation, by day, and night, during term, and vacation, they had been inseparable. Now, just on the eve of a long farewell, a cloud seems rising, and a storm gathering, to darken, possibly destroy their strong attachment. Ellingwood stands with one foot resting on a mossy log. His hands, when we first notice him, are folded on his breast, but they are soon moving in eager gesticulation. His face is flushed partly with excitement, and partly with the reflection of the cloud whose gold is changed to gorgeous crimson, so that the sky seems stained with its brilliant colors. Austin has his back toward the west, and his countenance is therefore shaded from the splendors burning behind. He is also on lower ground, but drawn up to his full height appears on a level with his shorter friend. Every feature of his countenance is glowing like the fires of Southern skies.

"Charles Austin," said Ellingwood, gazing steadily into the face of his companion and uttering his words in a subdued, but excited tone, "Charles Austin, it cannot be possible your people are so given over to madness. Why, my dear fellow, the movements you describe, mean war, mean blood, mean ruin."

"Ned," was the reply, "you will never comprehend us. Your conservative, and judicial, and judicious father, educated you in the antiquated lore of Kent, and Story, and Webster, and taught you to believe this Union eternal, and the stars of our flag really like the enduring worlds they represent in the heavens. Ha! ha! ha! the decisions of our own Southern Marshal are now with us as musty and rusty as the black letter of Coke. We have learned different lessons from our orators and statesmen."

"But, my dear Charley, will you sweep away the work of the Revolution, appropriate the national property, and strike down the national banner, turn the sword against your countrymen, and make our Republic, now united, and feared, and respected over the world, a mere collection of petty and warring principalities?"

"Ah! Ellingwood, that is the old strain we have been accustomed to hear from Professor Drilip, when he gets on the subject of the articles of Confederation, and the constitutional conventions, concluding with his customary eulogy on our perpetual stars, and the everlasting Eagle."

"Austin," interposed Ellingwood excitedly, "you

amaze and confound me. How is it possible that during the four years of our intimacy I have never discovered such opinions?"

"Because, dear Edward," responded his friend with a mellow tenderness in his tone, "our affection was too deep, and true, for me to permit a ripple on its clear surface. But before we part candor compels this disclosure. If any men from North and South could harmonize in sentiment and action it would be you, and I. Yet after all you perceive a radical difference, great as that between the bloom of the orange, and the blossom of the apple, between the pine of Maine, and the magnolia of Georgia, between Connecticut rocks and snows, and Carolina swamps and suns. We expect to make cotton and slavery the foundations of an empire, noble as our blood, rich as our soil, and splendid as our climate." As the young man spoke these words his face flushed, and his form dilated with sincere, and eloquent enthusiasm.

"But," returned Ellingwood, "can you really mean to say that the South is organizing and drilling, and determined, if the coming election does not accord with her wishes, to withdraw from the government? Depend upon it, the hand in this country, from whatever section, which dares first draw the sword, will perish by the sword. Besides, you will destroy the only possible security for your favorite institution. Now, each Federal Judge, under the solemn responsibilities of his office, in the face of mobs, and supported by the whole army of the Republic, is ready to deliver your fugitives. Commit yourselves to this movement, and every chain will be rent, and every slave be free, but not until this land is deluged with blood, and filled with corpses."

"No, no," rejoined Austin, smiling, and with the

slightest possible sneer on his lip, and contempt in his tone, suppressed by his real love and respect for his friend. "No, no, Ned. You know we Southerners are trained to pistol and bowie-knife and rifle, and when you see us armed, and panting for battle, you will submit on the field, as you have always succumbed in the cabinet."

These words, jocularly uttered, struck fire from the eyes of Ellingwood. His cheek grew red as the berries flushing above his head. His whole form expanded into youthful majesty. His voice trembled with his deep agitation. As the two students stood face to face, with equal sincerity, equal talent, and equal spirit, they seemed completely to personify their respective opinions.

"Charles," said Ellingwood, "Is this a delusion? Can you not understand? Can you not know us even from myself? Although we love peace, we are capable of war. That conscious strength which endures long is most fearful when aroused. A loyalty slumbers in the North which will resemble the great river suddenly thundering into the resistless cataract. You may strike down our flag, but before it reaches the earth millions of arms will be outstretched to raise it towards Heaven. The blood of heroes is in our veins. The fires of the revolution may be concealed beneath the ashes of selfishness and faction, but they will burst forth, and fill the world with their blaze."

"Stop, stop," responded Austin, with the passionate eagerness of alarmed friendship, "I have touched your pride, Ned, by questioning your courage. But my dear fellow, I intended no insinuation against you personally. You showed your daring, when you rushed forward and caught my frightened horses and saved my life, at the risk

2*

of your own, while my own Georgian cousins stood bewildered and aghast. God bless you, Edward, you are true as steel, and brave as Washington. But," he added archly, "you little knew what a rebel you were rescuing, or perhaps you would have let Joe and Tom dash me over the rocks, and drown my treason beneath the peaceful waters of the Vernon."

The young gentlemen both smiled, and cordially shaking hands, by the grasp of friendship, allayed the rising storm, which nevertheless was gathering, and muttering over the entire country too soon to burst forth in its fatal fury.

"Charles," said Edward, affectionately, still holding, and pressing the hand of his friend, "have you reflected that in the event of a war, you and I, now standing in this still evening, above this placid stream, eye to eye, and heart to heart, may hereafter meet in opposing ranks on the murderous field, and one become spotted with the blood of the other?"

Ellingwood shook as he concluded the sentence. This thought had evidently never crossed the mind of the impulsive Southerner, and his lid moistened, and his lip quivered at the very apprehension of such a possibility.

"Moreover," continued Edward, "how can you separate by the carnage of battle, and the wrecks of states, those two devoted girls?"

Charles looked in the direction indicated by the face and finger of his friend. On the top of a hill rising above the opposite bank of the stream, and distinctly traced on the illuminated sky, were two female forms, even in the distance conspicuous for their symmetry and elegance. As the crimson of the cloud rested on them they seemed almost transfigured in a supernatural glory. Walking swiftly down the hill the ladies soon stood in the shadow of the trees. Mary Ellingwood showed a lip and cheek brilliant as the rose. She was small, but inexpressibly graceful. Her forehead was somewhat square, and her nose had a slightly upward tendency, yet her mouth was perfect, and her eye beamed with animation. Miss Austin was an image of her brother. Her complexion was indeed usually pale, but the graceful proportions of a tall figure, a classic nose, a large, lustrous, splendid eye full of gentle light and love, a low voice soft with Southern languor, and a countenance exhibiting mingled culture and kindness, adorned her with all that can be expected in a woman. As the girls, animated by their exercise, stood together above the stream—

"Ah, my angry knights," began Mary, "It is well the exciting scenes of this august Commencement have brought us from neighboring Massachusetts and remote Georgia, to separate you in your wrath, and stop the effusion of your blood. We saw your rapid gestures, and your threatening attitudes, and rushed like angels of peace to breathe love into your hearts. We appear, and lo you stand meek as when Freshmen you were caught pilfering a Professor's orchard, and afterwards—more dreadful crime—murdering in your President's hen-roost."

"Or rather you resemble," added Anna, "two dignified Seniors, crowned with prophetic laurels, who having exhausted their rage and their arguments become quiet sheep because they have nothing left to preserve them rampant lions."

"Nay, nay," cried Ellingwood, laughing, "we pause as did the earthly choir of St. Cecilia gazing into the cloud of heaven, that they might hear strains from the sweeter angels."

"Or," interrupted Austin, "as garrulous young ladies subside before the more experienced tongues of gossiping spinsters, charged with the secrets of families and welfare of neighborhoods, and who while plying the needle to clothe orphans, are plying the tongue to uncover the faults of their friends. But, Ellingwood, before these girls retort with their woman's wit, jump into this boat, while I loose the chain, and we will ferry the angels over these waters of peace and let them drop concord from their wings."

The young men with a few vigorous strokes of the oars pulled the skiff to the other bank, where their sisters entered, and were soon brought over, while the boat left behind it circles of gold made by the beams of a summer moon just lifting her full orb into view. The gay voices of the retiring party were soon lost as they disappeared amid the trees, whose shadows interspersed with waving light lay along the hill. Still contrasting with the merry sounds was the solemn cry of a hooting owl. And although in one direction the heavens were bright and serene, in another were rising portentous masses of clouds, crossed with lightnings, growling with thunders, black with tempests.

CHAPTER II.

THE storm passed away with the night, and the morning of the commencement dawned in cloudless brilliance. An American mocking-bird, whose cage hung in the piazza of President Cleveland's house, catching inspiration from the sun, poured from his throat a flood of melody to salute day's welcome king, and rival the flood of beams streaming from the face of his ascending majesty. The notes so varied, so exquisite and so powerful, made the ear insensible to all more modest songs, and drowned the orchestral chorus bursting from every bush and field and forest over the wide landscape. Thus nature herself gave omens of happiness on this occasion of annual joy. Mary and Anna stood together on a porch, covered with a bloom of roses made fragrant in the morning dew. They were speculating in regard to the exciting topic which had evidently agitated their brothers on the preceding evening, and about which had been thrown a studious mystery.

"What," said the former, "could have caused the violent gestures we perceived in the distance, and the tumult of emotions they so plainly sought to suppress? Surely Damon and Pythias are not going to quarrel. Should this happen, Anna, we will soon suspect our own constancy."

"Oh, never, Mary, never!" was the quick response, while the eye and face of Miss Austin were at once softened and brightened with affection. "I greatly fear," she added, "that the discussion was in reference to the state of the country," and then, while her countenance indicated the utmost alarm, she concluded by saying, "There is sometimes on my heart an oppressive weight. A sadness steals over me I cannot explain, since I noticed, before leaving home, my cousin, Major Worstal, often in consultation with men who seemed military. Frequently loads of arms passed through our village, and our servants were continually reporting marchings in the grove and drillings in the swamp."

"Oh, Anna, Anna," responded Mary, "surely, surely the South will not rush into war. Dark visions sometimes cross my own mind. How fearful too would be the barrier dividing our own lives! But, nonsense! we will soon make ourselves old women with our gloom. Let us be happy to-day as the President's bird."

With these words the girls ran gaily down the walk, and warbled together the stanza of a merry song. While thus pleasantly engaged, musical with youth and health and hope, their attention was arrested by observing through the trees a man acting as if wholly beside himself. He danced; he leaped; he tossed his cap in the air, and caught it when it fell in a species of absurd ecstasy; he flung himself on the grass, and rolled over and over, evidently seeking relief from some long-suppressed emotion, while his face worked fantastically and his form shook almost convulsively.

"Is it possible," said Mary, gazing and smiling at these antics, "that the man is Silent Dick, of whom the boys speak so often? Whatever prank is played by the students, his invariable answer to the faculty is, 'don't know.' He sees nothing, hears nothing, says nothing, and yet is supposed to be a species of ubiquity whenever mischief is in progress."

"He is doubtless now," replied Anna, "refreshing him-self for the ignorance and silence of many years. He greatly resembles my Uncle Brompton's horse turned suddenly into pasture."

The girls laughed heartily as they still continued to observe Dick's ludicrous actions. The truth is, the simple janitor, from an instinct of self-preservation, practiced the most profound taciturnity both as regards faculty and students. By his wise policy he retained his place from year to year, fixed as the college-pump or the college-steeple—ay, more fixed; for the first of these had not long before taken a strange freak of exploding itself to shivers; and the second, on the same calm night, had suddenly lost its gravity, and most indecorously tumbled down the roof, and, after sundry absurd motions, leaped jocosely over the eaves, and assumed a plebeian posture on the ground, sin-gularly contrasting with its former aristocratic stateliness. Thus all the silent dignitaries of the place were at once whirled away from their customary propriety. Dick had for years, at a safe distance, seen class-rooms emptied, and bed-rooms packed, and hen-rooms plundered, and dogs, and geese, and calves, and once even a monkey, noisily discoursing or solemnly presiding in professors' chairs. During twenty seasons he had been a silent witness to all the mad pranks of American boys. Now, affected by the contagious antics of pump and steeple, he is exhibiting his superior Irish mirthfulness. Yet his frolic was occasioned by a most sober fact. The morning-bell had awaked from drowsy slumbers lazy students and growling professors. Entering the chapel, they saw, in the dim light, over the very desk of the president, a suspended form, grim, hideous, spectral, flinging around its skeleton arms, rattling its loose limbs, and pointing its bony fingers in a manner the

most startling and grotesque. Such a sombre vision of
death had produced laughter in a living man usually
grave as those eyeless sockets and that round white skull.

While the girls were enjoying their fun in observing
Dick the surrounding country began to be in motion.
Along the roads of the hills were discerned vehicles, like
black specks, descending into the valley, filled with men,
women and children, and, as they arrived, emptying themselves beneath the sunny branches of spreading trees
casting their morning shadows over the college lawn.
Occasionally a carriage, with a Hibernian or an African
coachman, brought the family of a wealthy merchant, or
physician, or lawyer, from a neighboring county-seat. In
a few instances city horses drew city people in city splendor to the door of the chapel, and then the conscious
animals, after pawing in their pride, whirled away with an
aristocratic dash. By way of contrast might have been
seen meek clergymen, with their meek families, descending
from meek weather-worn conveyances. The village was a
type of the country. It contained representatives from
every part of our republic. Fathers, mothers, brothers,
sisters, uncles, aunts, cousins, friends, had made weary
journeys from far States to hear some mere boy deliver
his rude speech, and see him receive an undeserved sheep-
skin. Men of the highest culture and distinction in
America were drawn to this retired place by an invisible
attraction. North, South, East and West assembled in a
manner belonging to that period of our national history
when Calhoun, and Clay, and Haines and Webster debated
with matchless power and eloquence in our Capitol. How
striking the interest thus excited by youth, as they stand
for a moment, gilded with hope, on that brilliant summit
separating the land of dreams from the land of realities!

Age loves the contemplation, because it excites so many bright images of its own former joys and aspirations.

But while we are philosophizing, notes of music swell upon the air. President, and professors, and seniors, robed in their black gowns, are beginning to march, followed by sober trustees, solemn dignitaries, and indiscriminate individuals. Behind comes the laboring band blowing with puffing cheeks as if the important occasion was one of wind rather than of ideas. The pompous procession moves along the gravelled walk, and entering the chapel is succeeded by a pushing crowd distributing themselves according to assignment, or caprice, or necessity. Then there is prayer, and then there is music. Speeches are announced, and delivered in the usual student style. Only a single incident has occurred to separate the occasion from what seems to those not specially and personally interested but a dismal return of annual platitudes. An ambitious orator had described the American eagle soaring above the clouds with his eye of fire undazzled by the sun. Just as the sublime creature had reached its noblest altitude, and the audience with eager gaze, and in breathless stillness, were following the upward gesture of the impassioned youth, at the climax of the figure, a mischievous ventriloquizing Freshman, who had watched the flight, and cruelly waited its culmination, uttered a shrill crow like the clarion of a victorious rooster. The sound seeming to issue from the very beak of the imperial bird, filled the building, and convulsed the spectators, whose peals of laughter sounded strangely in contrast with the previous hush of the assembly. The only composed face visible belonged to the urchin who wrought the murderous mischief. The victimized speaker slunk away like a crest-fallen cock. When he has retired a sullen stillness

3

is observable. Soon the flutter of a fan becomes painful.
A tall youth having crossed the platform, makes a graceful bow, and even by his presence fascinates with a quiet,
mysterious magnetism. Eye, mouth, forehead, form, attitude denote the native orator. His first silvery utterance
charmed the ear, and fixed the attention. As Charles
Austin stood before his audience, expressing in clear,
beautiful, impassioned words, and with the pathos of an
inimitable voice, assisted by a gesticulation of easy grace,
the fancied wrongs, and imagined rights of the South, he
glowed, and burned with the convictions of a persuasive
eloquence. The hush of interest was soon intense. At the
close, when he advocated secession in principle, and in
policy, there was a climax of excitement. Southern students burst forth into screams of applause. Southern gentlemen looked pleased. Southern matrons smiled sunnily.
Southern girls waved their fans, and nodded their heads
in delight. Even Southern negroes grinned with a species
of sectional sympathetic pride, and satisfaction. Bouquets
were flung upon the stage, and the young orator retired
amid storms of applause. The Faculty, and Trustees,
and the Northern portion of the audience sat under a
cloud of surprise, and sullen mortification.

Edward Ellingwood followed Charles Austin, having,
as valedictorian, the closing speech. He was not, like his
friend, an orator. His voice had no special music, and
his manner had no special grace. His person was rather
pleasing than commanding. Still, the noble forehead, the
firm mouth, the manly tone, the clear eye, the lofty purpose of a generous soul illuminating the intellectual face,
and giving dignity to the erect form, won confidence, and
compelled attention. When Ellingwood parted from
Austin on the preceding evening he read in the conversa-

tion of his friend the tenor of his speech, and he had
spent many hours of the night in shaping an answer. He
now described the struggles of the Revolution, the glory
of the Constitution, the vastness of the Republic, its influence for freedom, its weakness divided, its power united,
and sketched, almost with the glow of prophetic inspiration, its future, when, collecting 'and fusing the nationalities of the world, it should be a centre of universal
light, and liberty, and perhaps exhibit humanity in its last
and noblest development. Yet there was no pompous,
sophomoric, American exaggeration. Ellingwood never
passed the limit of a clear, forcible, manly argumentation.
His audience, however, caught fire from the sparks of his
calmly-earnest soul. Soon the Northern enthusiasm surpassed every limit. Even a venerable Bishop was seen
clapping his hands. Sober Trustees were surprised into
sudden smiles, and approving nods. One member of the
Faculty so far forgot his dignity as to stamp on the platform. An old Clergyman extending his arm in a rapture
knocked over a stand from the stage, and a descending
flood from a falling pitcher consequently quenched the
zeal of a stout farmer sitting below, who, not pleased with
a public shower-bath, brushed away the unwelcome drops
with his red bandanna, and muttered curses against cold-
water parsons. The Northern students broke forth into
loud, long, vociferous hurrahs. Ebony faces showed rows
of shining ivory. As Edward passed away over the platform he was showered with roses. One delighted Senator
stooped down, and snatching a garland of evergreen from
the stage crowned the Orator. This circumstance intensified the excitement, and the assembly seemed swayed by
a tempest. The jubilant strains of "Hail Columbia,"
pealing from horn, and trumpet and bassoon crowned the

triumph of the occasion. Yet the glowing victories of the two young speakers rent the Institution in sunder forever. Northern and Southern students parted with kindness, and yet with a conscious alienation, and a boding apprehension. The scene at the termination of this commencement was a picture in miniature of a war which was to divide the Republic, where bullets would be substituted for words, and where instead of peaceful plaudits would be heard contending armies.

CHAPTER III.

THE PARTING.

"Ha, Mr. Ellingwood," said Anna Austin, as she and the gentleman addressed stood on the President's lawn, under a large elm, "unfortunate is it for you that we have been detained here by the accident on the train. The village is in arms against you and Charles for destroying, by your speeches, an institution which the people love as they do their own flesh. The glow of the Commencement has vanished, and its victors are to-day victims. Such is the fickle populace. They, or the Faculty, led by indignant Dick and other disinterested officials, supported by a crowd whose patriotism dreads starvation, will pluck your garlands from your brow."

"Yes," said Edward, laughing, "our eloquence was certainly wind to have made such a storm. Curious, isn't it, Anna? What does Charley say?"

"I am afraid to tell you."

"Don't be alarmed, and I shan't be offended."

"Brother avers that Yankee patriotism is in the pocket, and not in the heart; and that in your farmers especially it is a fierce flame until it reaches their poultry and their crops."

"Yet," replied Edward, "in the Revolution it singed King George's lion."

"And in the event of the war," rejoined Anna, "you and Charles have brought on the country by your Commencement oratory, the royal beast may growl again at the recollection of the fire, and strike down your flag with his paw. It is dangerous to use rashly on such august occasions your extensive influence."

Ellingwood was somewhat staggered at this unexpected thrust. The truth is he had intended this interview to take an entirely different direction. He loved Anna, and he knew that Anna loved him, and before parting he hoped they would be bound together during life. In his embarrassment he blushed and pulled a cigar from his pocket.

He was ten years before his era. In the present age he would have opened his match-box and lighted his Havana, and declared himself under a wreath of tobacco smoke. Bold that man who ventured his first puff in the presence of a lady! Memorable that youth who, with the delicious weed glowing in his lips, forgot the shining stars, and on the thronged avenue, arm in arm with his *fiancé*, whispered in her ear his perfumed vows! Immortal that hero who, beneath a circling cloud, while whirling through the crowded park, jauntily knocked off his ashes with his finger and improved the interval by avowing, amid the roll of wheels, a passion hot as the coal he so gracefully exposed!

At the period we describe, Young America was several years from a millenium produced by the war, when a gentleman could smoke in a drawing-room, smoke during a drive, smoke on a sidewalk, smoke in making love, and smoke in breaking love, and feel that the fragrance of tobacco in his clothing was more delicious and acceptable than the odor of the rose.

Ellingwood in his confusion really bit off the end of his cigar, and returned it to his vest pocket with an embarrassed apology. The conversation would probably then have taken a more serious turn, but just at this important moment Mary Ellingwood, followed by Charles Austin, came running gaily along the walk.

"Oh! Edward! Edward!" she cried merrily, "you have ruined yourself, your institution, your country. The Faculty, so delighted on yesterday, would to-day rob you of your sheep-skin. The Senator who crowned you with the garland would now take off your head. Every old lady of the village regards you as she would a wolf in a famine."

"Yes," said Charles, coming up, "Ned, we have made a pretty muss. Did you see the farmer whose enthusiasm was extinguished by the pitcher Mr. Brinton knocked over on his head? He swears 'them sassy fellers will spile the nashun, and fetch down butter two cents a pound. Geese, ducks, chickens, cows, calves, mules, and hosses,' he thinks, 'won't be worth the raisin'.'"

"Possibly," responded Ellingwood, slyly, and with the slightest possible approach to a sneer that his friendship would allow, "should our eloquence really provoke a war, the same might be said of another class of more valuable animals in a more remote section of the country."

This remark would have provoked serious feeling; but Mary showed alarm and adroitly changed the conversation. Where there is a real affection storms are easily avoided.

While the young people were indulging their fun and banter on the very eve of a separation which was to terminate in tears, Judge Ellingwood and General Brompton were engaged in more serious discussion on the piazza of the President. The moon had now risen in her fullness. A mellow light over nature seemed to bathe her in its peace. The leaves on elm and maple shimmered in its gold, and rose and honeysuckle waved and blushed in the brilliance as it streamed from the room through the lattice. The scenes of the Commencement on the previous day had somewhat embarrassed the relations of the gentlemen; but radically different as were their opinions, they had too much sense to permit any estrangement.

"Really, General," said Judge Ellingwood, "I have never heard anything approach the eloquence of your nephew. You Southerners have a genius for oratory which he has inherited in its perfection. His style is figurative without being ornate, and always pervaded by a glow which gives interest to his argument. Then he possesses that magnetism of voice and manner no art can attain. I confess I admired his eloquence more than his principles. I could scarcely myself resist the spell of his inspiration. He does credit to your training."

"And yet," responded General Brompton, "your son has the more available talent. Our age is too sharp for oratory. Tropes must yield to facts. Statistics are destroying the rhetoricians. Edward will be better suited to his era, and I predict for him the highest eminence at the Bar and in the Senate."   .

"Let us thank Heaven for the promise of our boys, instead of contrasting their gifts. But do you deem it possible that the South will be carried away by the species of enthusiasm which Charles excited yesterday?"

"My abstract opinions, you know, have always been on the side of secession. No man living has ever so commanded my admiration as John C. Calhoun. I was a pupil in his law office and was educated under the fascinations of his presence. Still I have dreaded the immediate consequences of my own opinions. While I am transported with the prospect of a Southern Empire, I stand trembling over this chasm of separation, and have done all in my power to hold back our people."

Judge Ellingwood paused suddenly as these words were uttered. He seized both the hands of his old friend and looked him steadily in the face. They stood illuminated with the radiance which was pouring through the window over their persons. The voice of the Judge trembled and his whole person was visibly agitated.

"General," he cried, "we know each other too well, and our attachment is too long, to be shaken by antagonisms of opinion. We are both too old to have any selfish interest in a sectional contest. Let me beseech you when you return home, use your great personal influence to resist this popular frenzy. A civil war in this republic will shed blood enough to float its navy. It will shake the hopes of the world. In the end it may obliterate slavery and change the whole social aspect of the South."

"Judge Ellingwood," quickly responded the General, and with equal emotion, "we will not now disturb our friendship and embitter our farewell by political discussions. The conflict is inevitable. Five years will loose the earthquake. Human power is vain to arrest what Heaven has decreed. My fears, against my judgment, have sought to avert the coming strife. The task I have found impossible. Whatever the result, let no opposition of sentiment destroy that esteem and affection which have brightened so many years of our lives."

The noble old men, moving away from the light, grasped each other by the hand, and then, with the strongest protestations of friendship, warmly embraced before separating.

Just as they parted younger and gayer voices were heard approaching, and soon there were partings equally tender and affectionate.   As they withdrew to their several places of repose, the moon, which had been pouring over them a mild glory, was seen struggling in a gigantic cloud, whose ominous shadow, flinging itself over their receding forms, was followed by a burst of brilliance as the queen of night, disengaged from the blackness, rode in silent triumph over heaven.

CHAPTER IV.

THE LIFE TEST.

"My dear," said Mrs. Cleveland to her husband as they sat together in his study, "there is a shadow on your brow." Then taking his hand and tenderly kissing his forehead, she continued, "Do tell me what troubles you."

"Everything, Emily, everything. God and man are against me."

"But, my love," she answered in a tone of reproving affection, "have you no trust in Heaven? Surely we can commit our trials to Him who has promised support, and guidance."

"Heaven," burst forth Cleveland, bitterly. "Heaven," he repeated almost frantically; "has not Heaven permitted these Trustees to crush me, my Faculty to desert me, my friends to betray me? One year since they brought me here in triumph. Now, not a dog in the village but would bark me away, and bite me as I ran. Nothing so detestable as this miserable Protestant treachery. Our schools breed only small serpents. Every parish is a nest of petty vipers. Our colleges are full of imps and devils."

Mrs. Cleveland arose alarmed before this unusual tempest of passion.

"My dear," she whispered softly, "Do curb your indignation. Be careful how you talk! Even at this late hour of the night some treacherous ear may treasure these words to your injury."

"Leave me, Emily," he pettishly replied, "I wish to be alone."

As Mrs. Cleveland withdrew from the study, and passed into the hall, and up the stairs, the low light of the lamp may enable us to observe her face, and person. Everything about her appeared to have been arrested just as it was passing its natural limit. Her nose was beautifully round, and regular, yet with a tendency towards prominence. Her eye, visible an instant in the light, was just on the verge of being too large, too black, and too full. Her forehead was exquisitely formed, and looked like white marble delicately veined, but was rather high. Her red lip was chiselled just beyond perfection into an excessive firmness. Her form, admirable in size, and grace, and proportion, would have been a sculptor's model, had it not been evidently destined to a premature embonpoint. She was a woman of superior charms, and gifted mind, Scotch-Irish in her blood, highly educated in a rigid Presbyterian school, noble in her nature, and who, according to circumstances, would have been equally fitted for drawing-room, or lecture-room. Having afforded us time for our hasty observations, while ascending the stairs, she walked rapidly along an upper hall, and entered a front chamber.

"Is there any change?" she eagerly inquired of a negro-nurse who held in her arms an emaciated child about three years old.

"Not none, Missus," was the reply. "She be berry powerfu' weak."

"Heaven," cried Mrs. Cleveland, kneeling beside her little girl, "spare us this blow. It will drive Arthur mad."

"No, Missus, what massa Cleveland preach, dat he believe. If he tell de folks in de pulpit de Laud help 'dem in 'dar troubles; when dey come on him, he'se trus' de Laud."

"Oh, Eliza," exclaimed the afflicted mistress, "you can little understand the sufferings of such a spirit. I sometimes think believing ignorance is better than educated doubt."

"We'se niggas poor," said Eliza, "but we lub de Savya, and de Bibul, and de closet, and grace make us rich, Missus. Five chil'ren went from dese ole arms. Dey be anguls, bright anguls, anguls like de Laud. Bress Hebben, Missus," said the faithful, happy creature, looking upward with the glow of a seraph on her black face, "'stead of dis sufferin' chile dar soon be anudder 'joicin' angul."

"Oh," ejaculated Mrs. Cleveland, "that my dear husband had your simple faith! Far better would it be in this hour than all his wealth, fame, and learning."

Yes, there sat Arthur Cleveland in his study, with his hands pressed on his brow, and bending over his table in an agony of rebellious doubt. He had been born to riches, and high position. All his impulses from childhood had been scholarly, and he had possessed every advantage which education, and travel, and association could bestow. His talents, and social influence had elevated him prematurely to the brilliant Presidency of a New England College; a fatal and unforeseen defect had soon developed his unfitness for the place, and with all his shining gifts, it was evident another year of unpleasant struggle would terminate his present relation. While his intellect had been disciplined he suffered from the very excess of his advantages, since his will had never been trained in those hard contests which give poverty often a superiority over wealth. His appearance was an exact

4

index of his character. He was tall, graceful, almost femininely slender, with feet, and hands and limbs most delicately shaped and rounded. His nostril was that of an Apollo. His black hair fell over his neck in shining curls, and his brow seemed the throne of intellect. But his small mouth and jaw indicated weakness, and his gray eye, although lustrous, often wandered with an uncertain gaze. Fortune in him dwarfed the development of a superior nature by the very lavish expenditure of her gifts. He was like a tree, which would have been sturdy and stately amid the storm of its mountains, but transplanted to the culture of the plain, disappoints expectation by its slender trunk and sickly bloom.

."I can't bear it!" murmured Cleveland, striking his hand against his forehead. Then rising, and standing in the centre of the room he said desperately, "And I *won't* bear it!"

His heart had reached a bitterness of rebellion. Everything in the study seemed a contradiction to such passion. The books were in the most tasteful covers and the most regular rows. The lamp hung supported by bronze cherubs and shed down the softest light. The form and arrangements of the table, ink-stand, paper-folder, knife, pen, chair, all—from the pattern of the carpet to the fresco of the ceiling, busts, engravings, medallions—displayed a taste too delicate and sensitive to be masculine. There was scarcely a country in the world not represented there by some minute and precious relic carved into a useful form. The rich and exquisite gown of Cleveland alone indicated his character. Known to wear such a garment, he could never govern an American College. In fact, the man unconsciously had become Europeanized. "It is too much," he exclaimed, "for any one mortal to endure. They solicited me to accept this detestable Presidency. **They** brought me **here in** triumph. **They** flattered me like parasites. Now, all—Trustees, Faculty, villagers—are on me like wolves. The students would support me, **but their** young enthusiasm **is quenched by** perpetual **lies.** First idolized, **and** then **tolerated, and** then execrated! **Cursed be** Protestantism **for its treacherous** fickleness! Rome rises like a calm, venerable **temple of refuge** through the storms of earth. Thank Heaven **I sent for Frances!** Why is he not here? And then "— he wrung **his hands** in agony while he uttered his daughter's name—"my Ella! oh, my Ella!"

As he spake these words, a gentle step **was heard, and** Mrs. Cleveland, in her white undress, glided **to his side like a** beautiful apparition. Laying her hand on his shoulder she said, in a low, earnest tone, full of suppressed **anguish:**

"**Arthur;** oh, Arthur! Come! come! quickly! quickly! Ella seems dying!"

The President arose without a word and followed his **wife** up the stairs to a bed-room. **On an elegant table between** two windows was a shaded lamp casting subdued rays **on the sad scene. Several vials were scattered over the** bureau. Here and there in different places of the apartment was a spoon, or a cup, or an untied package which had **in its** turn been employed to relieve the sufferer. There was also **a** sickliness in the apartment not removed by an opened window, through **which the breeze was** waving the curtain **and lifting the** golden **hair falling** about a child's brow. Ella lay on a pillow placed over Eliza's knees, and the pure **white of her thin hand, and** sunken cheek contrasted strangely with **the black skin of the negress. The** face, now peaceful in a celestial beauty, seemed a sculpture from the vision of an angel. Mr. and Mrs. Cleveland stood, hand in hand, before their little girl, gazing in silent awe. A light from heaven was over the pallid features, and a smile was parting the lips. They looked, and looked, and looked until that picture was traced on their souls forever. The tick of a clock in an adjoining room became so loud in the stillness that it seemed beating the stern alarm of death. Suddenly there was a gentle heaving of the breast, just disturbing the folds of the open gown which fell back from the bosom of the child. Then a blackness spread from the neck to the chin, diffusing slowly along the cheeks until it reached the forehead, when the whole face was covered with an inky hue. Now the mouth worked convulsively, the features became distorted, the fingers were closed tightly against the hands, the tender limbs writhed in agony, and there was a low, spasmodic cry which cut into the very heart. The mother's whole being was wrung with a sympathetic suffering only the more intense because subdued and tearless. Cleveland was in a tempest of uncontrolled anguish. He dropped his wife's hand and, pointing wildly to his child, burst forth in a tone of an impotent and rebellious despair:

"Emily, this is too much! too much! God inflicts pain which man would relieve! Our human eyes fill with tears and Heaven seems adamant. That tortured child shakes my faith not only in Christianity, but in God. Creation seems like a great rack managed by an executioner. How can love and wisdom torment the innocent?"

The simple, pious negress lifted her eyes and hands in horror at sentiments so different from what she had heard from the same lips when the President discoursed so unctuously in the College-Chapel.

Mrs. Cleveland experienced acute pain, which intensified her suffering in the presence of her dying daughter. She said, looking on her husband with an expression of unutterable grief, "Arthur, earth is a mystery; our only hope and guide is our faith."

"I can understand," cried Cleveland, "how justice may inflict eternal punishment on obstinate guilt. But, there! oh! see there—that sweet face in agony! Why should purity be thus convulsed with pain? Why should our bright, joyous, sinless Ella lie there, while every feature and limb is thrilling and twisting in spasmodic throes?" Then casting himself on his knees before the attenuated and convulsed form, he exclaimed, "Ella! oh, my Ella! thy father would help where Heaven seems delighting in thy pain."

"God is Love," whispered Mrs. Cleveland, in the clear, firm, calm tone of an unalterable Christian faith.

"Bless de Laud," said Eliza, solemnly, as the blackness faded from the face and the features became still in the peace of death, "Hebben hab annuder angul."

Cleveland arose awed into tranquility. There was a calm in his breast like the hush which would follow the sudden subsidence of a cataract whose roar had been shaking earth, and sky. Both parents stood gazing on the face of their child breathing gentleness sublime in its repose. But soon the storm came back over the heart of Cleveland. He turned, and fled from the room. As he entered his study he was startled by the presence of two men, with whom at this late hour he had an engagement—forgotten in the sufferings of the death-room.

"Bishop Frances! Father John!" he exclaimed, "pardon my abruptness. My child has just died. Call in a few days."

4*

The Bishop was a tall, spare, gaunt man, with high, narrow forehead, projecting cheek bones, immense aquiline nose, and a restless, piercing, burning eye. His jaw and mouth evinced a commanding will. His whole soul was surrendered to a single object. He was a Jesuit, sold to the Pope, and the aim of his life was to subject the world to the Vatican. Every motion of the man tended to this end. There was no circumstance, however trivial, in the history of individual, or family, or neighborhood, which was not dignified with solemn importance when connected with the controlling purpose of his life. All the resources of a vast intellect, vast learning, and vast energy were consecrated on the altar of the Roman church and placed as absolutely at the disposal of the Pope as if he were a visible God. Bishop Frances was a single, concentrated, intense purpose.

Father John, on the other hand, was a large, rotund, jolly, joking priest, whose cheeks stood out with fatness, and whose eyes sparkled with good humor, and whose heart, fully embracing the religion of his ancestors, was yet divided between allegiance to His Holiness and a desire for the independence of Ireland. He was a constant vacillation between Romanism and Fenianism.

The two priests perceived with instinctive tact the peculiarities of their position, and with a few words of appropriate sympathy instantly withdrew, leaving Cleveland standing in his study, with his arms over his breast, white as a marble statue of despair.

His wife in the room above had just arisen from the cold corpse of her child, and as she stood at the window she perceived two retreating forms, which she recognized in the pale light.

"Oh, God!" she exclaimed with clasped hands and a

face turned upward in pain, "here is a sorrow greater than death." Turning away and bending over the body of her little daughter, she continued, while the tears streamed from her eyes: "Oh, Ella! it was hard to see thee suffering on this bosom which gave thee life; it was hard to see thee choking and gasping and black in thy great anguish; it will be hard to shut thee away under the coffin-lid, and cover thee beneath the cold earth, and come from thy grave to the desolation of this room, where every object will recall thy image. But, oh! it is more painful to know that thy father has kept from thy mother a secret which must separate our hearts and lives. I read his soul and his peril."

Mrs. Cleveland then knelt in silent prayer over her Ella, and remained an hour buried in absorbing devotion. She arose with the glow of calm faith beaming from her eyes and irradiating her face. Her being was consecrated, over the body of her child, to the rescue of her husband. In that still hour and awful place there was a solemn transaction between her soul and Heaven. She was assured that in despite of every Romish subtlety and appliance Arthur Cleveland would be saved.

The funeral took place on the third day after the death of Ella. Mrs. Cleveland indeed wept as she stood with her husband above the coffin, gazing for the last time on the hands folded over the breast and the childish face sweet with the peace of Heaven. Her fingers instinctively seized a half-opened rosebud lying on Ella's bosom, whose fading leaf resembled the young life so prematurely darkened. The coffin-screw pierced her heart, and the clod-rattle made her grasp convulsively the hand of her daughter who stood with her looking into the fast-filling grave. But no sorrow was so agonizing as that caused by her relation to her husband. Her arm was leaning on his arm, but her heart could no longer lean **on his** heart. A studied concealment had darkened their lives. The confidence of love had been rudely shocked. Between **Arthur and Emily** Cleveland the grave of **Ella** was now **rather a barrier than a bond.**

CHAPTER V.

THE PERVERSION.

A FEW days after the events recorded in the last chapter, President Cleveland might have been seen leaving his house in the dusk of the evening. His path lay through a beautiful grove of beech and maple, declining gently towards a stream, from a lovely spot where the college buildings, surrounded by the dwellings of the professors, were situated. In a grassy opening of the wood he encountered Dick, who had been seized a second time in his janitorial life with a fit of uncontrollable laughter, contrasting strangely with the sombre mood of the President.

Just before the amused Irishman was an antiquated white horse, whose tail, with the surrounding hair, seemed singed and blackened by fire. The venerable animal, now spotted by age, had been the property of Arthur Cleveland's predecessor in the Presidency. The old clergyman, owing to his popularity and his position, was frequently called to funeral services, and "Gray" was uniformly driven by him at the head of the procession. When the excellent man himself died, as his body was conveyed in a hearse to its resting-place, the faithful horse was grazing on the lawn. He stood for a moment eyeing the mournful company, and then deliberately assuming his customary position in advance, marched in solitary solemnity to the open grave. This act had touched the community and made the aged creature a species of public property, with a life insurance. Notwithstanding these sad associations, he was the subject of the janitor's merriment, which thus appeared always strangely connected with death itself.

"Well, Dick," said the President, "what possible thing could ever make you laugh? I shall expect after a while the graves to be opening."

"Oh, Mishter President," replied Dick, taking off his hat, and ducking his head, and showing teeth white as his peeled potatoes. "It's agin I've clane gone from mysel'. I beg yer's pardon for makin light fornenz yer' grief."

"But Dick, I am puzzled at this strange change in your conduct. It is a phenomenon I wish explained."

"Och, Mishter President, I'm call'd grave Dick, and grave Dick I am. The grave skiliton made me laugh, and auld grave Gray makes me laugh, and well I git my name."

"Go on, go on," interrupted Cleveland, "it grows late, and I am in haste."

"See there, yer honor," said Dick, pointing to the horse, who was looking with his head turned as if conscious he was a subject of conversation, "jist that sing'd tail of auld Gray, and that burnt patch of hair fitched these same laughs a risin to my lips, to show my Irish natur, as you know the pond, as green and still as Erin's shamrock, has gas below, when bubbles come a glitterin' up."

"But what possible connection between those unfortunate marks made, I fear by fire on the poor horse, with your unusual merriment?"

"On my faith, yer honor, a clare connecshun. And two on your frisky frishmens cautched the crittur, and haltered him till night in yer own stable. Then jist as

I was rinning to pull the bed-bell, they tuk him, and tied him to Profisser Thamson's knocker with some fire-crackers to his white tail, and they fizzed, and they blizzed, and they spit, and they popped, like laughin' flame-imps, and auld Gray jerked, and the knocker sthruck, and up flew the winders, and the students poked out their noisy heads, and bawled and yilled, and the Profisser in his night-cap, with a candle in his hand, cum to the doore to see the muss, and thin sich a shoutin, and screamin was never heard onny place only in Amirica. That singed tail and hair jist made me see the Profisser's night-cap, and hear the yellin over agin."

Here the Janitor could contain himself no more, but, as the vision passed before his eyes, he burst forth in a succession of guffaws, for which he had to beg pardon of the President with his awkward Irish politeness.

"Well, Dick," he said smiling, "you are certainly excusable for your merry mood. I must bid you good evening."

He then passed rapidly on refreshed by the janitor's simple hearty amusement, which had for a moment made him forget his own dark, and unhappy heart. How strange that such sympathy with the humblest natures will often assuage the sorrows of a lofty spirit when insensible alike to the arguments of philosophy, or the consolations of Religion!

But now as the shadows of night were gathering, Cleveland hastened forward with a swifter step. Soon his tall form was moving along the summit of the opposite hill. Descending its side by a winding path he stood before the door of a house which rose beneath a stately Cathedral. One vigorous pull of the bell, with its sharp ring, at once brought out a servant.

"Is the Bishop at home?" was the impatient inquiry.

"He is, yer rivrince, and expects you in his study."

Cleveland crossed the threshold with a beating heart and a timid step. He felt he was passing into a mysterious domain, from which return was difficult. The brogue of the servant had awakened the thought, that Rome was, after all, a foreign domination. But as he ascended the stairs he grew more composed and determined.

Bishop Frances had heard his voice, and met him in the upper passage. Smiling and grasping his hand with great warmth, he said:

"Thank you, President Cleveland; thank you, for such a mark of your confidence. Nothing, I am certain, but an earnest inquiry for the truth would have ever brought you beneath this roof."

Cleveland returned the salutation with equal cordiality and replied, "Indeed, Bishop, I venture everything in keeping this engagement. But in the path of duty the heart is bold."

"Come in, come in," exclaimed the Bishop; "here in my study, surrounded by holy books, and beneath the spire of that venerable Church, is the very place to find the will of Heaven."

The two men seated themselves. The Bishop occupied his chair, and Cleveland a sofa. A few coals burned in the grate to remove the evening chill, and dim shadows rose, and fell over the massive volumes which lined in rows the sides of the room. An immense silver crucifix was on the table. In carved niches, stood sculptured forms of the Apostles, and in several places were paintings of angels, and martyrs. More conspicuous than all was a large photograph of Pio Nono, whose benevolent countenance was smiling immediately opposite

Cleveland. Through the large window were visible the outlines of the majestic Cathedral. The President was in that nervous state produced by agonizing sorrows when his sensibilities were impressible, and he shrank with recoil from argument. Such being his condition, under the influence of a superior will, he seemed a tiny bark dashing fitfully on the waves beside a stately ship, riding unrocked by billow, or tempest. The practiced Jesuit read at a glance his mental, and moral state, and knew the stronger his positions the more probable his success. After a brief silence, just beginning to produce embarrassment, he commenced:

"How thankful you should be, Mr. Cleveland, that even by persecution, and bereavement you have found that your life has been a continuous error!"

"I trust I am grateful," he replied, "for my illumination. Baptized in the Protestant faith, a preacher of the Protestant Gospel, a minister of Protestant sacraments, I have ever tossed on a sea of doubts. Now Protestant treachery, and meanness have shown me that where morals are unsound principles must be untrue. I need the rest of the true Church."

"By the grace of the Saviour, and the merits of the Saints, she has purchased peace for all her children. But there is an indispensable condition. Shall I name it, Mr. Cleveland?"

"Keep nothing in reserve. I beg you above all things be explicit, and be decided."

"But perhaps," responded Bishop Frances, "I may startle you by the demand, which truth makes upon your faith."

"Never, never," burst forth Cleveland impetuously. Then rising to his feet he exclaimed,

"I have from my youth been familiar with the evidences of the Christian Religion, and with the claims of the Anglican Communion. I am the sixth youngest son in a line of Clergymen beginning almost with the birth of the English Prayer-Book. I am tired of investigating, tired of doubting, tired of suffering, tired of earth. I only beg for rest."

"Dear friend," answered the Bishop, "the Church comes to you not with argument, but with authority. She does not reason—she commands. As the representative of Heaven, she has but one requirement—submit. Argue no inferior point. The Pope is the Vicar of Christ. As the Head of our infallible Church, he must himself be infallible. To him even now yield your being, and your salvation is more secure than the perpetuity of that world twinkling through your window. It will fade into darkness—you will shine forever."

As he spoke he pointed to the evening star shining down on earth with the tranquility of heaven. Cleveland lifted his eye, and caught that light of beauty. Instantly his soul appeared to float in an atmosphere of holy serenity. His whole system, overstrained by excitement and sorrow, gave suddenly away, and he was convulsed with the power of his emotions. Tears which he had refused to drop on the coffin of his child streamed down upon the floor.

"Oh," he cried, throwing himself reverently on his knees before the image of the Pope, and lifting up his eyes and hands, "years since, I saw that divine face smile from the throne in St. Peter's over the prostrate adoring crowd. Those holy hands were stretched out in blessing. Those sacred lips uttered words I can now recall. The vision shines through years with the radiance of yon star, or the glory of an angel. I bow at the feet, I then desired to kiss. I follow my destiny. I submit body, and soul forever."

Cleveland remained long prostrate in a rapture of devotion.

The Jesuit stood over him with a sly twinkle of surprise in his eye and a slight curl on his lip, occasioned by the ease with which he had won a College President and a Doctor of Divinity.

Yet, when Cleveland arose, even after this burst of feeling, a shadow of doubt, like a cloud, crossed his soul. The brightest glow of his emotion was dimmed by the reflection that he might err in making sentiment his guide instead of reason, and man his oracle instead of God. Perhaps, had he seen the expression of the Bishop, he would have been recalled to his former faith. As it was, he passed the threshold in his consciousness a Papist. Still he would have hesitated immediately to have openly committed himself to Rome had not circumstances occurred to precipitate his action. When leaving the Bishop's house, he noticed the shadow of a lurking man passing towards the grove. He perceived that he was watched. His suspicions had been previously excited when the visit was made to him in his own house on the night of his child's death. He knew that his concealment from Mrs. Cleveland could not be much longer maintained. Every tie binding him to the past seemed breaking. At last the conduct of his former friends, and associates became so marked by chilling, and embarrassing restraint, that he felt like a suspected traitor. His sensitive nature was thus constrained to find relief by a decided and final step. He was soon baptized by Bishop

Frances. Then, after his novitiate, amid clouds of incense, and peals of music, and the blaze of candles, while the dim light of painted windows solemnized the pageant, he made the canonical vows of faith, and obedience in the venerable Cathedral, and became a member of the Roman Catholic Church.

CHAPTER VI.

WILLOW-SHADE.

"Edward, behold your destiny," said Mary Ellingwood, as she stood with her brother on the piazza, and held before him a letter which had just been taken from its envelope.

"Why, Mary, what do you mean?" he replied, coloring with a slight embarrassment.

"I mean, brother, you have made a great mistake. When the rose hangs blushing on its stem, willing to be transferred to your button-hole, and you neglect to pluck it, do not be surprised to see it on another's breast."

"Explain your riddle, Mary! what conceivable connection is there between a rose and that letter?"

"Ah, Ned, prepare for battle! Examine your sword! Load your revolver! You will have something to fight for besides the Constitution. Your rose is in danger as well as the stars of the flag."

Mary here shook the letter playfully in her brother's face and laughed heartily at his evident confusion.

"Your fate," she added, "I fear was sealed when a pretty pair of lips were breathing perfume over this envelope."

Then holding the epistle before him gracefully, and mischievously between her delicate thumb and finger, she exclaimed,

"Sea-Side, Ned; Sea-Side."

Ellingwood's face became red as the morning cloud in

the opposite sky. There was a visible tremulousness in the smoke-circles as they curled away from his cigar and floated off quivering to vanish in the air. The wreaths above him were evidently multiplying and thickening with the intensity of his feelings. After a few moments of silent thought he exclaimed, with a sudden burst of passion and an abruptness of manner indicating a most resolute purpose, "By Jove, Mary, she shall be mine! It is predestined above. No man shall step between us."

While he spoke his hand went down instinctively to where he had for some weeks been accustomed to find his sword-hilt.

Mary laughed still more at this soldierly explosion. "Brave, Edward; brave, while your rival is a thousand miles distant. When you meet on the battle-field it will be the contact of billow and tempest! I tremble when I think of you and Major Worstal,—a magnificent Southern giant—standing eye to eye and breast to breast, in patriotic contest for the Rose of Sea-Side."

Ellingwood started when his sister mentioned the name of his rival. "Worstal! Worstal!" he exclaimed., "why he is a country cousin of Anna Austin, and, if reports are true, a splendid plantation booby."

"Cousins, Ned, are the most dangerous rivals possible. They have many of the privileges of brothers. How often have Anna and the Major, when boys and girls, in play, whispered their love, and perhaps stood together in mock marriage before some lad unmentionably surpliced! What tender associations of early years are in his favor! He is near and a relative! You are separated by distance and by war. Ah! Ned, when the rose was in your power, on that auspicious evening after the Commencement, you should have placed it on your bosom, and over your heart. I know that it was only awaiting your will."

Ellingwood could endure this banter no longer. He grew red with absolute vexation. He was angry with himself and angry with his sister. He pettishly tossed away the remnant of his cigar over the railing of the piazza, and was reminded of the awkward confusion in which he had bitten off his Havana during his last interview with Anna, and returned it to his vest pocket with a blundering apology. "Confound you, Mary," he said in his vexation; "you have, yourself, caused all my troubles. You and Charles interrupted me just as I was about to decide the question of my life. Mountains now seem to stand between Anna and myself. But they shall be overcome! No earthly power shall prevent our union! 1 beg your pardon, sister, for my rudeness."

Mary was amused rather than provoked at the earnestness and violence of Edward, and going towards him, took his hand and gave him a kiss.

"Mary," said her brother, tenderly, "you are a teazing creature; but the best girl in the world—except one."

"And she," replied Miss Ellingwood, with a twinkle and a smile, unable to resist the temptation, "is in a far country, surrounded by splendid Confederate gallants, above whom towers the epaulettes and plume of Cousin Hercules, while Edward Ellingwood, having neglected his opportunity, is fighting to tear down the very banner under which Anna Austin lives."

"Mary!" burst forth her brother, "this is absolutely unbearable. You are provoking beyond endurance. A treaty of peace, sealed by a kiss from your own lips, and offered by yourself, is no curb to your mischief."

While Ellingwood was uttering these words a servant

announced that his father wished his presence in the study He was glad of an opportunity to withdraw and hide his vexation; while Mary, with several profound and graceful courtesies, bowed herself laughing through the hall.

During the time required for Edward Ellingwood to become seated by the Judge, we may be making a rapid survey of Willow-Shade.

The house was one of those plain, but respectable, and even stately stone mansions not uncommon in New England, and now seemed invested with a species of autumnal solemnity as it stood amid an October haze, which was curtaining the earth and reddening the sun. A vine along the porch was already dropping down its leaves and exposing to the passer's eye clustering grapes in their purple lusciousness. The peach blushed on branches partially denuded; the pear no longer hid its yellow amid the green, and the red apple hung heavily on its stem. A late rose still lifted its fragrant beauty above a faded sisterhood, so mournfully indicating its own decay. The distant hills were gorgeous in that sad glory which only makes the coming ruin more dreary and more dreaded. The shy squirrel gambolled fearfully with the disappearance of the concealing verdure; and with the vanished brilliance of the sun the voice of the dove had become increasingly mournful. Even the rivulet stole sluggishly through the grass with a subdued murmur, and the river rolled towards the sea in a solemnized majesty. Perhaps also the painful condition of the country imparted even to nature a deeper tint and a darker shade. The great willows at the edge of the garden waved their yellow limbs and leaves with a species of sympathetic sadness. Youth only could experience merriment amid such scenes.

Edward Ellingwood was conscious of an entire change

of feeling when he passed from the piazza and the jests of his gay sister into the still study of his venerable father. As he entered the room, the old lawyer laid down his pen and closed a volume he had just taken from a shelf of the library. Looking on his son affectionately, he exclaimed: "Good morning, Edward; good morning."

The salutation was returned with the utmost love and reverence.

"Why," said the Judge, "how well your military coat becomes you! I little thought when I taught you in Story, and Kent, and Marshall, I should ever see you in a captain's shoulder-straps and preparing to test in battle what you learned in this old study of Willow-Shade."

"Father," Edward replied, with deep emotion and in a tone of manly resoluteness, "what I received from your lips I trust I will be ready to defend with my life."

"I know, my boy," the Judge said, with an evident paternal pride, "you do not regard your uniform as a silly miss admires the last fashion; but esteem it a badge of principles for which you are willing to die."

"I hope," responded Edward, "that I have pondered your instructions, and that I shall go into battle knowing for what I fight."

"Ever keep in view," replied the lawyer, deliberately removing his spectacles and laying them down on the opened book, "the true issue of this strife. Slavery is not the primary question. The cannon aimed against our flag on Sumter assaulted our national sovereignty. A people callous to the wrongs of the negro have arisen to establish their unity. The compacts of the Constitution solemnly bound us to respect the rights of the South, and I, and every Federal judge, would have been supported by the whole army of the Republic in delivering pursued fugi-

tives. In no instance has the nation violated its pledge.
A war commenced for the freedom of the slave would
itself involve the principle of secession, and overthrow
the work of our Fathers. But when the standard of our
country is assailed from whatever section, the President
must obey his official oath, and defend, by sea, and land,
our integrity and sovereignty. Possibly, as an act of war,
the slave may be proclaimed free. This, however, will be
only an incident of the contest. Always have in your
view, the object for which you fight, and your course will
be true, and honorable, and generous, and patriotic. Let
you motto be 'The country, the whole country, and
nothing but the country.' "

As the old man spoke, his eye kindled, his countenance
beamed, his lip quivered. He glowed with that ardent,
yet temperate emotion characterizing cultivated natures,
whose impulses are ever subordinate to reason.

Edward caught inspiration from his father, and stood
before him a youthful representative of the genius of his
country. He exclaimed with strong feeling, "I thank you
dear father, I thank you a thousand times for your wise
instructions. They have both fortified my intellect, and
animated my heart. Ever may the guides of my life be
the Constitution of my country, and the Bible of my God!
For these may I be willing to shed my blood, when any
foe, domestic, or foreign, political, or religious, may strive
to overthrow the one, or to fetter the other."

"My son," answered Judge Ellingwood, taking fr m
the table a beautiful little silken flag made by his daughter, "Here is, in miniature, the representative of that
banner which floated over Washington, and inspired the
Revolution, and was flung from Liberty Hall when its
old bell pealed forth the first notes of our national ex-

istence. Guard its eagle! Love its stars! Defend its folds! Place it on your heart! There wear it during life! Kneel, Edward, kneel! Kiss the Constitution of your Country, and the Bible of your God, and vow yourself for ever to their defence."

As he spoke the noble old man arose from his chair. Although not tall, his stature appeared majestic. His gray locks trembled with the excitement of his patriotic soul as they fell around his venerable face, and forehead. He moved to a shelf and took down a worn copy of the Constitution, and lifted from the table a beautiful Bible, and stood holding the first in his left, and the second in his right hand, the ideal of a dignified and commanding age.

Edward experienced an electric thrill darting through his being. He flung himself at the feet of his father, and grasping and kissing in turn the extended volumes, and reverently placing the flag on his heart, felt that his existence was consecrated to his Country and his Religion.

CHAPTER VII.

NOT long after the events we have just recorded some very different circumstances were transpiring in a distant Southern mansion. Two persons sat on the broad verandah by which it was surrounded. Immense doors and windows, communicating with the adjoining rooms, showed by their width, and height, and numbers an evident design to invite the cooling breeze, and mitigate the tropical heat. A peculiar languor pervaded nature. The sun had passed his meridian possibly three hours. The siesta after an early dinner was over. The blaze of the sky, however, was scarcely diminished. On the right, in the distance, was a cypress swamp, above which rose a gigantic tree lifting its branches festooned with vines to the heavens, while towards the left, through an avenue of the pine-forest, might be seen the blue ocean, gemmed with islands, and flashing with sails, and stretching away until it met the encircling sky. The oval lemon and the round orange glowed beneath their leaves, and the fig stood loaded with heavy burdens. Negroes—male, female, young, middle-aged, old—of every hue from suspicious yellow to blackest ebony, and of every feature, figure, and variety—under the shade of trees, and beneath the glare of the sun—lounged, worked, talked, laughed, grinned, crawled, tottered—free from care, and in the happy consciousness that a kind master was always considering their temporal, and their spiritual wants. Everything indicated slavery in its boasted, peaceful, patriarchal glory, and had there been no other side to the picture, theorists would have found it hard to convince the world that the institution was an injury.

But we are chiefly concerned with the persons on the balcony. The lady we at once recognize as Miss Anna Austin. Her cousin, Major Worstal, was the gentleman. In size he was a Hercules, and in form and proportion he had been manly perfection until his premature rotundity had become excessive, and a repulsive beefiness monopolized his hands and cheeks and neck. Still his great strength and stature gave him even yet a certain majesty. A stranger introduced into his presence would have felt a species of awe, if risibility were not excited by the rapidity of his motions while engaged in the very feminine occupation of fanning his oily face. Streaming with perspiration, he was looking down love on his fair cousin from two small animal eyes.

"Anna," he said, while puffing and panting and fanning with an embarrassed violence, "I have received an order from my Colonel, and I must leave within an hour through this infernal heat. Can I see you a few minutes alone?"

"Why, Cousin Henry," she replied, "are we not alone on the verandah?"

"Alone," he rejoined, somewhat peevishly, and making more vigorous his exertions to keep cool. "Alone, with Charley there smoking under that tree! the General in yon door reading his paper, and twenty niggers peeping and listening about!"

"But speak low, Henry, speak low, and I will promise to hear every word of your important communication."

"My voice, you know, cousin, is like a conch-shell, with

6

only one note, and that loud enough to rouse all the lazy black devils on a plantation."

"Well, what do you propose?" inquired Anna, laughing.

"Let us go down," he said, rising from his chair, and moving his fan with a furious rapidity, "to the ocean-seat."

"You do not seriously ask me," exclaimed Anna, in assumed alarm, "to expose my complexion and my life in the blaze of such a sun? Why, Jim and Jumbo would scarcely dare such a peril."

The Major, however, insisted, and would take no excuse. He had from childhood regarded Anna as his future wife. He had taken it for granted that she would be the presiding mistress of his great desolate mansion. He had never until lately conceived that a rival would cross his path. But the war had excited in his breast unexpected anxieties. General Brompton's house was now often filled with gay, dashing, splendid Confederate officers, and the brilliant scarfs, and the gilded epaulettes were disturbing his old confidence. He had repeatedly broken down in the effort to declare himself. Now, however, his apprehensions forced him to decide the question, and he had only one burning hour to spare. Nothing could have been more absurdly unpropitious than the amusing spectacle of his cousin and himself, moving arm-in-arm beneath a huge umbrella, and amid such a blaze, to such a place, and for such a purpose. Arrived at the spot the difficulties were not diminished, and their exact measure was given by the accelerated violence of the fan. The situation of Miss Anna was by no means agreeable. But what surpasses the endurance of woman! Nothing in love is so embarrassing as premeditation, and the Major had neither volubility nor confidence to spare. He soon became red with heat, and red with confusion.

"Anna, dear Cousin Anna," he stammered in an amusing bewilderment, "you know what I mean."

"And I know, Henry," she answered, playfully, "what that dreadful sun means. How the perspiration streams from your face!"

The Major bent over, seized her hand tenderly in his great fingers, looked upon her softly from his diminutive eyes, brought near her cheek his huge, hot, beefy face, and was summoning all his energies to make her the mistress of his heart, and life, and home, when a mischievous, ragged negro-urchin, who had been peeping, and grinning in a thicket, climbed a neighboring tree like a monkey, and sat peering down from a branch with impish gaze. At the same moment there was the shrill crow of a cock, and the loud bray of a donkey. Apollo could never have overcome such obstacles.

Miss Austin, rising hastily, said: "Cousin Henry, the General and Charles are standing on the verandah and beckoning our return. We had better go."

Worstal was thus saved the mortification of a refusal, and was as much relieved as Anna to be extricated from an awkward position. When they reached the house, the Major's horse, held by a negro, stood saddled for his master. Worstal drew on an immense pair of gloves, took his whip, drank a stiff glass of brandy, and mounted. The moment he touched the animal he was transformed. Instantly the dejection caused by his discomfiture vanished. Fire came back to his eye. His form dilated into grace and dignity. His head sat proudly, and even nobly on his neck. On his beautiful horse pawing and prancing, with curved **neck**, and expanded nostril, and flashing **eye**, he seemed an equestrian god.

General Brompton, standing on the second step of **the** verandah, with Anna and Charles above him, said, "Major, you must pardon my apparent urgency in hastening **your departure.** I knew your command was peremptory, and perceiving that you had forgotten the time, **I** ventured to **order your horse, and** beckon you to the house."

"I thank you, uncle," he answered, "for your thoughtfulness. Minerva will soon make up my lost time. You **see** she is full of lightning this afternoon."

"And now," returned the General, "I have such confidence **in** her heels and fire, I shall detain you by saying what I was about to urge on Charles, just **as you came** with Anna on the verandah."

"Speak," he replied, "as long as you would to a country jury **or** the Georgia Legislature," and then pointing to his splendid mare with a proud glance downward, he added, "here is security in flesh and flame that **my** order will not be violated."

The General drew himself up on the step very much **with the** air **of** a Judge looking down from his bench with satisfied dignity before commencing his charge.

"Young men," he began, "**I** perceive the South is about **to** misunderstand **the entire** principle involved in this war. Philosophically it may be a contest of antagonistic **races, but practically it is a conflict** of constitutional interpretation. **Slavery is** a mere incident in the struggle."

Charles **Austin looked** delighted, and Major Worstal looked disgusted, and **Anna** looked amused as she compared the different expressions **of her cousin and her brother.** The former drew his legs **close under his horse's** body, as if about to spur away in his surprise, and chagrin, and roared out, "General, I fight for the nigger, and to carry slavery into that hell of a New England, and to kill or cure its infernal abolition Yankees."

As his mare pawed and snorted beneath his gigantic form, he added, with a fierce laugh, "I have trained Minerva so well that she is mad when she hears about a nigger, or a Yankee."

General Brompton would not have expended more breath in his argument had the Major been the only person in his audience. He had, however, Charles Austin in his view, and knew how important it was to impress, at this exciting crisis, on his susceptible and superior mind, principles he had been taught from his youth.

"I know, Henry," he resumed, "that your opinion prevails through the South. But do we not degrade ourselves to fight for negroes and cotton-bales? Are not our rights secure by our constitutional compromises? Can we justify war by mere antagonism of blood? No, the question, as Mr. Calhoun taught, is one of liberty. We fight to establish the freedom of a sovereign State by her sovereign act to secede at her sovereign pleasure. On no other principle can we defend the confederacy."

"Thank you, uncle," exclaimed Charles Austin, while his body and soul kindled with that oratorical fire whose sparks had flashed his audience into flame when we heard him on the platform of the commencement, "thank you, uncle," he repeated with glowing earnestness, "I should think myself degraded to fight merely for the chains of the slave, or the conquest of the North, where I have seen so much to admire and love. But I exult to cast myself on the altar of my State, and give my blood for her glory."

6*

"Charles," answered General Brompton, with a pleased smile of satisfaction, "for this I have educated you from childhood. I surrender you to Georgia. God bless her sovereign star!"

Worstal could not comprehend the argument, but he caught the enthusiasm. Sitting loftily on Minerva, now almost frantic with the contagious excitement, he waved his cap, shouting, "Hurrah for Georgia!" The General and Austin joined the cry, exclaiming, "Hurrah for Georgia!" Negroes, great and and small, young and old, male and female, of every shade, form, and dignity, in bass, treble, and tenor, with waving hands and shining ivory, yelled, "Hurrah for Georgia!" The slave in cotton-field, rice-field, and sugar-field, catching the sound, and pausing over his hoe, repeated the words, until far and near, from earth to sky, swelled the shout, "Hurrah for Georgia." Here was struck the key-note of secession.

Sweet Anna Austin, whose gentle nature living in the higher world of the affections, knew nothing, and cared nothing for the political principle, yet, amused with the spectacle, as the notes were dying away in the distance, took off her hat, trimmed with a Northern rose, and waving it gracefully over her head, said, merrily, and musically, "Hurrah for Georgia." Worstal, now mad with brandy, and excitement, put spur and whip to Minerva equally frenzied, and saying farewell, dashed wildly forward, with his trumpet-voice yelling for miles "Hurrah for Georgia," while he, and his mare, seemed one flying fiend rushing over earth with the havoc-notes of war.

CHAPTER VIII.

ARTHUR CLEVELAND, by his sudden defection, had certainly made himself liable to the suspicion of weakness and of perfidy. Yet he believed himself sincere. His was in truth an undeveloped nature. No early struggles had ever awakened in him a true manhood. He was merely a spoiled child of wealth. In his soul was a concealed mine of genius, and of power, whose treasures coming years might expose. Life's ordinary trials, which in hardy natures would have provoked amusement, or resistance, were by him magnified into peculiar sufferings. He had great capacity to acquire, and little ability to apply. His erudition was always overmastering his logic, and oppressing his common sense, so that he was a dreamy clerical scholar. At College he had been remarkable in the languages, and brilliant in his essays, but lame in Mathematics, and confused in Metaphysics. As a Professor he had been a good instructor, and a bad disciplinarian. While President he was popular with boys, and unpopular with men. A certain effeminacy of appearance, and mind was destined to be visible even under his gray hairs unless struggle finally gave vigor to his will, and power to his face. A few years in the manly study and practice of the Law, before he became a Clergyman, would probably have placed him beyond the arts of the Jesuit. Beneath his entire character was also a latent ambition burning like fire, yet disguised by the habitual, and unconscious sanctimoniousness to which he was liable from his ministerial position. He resembled a carved and gilded yacht, navigated by confident amateurs, and circling ignorantly about the expecting whirlpool.

Bishop Frances read his man with the glance of priestly intuition. He had known him for years better than he was known to himself or his friends. These suggestions will explain a conversation between the Jesuit and his pervert, as they sat together in a grove just before the Cathedral.

"Mr. Cleveland," said the Bishop, fixing on him a pair of black, glittering, fascinating eyes, and speaking in a low, earnest voice, "there is a vast field before you in this country. Your usefulness may be without limit."

"O, my best friend," he replied, "all my aspirations have vanished. My only desire is to serve the Church as an obscure and humble layman."

"But," returned the Bishop, "you have no right to bury your talent. A great work is to be achieved in America among the more cultivated classes. Your genius, your learning, your social position, your wealth, all mark you as the man to. win and mould numbers within the influence of no other."

"You forget, however, that barred forever from the Priesthood by my marriage, it is impossible for me to move in a large sphere."

"Ah! Mr. Cleveland," said Bishop Frances, with a most mysterious and significant expression, "I have a plan, sir, I have a plan. The Church shall never lose such distinguished gifts. Will you not promise to commit yourself to my disposal?"

"I am infinitely indebted to you as my guide and father, and I willingly will submit to your advice."

"And now," replied the Bishop, "study the English movement! Especially consider two types! Professor Oldman will never accept the Roman Church. He is restless, and therefore useless. His apologies are more for himself than for others. We can never safely employ a tool, however valuable, which may at any moment fly off, and cut our own fingers. But Archbishop Planning has submitted wholly. He will be the staunchest advocate of Papal Infallibility. His knowledge of Anglicanism and Anglicans has been a golden treasure to the Church. Strong himself, he persuades others. Unqualified surrender is the secret of his magic power. Hence rectors, professors, doctors, nobles and their wives, their children, their titles, their estates, have followed him to Rome."

"Bishop Frances," quickly interposed Cleveland, "you amaze and startle me. I have never conceived of exerting such an influence. Why do you present before me an example, when the obstacles to my imitation are eternally insuperable?"

"Leave yourself with me, Mr. Cleveland, leave yourself with me," rejoined the Bishop, taking him by the hand, and looking on him with a paternal smile. "The Church in America is to be shaped for all future time. Before many years a Cardinal will be required. Of course, as the Pope has the tiara because he has the mitre, he must cling to his Bishopric. Besides, we need the prestige of the Eternal City, the splendors of the Vatican, and the magnificence of St. Peter's. But storms are rising, my dear friend, storms are rising, thrones are trembling, the liberals are multiplying, and his Holiness may yet seek a refuge in America. With such possibilities in the future, there can be no bounds, no bounds whatever, to your influence. Plant yourself firmly and forever on the Papal Infallibility, and I predict for you a career of unsurpassed brilliancy."

Cleveland was fascinated into silence by the tone, and manner, and suggestions of Frances. A new world was opened in his heart. Glittering visions for a moment rushed dazzling over his soul. He saw, as never before, the strength of his own ambition, and trembled with alarm. Looking imploringly towards his adviser, he exclaimed, "Bishop, my dear Bishop, I beseech you, drop this subject, and let it never be resumed. It will be my single aim as a simple laic always to humbly labor for the Church in the most retired sphere. Never, I pray you, never place before me any position of exalted influence."

"You have agreed," he replied, "to submit to my advice. I will venture one suggestion on a delicate subject. There can be no distinguished usefulness without distinguished holiness, and no distinguished holiness without distinguished self-denial. Guard your relations with Mrs. Cleveland! Uxoriousness is the curse of piety. Woman blasted Eden."

Cleveland felt his natural paleness flushing into scarlet, and was about replying in a state of the most intense excitement, when Bishop Frances again seizing his hand caressingly, and dropping his voice to an affectionate whisper, anticipated him, and said, "Let me add one word more of counsel. Write a book, Mr. Cleveland, write a book. Declare your conversion before the world. St. Paul obtained strength when he proclaimed to people and kings the miracle of his change."

"But how is it possible for a mere neophyte to discuss questions which require the labored investigations of years, and which a life-time can scarcely comprehend? You urge me to a task wholly beyond my ability."

"Seek the grace of Mary," answered the Bishop. "I will give you every needed assistance, and with the sanction of his Holiness, you may help the Church and advance yourself."

The resistance of Cleveland was easily and speedily overcome. He had abandoned a brilliant position, where, as a Clergyman, he had been always in the public eye, while the Presidency of a college greatly widened the circle of his influence. It had been with a severe struggle that he resolved to abandon his honors, and be contented in an unnoticed private sphere. His latent ambition was soon excited by the suggestions of one to whom he felt so much indebted, and aspiration was disguised under the plea of duty. As his conversion had attracted universal attention his book would be assured of circulation, and promote his reputation. The volume was prepared with a rapidity which seemed marvelous, and almost amusing when the magnitude of the topics was contrasted with the recency of his change. However, Frances furnished the learning, and the argument, and Cleveland the style, and the enthusiasm. But if the book was suited rather for weaklings than for scholars, it accomplished the purpose of the Bishop by erecting behind his disciple a barrier to prevent his return. It charged that Protestantism was deficient not only in faith, but in morals, and defended Popish superstitions, Popish corruptions, Popish usurpations, Popish miracles, Popish persecutions, and of course, as the fountain of all, Popish infallibility.

Mrs. Cleveland was deeply tried. As she sat one evening with her daughter on her knee, and her husband by her side, she said, "Heaven forbid, my dear Arthur, that I should fetter your opinions, or obstruct your course. But I must tell you that certain assertions of your book have caused me great pain. I never intend discussing the questions which now separate us, and yet I cannot help asking, whether, when you assert that Protestantism is devoid of morals, you do not stain your own father, your mother, your brothers, your sisters, your associates, your friends, your very ancestors,—nay, me, your wife? Surely you know that the law of God is the rule of our lives, however imperfect we confess its observance!"

Cleveland blushed in painful confusion, and answered earnestly, and quickly, "I implore you, Emily, to remember that I refer to the tendency of a system, and not to the character of individuals. Before heaven and earth I assert the purity and sincerity of my Protestant friends."

"Enough, enough, my own husband," said Mrs. Cleveland in a tone of the most affectionate tenderness, "I accept your explanation, however I may esteem your logic. Oh, may nothing ever divide our hearts! Our early love, our marriage vow, the altar which witnessed our union, our Ella's grave, this dear child's future, our happy home—how many ties sacred, and enduring bind us together!" While she spoke, her voice, became tremulous, and tears gushed over her cheeks.

Cleveland stooped, and tenderly kissed away the drops, and assured his wife of his continued and increasing love, while Ada, throwing her arms around both her parents, and then stroking their faces with her little fingers, wept in childish sympathy. The moon looked coldly on that family group as she has on many similar scenes during the ages when every suffering of the human heart and every interest of human life united to invoke a warm and tender glance. Even the stars shed down a chilling lustre.

Notwithstanding the affections which had thus been elicited, Cleveland was far from satisfied with his present position. Indeed it was fast becoming to him insupportable. He had now resigned his collegiate position. His book arose like a wall to bar return to his former faith. His future stretched before him a wide, wild, uncertain sea. While attached to his wife, he felt daily more and more the embarrassments and complications of his life.

The Bishop had foreseen his involvements, and long before prepared a method of extrication. When they were once together in the study which had witnessed his conversion, he said blandly to his friend after a long conversation, "My dear President," as he still often called him, "have you ever considered that the cause of the marvellous successes of Rome is not so much the infallibility of her faith as the wisdom of her policy?"

"You surprise me!" returned Cleveland, "I had supposed her triumph was that of truth under the Divine blessing."

"Of course," answered the Bishop, smiling, "in the largest sense you are correct, and yet in another view her victories are traceable to the celibacy of her Clergy. You see," he added laughing, "how woman always appears as a disturbing element. Her evil did not end with Paradise."

"I confess," replied Cleveland, looking uneasy, and incredulous, "between the result and the cause you assign I perceive but little connection."

"Ah!" continued the Bishop, with a low significant chuckle, "I must express in turn my amazement at your philosophic obtuseness. Possibly I may be chargeable on this point with the prejudices of a celibate. But hear me patiently for a single moment. Look at a Protestant

7

Parson in a wealthy metropolitan Parish! He has a fashionable wife, and children innumerable. He must live on a principal avenue in palatial splendor. He must have a costly equipage, and establish his sons, and marry his daughters. All this demands a large revenue, which in a few years would build an asylum, endow a college, erect a church. Popular gifts must, of course, be secured to rent pews so that the salary may be paid, and mortgages be satisfied. Hence we have that law of demand and supply—so much eloquence for so much money—which blasts Protestantism by converting its worship into a mere rhetorical attraction. On the contrary we Catholic Priests with our small compensation, expend on the Church what these Preachers lavish on their families. Have I proved my point, Mr. President?" he concluded with an air of conscious triumph.

"I admit," responded Cleveland, "the correctness of your conclusions. I had supposed that the power of our celibate Clergy was simply in their privilege of single devotion to the Holy Church; I now perceive that the money-question underlies everything."

"True, true," answered the Bishop gravely, "money moves the world, money alleviates Purgatory, money opens Heaven. However, the consideration you urge is doubtless the one chiefly designed by the Church. Celibacy, by the suppression of the strongest passion of human nature, and the opportunity it affords for meditation and labor, has given her the most devoted servants, and the world its most shining possible examples of piety. I know of but one grace superior to it."

"Superior!" exclaimed Cleveland, "superior! Certainly nothing can be above the state of our Lord, and his Apostles. Explain yourself, my dear Bishop!"

"I hesitate," he replied. The subject has often occupied my thoughts, and yet I fear that delicacy forbids me even whispering it in your ears."

"You excite both my surprise and my curiosity," Cleveland answered, while his kindling face and eye showed the truth of his words.

Frances seemed to hesitate, as if alarmed at the consequences of what he had suggested. He placed his hands softly on the shoulders of Cleveland, and looking into his face with two dark magic eyes, he said in a mysterious tone, "My dear friend, we had better leave this subject. I cannot incur the responsibility."

"Speak, Bishop, speak," burst forth Cleveland impulsively. "Do you think I am a child? Be frank, and I will take the blame."

"Well," returned Frances, continuing his posture, and resuming his tone, "remember now and always that you forced my opinion from my lips. However, as I speak in the abstract I may comply with your request." He then looked still more earnestly on his disciple, and said with a slow, hesitating, and almost painful deliberation and emphasis, "That man, in my estimation, who, having lived amid the joys of the married state, abandons the nectar of Eden for the good of the Church, merits a glory only inferior to that of Apostles, and certainly equal to that of Martyrs."

Cleveland started as if a galvanic battery had shocked his system. He bounded from his chair. He stood before Frances. Trembling with surprise and agony, he confronted those cold, fixed, snaky eyes. "Bishop," he cried with the most vehement passion, "Bishop, you cannot, you *dare* not mean this hint for me. You would not cruelly rend the tie which binds me to my wife, whom I have vowed to love and cherish."

" I need not remind Mr. **Cleveland**," he replied, with a
steady voice, and gaze, " that the Church regards as void
a marriage where the service is performed by any but her
own Priests. In all such cases a Papal dispensation is. a
policy rather than a necessity. Nor would I advise you
to apply for a favor so distinguished, as it might be refused. Still it would delight me to hear you from our
Pulpits, and to see you minister at our Altars. Be seated,
my dear friend. **Compose your nerves**, and I shall never
again repeat the suggestion."

Cleveland obeyed with the movement of an automaton.
He was under the spell of a superior will—a fly struggling in the net of the spider. Nothing more was ever
advanced by his subtle adviser on the subject, and
nothing more was ever necessary. A seed had been
dropped into a prepared soil, and the penetrating Jesuit
knew that it would silently grow without further assistance.

Cleveland returned to his home another man. His wife
perceived the change, although she knew not the cause,
and made no remark. When her face was averted he
often gazed on her with an ineffable sorrow. For days
the sight of his Ada always moved a tear. Often he
found himself caressing those he loved with an anguish of
affection. He knew that he was about to break the heart
of his wife, to darken the prospect of his daughter, to
cloud the joy of his home. Yet, wherever he went, the
phantom of a Papal dispensation followed. It colored
his thoughts, and filled his dreams. His desire to preach,
his preference for clerical habits, his yearning for public
position, together with a mingled ambition for distinguished holiness and distinguished station rushed over his
soul like a march of successive tempests. The wretch

sometimes abandoned his dwelling, and then returned, lingering around it, yet unable to enter. He would stand concealed gazing through the window long and intensely on the sweet face of his Ada, and her blue eye and her golden hair, and as he looked entranced on the noble countenance and matronly form of his beautiful Emily, he shook with the struggles of his breast. He became in appearance a shadow.

One night he started from his sleep in horror, having dreamed that he was sailing over a sea of fire, on a phantom ship, whose sailors were ghosts, while grinning spectres on the flames flew beckoning onward to a blazing whirlpool. Frantically embracing his wife he kissed her in a frenzy of love. When asked the cause of his alarm, and violence, he could only utter a groan. However, habit gradually familiarized him with an idea once hateful, and he considered his struggles simply as a rebellion of the flesh, while indeed a secret burning ambition was in his heart. Besides, the suspense following his application for the indulgence served to blunt his sorrow.

In the end, when Frances brought him the fatal document, he grasped his hand, and in an ecstacy kissed the seal and signature of the Pontiff. He and the Bishop considered deeply and consulted often how to communicate the terrible information to his doomed wife. Circumstances, however, shaped the sad affair in a way their wisdom would not have determined. One day, in his study, when he and the Jesuit had an appointment, the parchment in its scarlet letters, and with its red seal, was taken from a secret drawer and left on his table. Being called suddenly away, and detained longer than he expected, the dispensation was forgotten. Mrs. Cleveland happened to enter the study, and the unusual character and appear-

7*

ance arrested her eye, and a single word flashed the whole truth on her woman's intuition. She saw but that word. That word burned into her soul. It marked on her face the wrinkles of age. It brought into her hair the white of winter. She stood with clasped hands, petrified by her anguish, like a statue consuming with interior fire. Cleveland, having remembered his carelessness, returned to the study, breathless with haste and fear. A glance revealed the truth. He trembled, and would have fled in wild terror, but was arrested by the voice of his wife.

Standing loftily while her eye flashed her just indignation, she pointed with her right hand to the parchment, and exclaimed, " Arthur Cleveland, there lies the secret of your struggles, and the proof of your delusion. There is a demonstration that Rome, to secure her purpose, would rend the altar of heaven. There is the seal of mortal man," and seizing a Bible which lay on the table, and holding it towards him, she said, "and here is the Word of an infallible God. You have withered these cheeks. You have blanched this head. You have pierced this bosom. You have crushed this heart. You have renounced your faith, your wife, your child. Behold the wreck made by your infatuation! But you are my husband. Human power is impotent against this Divine Law. Although I cannot permit your embrace, I here vow on this Bible and before Heaven to follow you through life and rescue your soul."

The smitten husband shrank and cringed before the burning gaze of his injured wife. He would have answered, but she commanded his silence with a womanly majesty which awed him into submission. At this moment, Frances, in pursuance of his appointment, made his appearance. Mrs. Cleveland stood before him like an angel of retribution. The strong man shrank before the gaze of the outraged woman. He would have retreated from the storm, but was arrested by her voice before he could escape.

"You," she cried, and her face and eye breathed and flamed with indignation. "You are the serpent who have wound yourself into this Eden to blast its joy. Your subtle breath is the poison of our home. You have come in the garb of Heaven to do the work of Hell. You are the emissary of the Pope, and the minister of Satan. You would dare separate those whom God has joined. You blasphemously place the dispensation of a worm above the will of the Creator. Heaven shall baffle your plans and save my husband."

Frances was too shrewd to attempt a response. Just then the bright Ada smiling darted like a sunbeam into the room. Mrs. Cleveland snatched the child convulsively, to her bosom, and with a look of anguish and reproof, but a step of majestic dignity, left the room. The Bishop, and Cleveland remained overwhelmed with confusion and dismay.

CHAPTER IX.

THE CAPITOL.

THE cannon which blazed against the flag of Sumter
was charged with the destinies of our country. Its roar,
indeed, connects itself with the future of the world.
Nothing but such thunder could have waked our nation
from its sleep of death. Immediately over every part of
our vast territory, men arose willing to sacrifice life for
that fallen standard which they regarded as representing
the sovereignty of the Republic. A contest was initiated
to decide forever whether our unequalled territory, in the
heart of the American continent, and so closely connected
with all the grand divisions of the old world, was to be
controlled by innumerable petty States, agitated in eternal
wars, or to be governed by local organizations under one
united power, whose flag should command the respect of
the nations as the emblem of human liberty. All other
considerations were incidental and subordinate. And
whatever the excesses and outrages of the war, and the
opinions, and cruelties of individuals, we are not to suppose that men on both sides were not sincere believers in
their respective principles. No purer statesmen ever lived
in the history of our country than the gifted Southern
band who battled against Clay, and Webster on the arena
of the Senate, and it was impossible that leaders of such
ability and eloquence should not leave behind them a
vigorous and enthusiastic school willing to defend their
views with both tongue, and sword. Questions of race

80

and slavery undoubtedly precipitated and intensified the contest, but independently of these, exaggerated opinions of the rights of States must always, and inevitably, terminate in conflict with the general Government. The intense face, and narrow forehead of Calhoun as certainly typified the sectional spirit of Secession, as the broad brow, and majestic proportions of Washington personified the genius, and the destiny of our undivided Republic. Leaving, however, these reflections we will return to the personal histories we have proposed to narrate.

Edward Ellingwood and Charles Austin, true to their education, enlisted, each in the army whose banner was the standard of his heart and his opinions. In the eye of the one floated the unbroken constellation of the Republic, and in the eye of the other the separated stars of the Confederacy. Neither was in the mutually-mortifying struggle at Bull-Run. Each, unconscious of the presence of the other, mingled in the fight which planted our flag on the walls of Fort Donaldson, and started General Grant in that military career destined to terminate in the triumph of his country. They were thus acquiring endurance and skill in the various contests of the war, and perhaps no young officers in either army had exhibited greater talents, or courage, or gave brighter promise of advancement.

During the interval we have described, it happened that Judge Ellingwood and General Brompton were to meet in the City of Washington, where the latter sought in vain to be recognized as a confederate commissioner that he might adjust certain important questions of policy. Both, as cultivated gentlemen and astute lawyers, comprehended the true issues to be settled before the country, and the world. The interview was anticipated with mutual interest, and ended with mutual respect. It took place in one of the private rooms of the Capitol. The Judge was already seated at a table covered with letters, and papers, when the General entered. Instantly laying down his pen, he arose with a somewhat stately and formal, but polite salute, which was returned in a similar style and spirit. The two gentlemen were soon sitting in their chairs face to face.

"Ha, ha, General," began the Judge laughing, "we have not met before since that famous commencement drew us together. How amusing the excitement in the old College-Chapel! You see Charley, and Ned have led us to war at last. I fear the young rascals were better prophets than ourselves."

"I have often smiled," said the General, "when I have recalled some of the incidents of the scene. Yet now memory invests it with a shade of gloom. The fellows may find an exchange of arguments more agreeable than an exchange of bullets. Had the boys, and women foreseen these troubles they would scarcely have been so enthusiastic."

"Well, my old friend," replied Judge Ellingwood, in a more subdued and serious tone, "it is indeed a sad matter. The result was destiny. Nothing but the sword can now adjust our disputes. We have been long sowing the seeds of war in our words, and we must reap the harvest in blood. But," he added with a flashing eye, and a quivering lip, "while I have always conceded sincerity to the people of the South, however I may have blamed some of their leaders, and attributed this strife to their education, I have been startled, and amazed by certain reports relating to your prisons. On this point, before our interview proceeds, I must know your private opinion."

While these words were uttering, Brompton started from his seat in great excitement. Lifting his large person to his full height, and folding his arms over his breast, he looked down on Judge Ellingwood with a powerful but suppressed emotion, and exclaimed, "I had supposed this unpleasant topic would have been avoided. No man more than I deplores the cruelties to which you allude. Our people have been, indeed, for the moment, misled, nor are your own soldiers guiltless of excess. As gentlemen, as Christians, as Americans, we must equally abhor every outrage in the hospital or on the field. You have met in other days Southern Statesmen beneath this dome, and you know well their chivalrous honor, which would have spurned inhumanity as cowardice. Believe me their sons are not degenerate."

Judge Ellingwood also arose during the delivery of these sentiments, and with a pleased smile and glowing countenance extended his hand to his friend, and replied, "Pardon me, my dear General, for introducing this subject. I knew too well your native nobility to suppose you could speak otherwise. Let us be seated, and be calm." The gentlemen resumed their chairs. "We," continued the Judge with studied composure, "as lawyers and politicians, unable through age to mingle in the strife of war, can more cooly study events, and comprehend the principles involved in this gigantic conflict. I have given all my remaining powers to my country, and sent my son to fight, perhaps," he added, with a tear, "to die, that we may establish forever the supremacy of a united Republic on this continent and before the world."

"And I," responded the General, "with equal honesty of conviction have devoted myself and my nephew, whom I love as my flesh, to maintain the right of every State to its sovereignty, and am willing to drain these aged veins, if necessary, to prove my sincerity by my blood. Whatever result the sword achieves I will accept during life."

"I know," returned the Judge, "that at present we must differ. Perhaps I am too sanguine. But I think, as this country is united by its history, its interests, its very rivers and mountains, and physical features, on which Almighty God has stamped eternal unity, so I believe it is the destined refuge of the nations, where all blended races are to lose their antagonism, and give humanity its noblest type, and spread liberty over our world."

"And I," said General Brompton, "hold that the North and the South, different by blood, and education, and climate, will work out a better future for themselves and for mankind under separate governments, and for this faith I have pledged my all."

"Permit me, without offence," replied Judge Ellingwood, "to say that this war will result not only in the freedom, but in the political equality of the slave. Without pausing to pursue such speculations, I think we will unite on certain great questions when the struggle has terminated."

"First, Judge, you must win your laurels before we shape our plans under their shadow," interrupted General Brompton; and then, with a mischievous twinkle of the eye, he continued: "I suppose you allude to certain theories now largely discussed in New England. Your women begin by claiming the right to vote and hold office, and will end by sending the men into the kitchen and into the nursery. Or possibly you refer to that Yankee facility for divorce which is fast allying Puritanism to Mormonism. I have heard that husbands now transfer their wives and children as they do their horses and cattle, so that a Court of Justice resembles a stock exchange."

"No, no, no," said the Judge quickly, and blushing slightly with vexation, " I detest as much as yourself the monster exhibited when the soul of an unmarriageable female aspires to masculinity, and treats life with disgust because she cannot unsex her body. To me, our modern departure from the old scriptural rule of divorce, as substantially embodied in the English law, is odious. I referred, however, to the Papacy."

"Ah," interposed the General, laughing, " our ancestral blood will show itself. You, as an hereditary Congregationalist, and I as an hereditary Presbyterian will never find it hard to unite our forces against Rome."

"I have been looking," said the Judge, "beyond the fierce struggles of our present war, and I see in the future a yet more gigantic contest. Heaven grant that it may be determined by the ballot, and not by the bullet! I have been studying the origin, the development, the genius of the Papacy. Its peculiar claims, unsupported by Scripture, must find their sole warrant in the authority of the Church. Now mark me, General—mark me—the infallibility of the body logically implies the infallibility of the Head. The Pope will be eventually declared the source of all truth, grace, and sovereignty. As the representative of heaven he will assert his right to the worship and the government of earth. While such a monstrous pretence will alienate the culture and intellect of the age, it may even increase his power over the ignorant masses, whose reverence for images and invocation of saints have educated them to prefer the adoration of a visible God. Well do the Jesuits know that a declaration of infallibility will compact their marvellous system and add to the

8

vigor of its conquests. A united Protestantism should defend our country from this spiritual slavery."

"I too," answered the General, "discern the tokens of this terrible battle, more convulsing than our present war. Not only all Protestants, but all who love human rights, and human progress, should seek to avert from this continent a dominion eternally inconsistent with human liberty. But, Judge, I assure you that if the Priests in council make the Pope a god, the Kings will soon make him a beggar. However, the loss of his temporal rule may only increase his spiritual power. And now, my old friend, we must cease our speculations, and busy ourselves with facts."

"Yes," said Judge Ellingwood, pointing down to a table piled with confused documents, and then upward to a marble bust of Washington, "that venerable face will soon look on us reprovingly for chatting like boys about the future, when so many grave interests in the present demand our attention."

We will leave the old gentlemen absorbed in the discussions arising during their interview, and return to persons and incidents of another description.

CHAPTER X.

A JESUIT.

THE agony of Mrs. Cleveland after her reproof of her husband and the Bishop was indescribable. When she retired to her solitary chamber a weight on her heart almost stopped its pulsations. Frosts of a premature age crept chilling through her veins. She felt herself bowing to the earth. Her deserted bed intensified her sense of widowhood, and she threw herself upon it, clasping her hands in a temporary despair. Suddenly, in her own home, a chasm had yawned between herself, and her husband. She was not bereaved by death, but by a power more remorseless. A grave is expected at last to separate mortals, and they are prepared for a common catastrophe. *She* was to endure a widowhood, made, not by the will of God—man's tyranny had caused her desolation. After the first violence of her grief had subsided, her spirit gradually settled into the peace which follows submission. Needing sympathy and counsel she sent a note to her Pastor, explaining briefly the nature of her sorrows. Dr. Elton was absent when the messenger arrived. He soon, however, returned, and repaired to the home Cleveland had deserted.

Entering the room of the abandoned lady he exclaimed with an assumed abruptness, intended to divert her from herself, "My dear madam you indulge a very great grief for a very small loss."

"What can you mean, Dr. Elton?" cried Mrs. Cleveland, lifting her eyes in astonishment, while her countenance indicated acute suffering.

"I mean," responded the Clergyman, "that a man who would be lured by a Jesuit from such a wife, and such a daughter, and such a home, does not deserve your tears. You might weep over his grave but not over his cell."

"Oh, Doctor!" she exclaimed, "he had many noble and shining gifts. Our hearts were united in a true love, and until now he has been an example of affectionate devotion. His wealth has been his ruin. Had he been born to struggle he would have proved a blessing to his race."

"Madam, I have no more patience with this thing," said Dr. Elton, with an expression of disgust in his face, and a quiver of scorn on his lip and in his nostril. "These fellows who love the paint of Babylon should go where they can flash in her gold and scarlet without sham or falsehood. We are thankful for their defection. Anything is better than a tinsel imitation. Esop's daw in peacock's feathers with me was never a popular bird. But that a man should desert his wife, is against every law of Heaven."

"Speak gently, my dear sir; speak gently!" interrupted Mrs. Cleveland, closing her weeping eyes, and clasping her hands for a moment. After a brief pause, she continued: "Mr. Cleveland will come pure from the flames. He will not be consumed, but saved." Then looking solemnly upward, and pointing with her right hand, she added: "On the Throne is One who answers prayer."

"But what on earth could tempt the man to forsake his home?" interposed Dr. Elton, impatiently. "To worship a saint is bad enough, but to betray a saint is abominable. How did Satan ever delude your husband into such folly?"

Mrs. Cleveland smiled despite her pain, and said: "If his treachery was to be measured by my saintliness, he would be quite innocent. The history of his perversion is sad, and brief. Its root was in himself. He seemed never to have had any comfortable faith in our holy religion, and his tastes became more and more æsthetical. His hatred of Protestantism was only equalled by his passion for union with corrupt and idolatrous communions. Thus weakened in his heart, the dying agonies of our dear little Ella were keen torments, which made him bitterly arraign Providence. While in this diseased and partially insane condition, he came under the influence of Bishop Frances, and soon leaped headlong into the arms of the Papacy. At last, in his madness, he applied for this dispensation, which has fallen like such a blight on our lives. Oh, our home! our home is indeed covered with a cloud." While uttering these sad words, Mrs. Cleveland for a moment was almost convulsed with a paroxysm of agony.

"Well, Madam," answered Dr. Elton, himself deeply moved: "I will seek, and try persuasion. Perhaps he may be brought back to your bosom, and this midnight be lifted from your heart and house. He may be a Romanist, and yet a husband and a father. I do not understand his Church requires such a renunciation of her children."

"I fear," replied Mrs. Cleveland, "that the disease has not yet exhausted its violence. Perversion seems like a fever, which has its period of contagion, then of frenzy, and then of prostration. My husband's system will, I am certain, at last cast out the poison, but my own faith will

8*

first be long tried. However, go in the name of truth and love, and do what you can!"

"With your permission," said the Doctor, "I will seek an interview with Mr. Cleveland, and without endeavoring to win him from his religion, I may at least try to restore him to his wife."

"Go, my good Pastor, go!" cried the weeping woman. "May Heaven give you wisdom to rebuild these shattered altars of our happiness."

The abrupt, but kind and manly clergyman, bidding her a tender adieu, left her in her tears, and proceeded at once to execute his ungracious and hopeless task. He feared his inability to control his indignation, but resolved to make a strenuous effort. A test of his self-command occurred sooner than he expected. As he passed homeward through a grove, he perceived Cleveland sitting at the root of a venerable oak, whose sturdy trunk was no emblem of an uncertain life, more fittingly seen in the shadow moving with the breeze, and changing with the cloud. After leaving his house, and parting from the Bishop, he had wandered forth in the keenest misery. His purpose was not shaken, but his heart was pierced. The picture of his agonized wife, and forsaken child, and desolated home, was traced ineffaceably on his memory. When Dr. Elton approached, he was absorbed in one last intent gaze, which seemed to carry out his very soul, and fix it on the images of the family group, as they appeared in all their beauty, and grace, and joy, in a photograph hitherto carried in his bosom—soon to be abandoned for ever. His solicitude concerning the dispensation, and his delight at its reception, misled him to believe that his human affections had been crushed. He was now learning that the roots of love can only be torn, by long violence, from the sacred soil in which they have been deeply imbedded. Hearing a step, he looked up, with a tear on his eyelid, and **anguish** on his face. Perceiving who caused the interruption, he hastily restored the **photograph** to his breast. **Dr.** Elton read the situation at a glance, and his indignation at once melted into compassion. **He** knew he stood before a tortured man.

As Cleveland arose, the Clergyman extended his hand in the kindest manner, saying: "My dear friend, we have met in a lovely spot, well suited to the calm of meditation."

"Yes," he responded in a tone of mingled sadness and confusion, "but there are storms of the spirit not to be hushed by the evening stillness of this grove." It was the embarrassment of the moment which elicited a reply, thus exposing the state of his mind.

Dr. Elton answered: "As an old friend, who feels a true interest in your welfare, and attachment to your family, may I not inquire whether there is not yet a remedy for your troubles? It is not too late to repair the ruin wrought in your home."

"Upon this subject," returned Cleveland, "I do not wish to converse. My heart may bleed while my purpose is unshaken."

Said Dr. Elton: "I will use no arguments to disturb your belief in your church, but surely, in the name of law, and of humanity, I may implore your return to a forsaken and anguished wife. Oh, Sir, recall your early love, your exchanged vows, the morning when in yonder church my own voice pronounced Arthur Cleveland and Emily Woodbridge one before God! Now on your very finger is an emblem of your union. Can you tear it away? Would you rob your wife of the name you have given? Will you cast her on the world? Will you consign to strangers the education of your daughter? Will you leave your home without its protector? Will you make a widowhood by being even more cruel than death? Think of the years which have come laden to you with their bliss! Think of the little grave, over which I saw you weep as I pronounced the solemn committal, and consigned your Ella to the earth! Think of your bright and beautiful Ada, whom you have brought into existence to desert! Think of your wife, who through long years of bereavement will drag along her desolate days, and live only to drop her sorrow into the grave!"

While Dr. Elton spoke, Cleveland was deeply and visibly agitated. After a moment's silence, he replied: "Our former relations, and your kind motives, will excuse this appeal. Only to Him who permits them, and to myself, can my sufferings be known. If I hesitate, it is not for what I endure, but for what I inflict. That faith, of which trial found me destitute, I am honestly seeking in the bosom of the infallible Church. I thank you for your sympathy, while I must reject your counsel."

These words were uttered in a tone indicating that further argument would be deemed an intrusion. Dr. Elton very politely shook Cleveland by the hand, and the gentlemen parted with mutual kindness. The latter hesitated for several days whether to have a final interview with his wife, or to address her a note of farewell. The latter course was at last resolved upon, after consultation with Bishop Frances. It was another arrow in a lacerated heart, inflicting even greater pain than a description in a newspaper of the magnificent pageant, during which her husband was ordained a Priest in the

Roman Catholic Church. Afterward she heard that he occupied a cell in the Episcopal residence. Thus the separating chasm seemed impassable. And yet she felt that her passion to reclaim him from his delusion became, by the very obstacles interposed, more intense than even his own alien and unnatural devotion to Rome. The thought of legal redress, Bishop Frances had well calculated, would never enter her lofty soul. She knew that while marriage was an indissoluble state ordained by God, any compulsory process of law would only complicate mutual miseries.

In the meantime Cleveland, to confirm his faith and peace, and conquer his lingering Protestant revulsion to certain dogmas and practices, was daily committing himself more and more to his Bishop, who rightly judged that no man could be used by Rome until perfectly subjected to the Pope. Frances was seeking daily in all possible ways to indoctrinate and mould his disciple. Coming one morning to the narrow room, or rather cell, which Cleveland had chosen to promote his mortification, he sat down on a wooden stool, while his pupil was seated uneasily on the side of his iron bed.

"Here, my friend," said the Bishop, "I have on this paper a curious calculation. You know statistics rule our age. This table is compiled from the registers of Irish and German immigration. I find that within a half century, simply by natural increase, Rome will govern this Republic."

"Yes," replied Cleveland, while his face beamed with pleasure. "Even the laws of creation are on the side of our holy church. The old birth is more certain for Rome than the new birth for the Protestants."

"How glorious the day," replied the Bishop, while his

eye kindled in anticipation of the triumph, "when we shall have a Catholic President, a Catholic Cabinet, a Catholic Congress, a Catholic Judiciary, and a Catholic Nation, as well as a Catholic Church. Yet that result is certain as the law of generation."

"And a Catholic America means a Catholic World," answered Cleveland, with the exultation of a recent convert.

"Yet," rejoined the Bishop, "it requires all our skill to counteract these republican influences. You know, however, that every movement of Rome is part of a system. One vast machinery stretches over the world, whose centre is the Vatican. Our organization resembles an army distributed over the globe, where every soldier has his assigned duty, and every order proceeds from the Pope as its commandant."

"This is to me," responded Cleveland, with a glowing countenance, "the glory of the system. While Greeks and Protestant heretics have broken away from our communion, our only Catholic Church is diffused over the earth, showing in her infallible head the visible image of her universal Lord."

"See," said the Bishop, rising and pointing through the small window. "See that Cathedral! What could exceed the beauty of its situation, commanding this entire valley, and first arresting the eye of every passer as the most prominent object of the landscape. That cross, lifted to the skies, proclaims the wisdom of the Vatican. Every village in this country is studied on a map at Rome. Every family is known through our faithful servants. Every individual heretic, at all within the circle of our influence, is committed to some special guardian. Every ecclesiastic over the globe has his prescribed task. Thus our organization, directed by the Pope, is wide as the battle-field of Satan. The reflection is grand, inspiring, sublime beyond expression. The result can only be victory," and the Bishop's face shone in the light of anticipated triumph.

"And here," responded Cleveland, catching the enthusiasm, "I perceive the necessity of infallibility in our Great Head. Even an Œcumenical Council would be a cumbersome annoyance. A system so vast requires one unerring sovereign will."

"Do you know," said the Bishop, turning toward Cleveland, and sinking his voice almost to a whisper, "that the Order of Jesus is the pillar of Rome? If our Lord saved the world, Loyola saved the Papacy. His followers, bound body and soul to his Holiness, support his throne, and achieve his victories."

"I am aware of the fact," answered Cleveland, "and the highest aspiration of my heart is to be a lowly member of your society."

"I rejoice over your desire," returned the Bishop, visibly delighted. "It will conduce not only to your usefulness, but your promotion. I have long marked you, even before your conversion, as the Planning of America. Your talents and position give you shining opportunities. I predict for you the most distinguished success among the higher classes of this country, and the most speedy and brilliant reward ever bestowed by a Pope."

Shortly after, in a deep vault of the Cathedral, dimly lighted by a single lamp, Cleveland was initiated into the Order of the Jesuits. Over the altar was a picture of Loyola, with a chain around his body, scourging his flesh, as he stood looking into Heaven, from whose light gazed

down admiring angels. Surrounded by monks robed in
black, Cleveland knelt before the image, and pronounced
an awful oath, binding him forever to the Pope in an
indissoluble allegiance, stronger than any obligation he
could owe to family, country, truth, faith, or life. Soon
after, by another impressive rite, was committed to him,
as the present work of his Priesthood, the conversion of
his former pupils, Edward Ellingwood and Charles
Austin.

CHAPTER XI.

Some weeks after the events just narrated, two men in a skiff were descending a deep and clear stream, winding along the base of the high hills of northern Alabama. The young moon was tracing in a line of silver her faintest crescent on the sky, and the navigation under the dark shadows of projecting rocks was principally by the brilliant light of the stars. A negro pulled the oars, and a round, portly, jolly personage sat steering in the stern.

The latter, at the time our chapter opens, was saying with the slightest Irish accent, "Are you certain, Jumbo, that Major Worstal and Miss Austin are now at Magnolia Springs?"

"Sartin, Massa Preese, sartin," replied Jumbo, resting a moment on his oar. "Dese eyes know Missus Ausson, and dey see dat ar lady dis berry mornin a ridin her white pony, and whar Missus Ausson am, dar spec ollers Massa Wossal. He am wunderful in lub wid de lady, like my Jim lub 'lasses.'"

"Lasses," said the Priest, laughing, "lasses! you mean girls."

"Law, no, Massa Preese. Ho! ho! ho! do gals grow in de suga field? Do gals spirt from de caue? Do gals bile in de kittle? Do gals stick to de fingers?"

"O Jumbo, I understand now. Your nigger wisdom has got at last under my Irish hair. You mean Major

"

Worstal loves his cousin, Miss Austin, like your son Jim loves molasses."

Jumbo, resuming his oars as if his purpose of instruction was accomplished, replied with a nod of approval, and a low, significant chuckle, "Dat am it, Massa Preese, dat am it. You's hit zackly de comprehenshun of de idea. My Jim's brot up on dat same lasses, and nosin now so make de light come from dat nigga's eye as de lasses in de suga-ladle, when de kittle rore. And 'nosin make Massa Wossal's eye bright as de mornin', like de face of Missus Ausson. He gib dis nigga quarta dolla for singin 'bout her in dis yer boat."

"Jumbo," asked the Priest, wishing to elicit some amusement for the hour. "Can't you give me that song?"

"Well, I mus tell carcumstans, Massa Preese," said Jumbo, deliberately taking the oars from their locks, and permitting the skiff to float down the dashing current. "De Maja, he cum from de camp, a glitterin' on his hoss, which fell, and sprain a leg, and walk limpin' to de ferry. He den want to cum to de 'Nolia Springs in dis yer skiff: so dis yer nigga row, and de Maja he steer. He's quire bout Missus Ausson—how she look—how she dress—how she sing—what gemmen visit de house—who dance wid her, and talk wid her—but," he continued with a grin, which showed his ivory to the stars, "he say 'nuffin 'bout de time he ride wid her."

"What do you mean, Jumbo?" interrupted the Priest, who saw, with quick instinct, that he was about to learn something amusing at the expense of his old friend.

"Go on, and tell me all the particulars of that ride. I am acquainted with Major Worstal, and I want to know all about it."

Jumbo drew himself proudly on the seat, and began with all the deliberation and importance of an ancient bard, or a modern orator. "I'se then tell de story fust, and den sing de song. Dar," he said, looking and pointing as if there was an actual person before his large rolling orbs, "I'se jis now see de Maja. He cum on his mar to Ginral Brompton's house at de sea-side. Hah! he look splendid as my ole Nell's Spanish rooster, wid his red crest, struttin afore de hens, pickin pleased roun dar laud, and massa. His shirt-bosom white as de cloud on dat baby moon. His epillettes bright as de yaller corn in Octoba. His sash red as de scarlet cactus in de big swamp. His sword, danglin' and janglin', as he sat proud on de prancin' mar, wid his toe just touchin' of his sterrup. He giant, Massa Preese, a growin' to dat hoss. He gets off, and he rings at de door, and he asks for Missus Ausson, and he strut 'bout jist like our Massa's peacock. Afta dinna Is'e ordered to git Missus Anna's pony, and Jim, he's ordered to git de Maja's mar. But her girt war broke, and dat 'tained Jim. Den de Maja he fly mad, and he cum puffin his seega like de smoke of our cabin chimbley. He run a roarin', and a cussin', and a strikin' at de niggas, specially Jim, and he say: 'Cuss yer Jim, put on dat saddle in a flash.'"

Said Jim, wid a wink at dis yer nigga, his 'spectable fadda: "Massa Maja, shall I put on de saddle zackly as it am?"

"Yes," shouted de Maja, swearin' awfu'. "Jim slap on de saddle wid de girt hangin by a little jibber. I bring out Missus Anna pony, and she look like de picter in Massa's parlor, ob de angel sailin' on de cloud up into de hebbenly light. Den Jim hole de Maja's mar while he mount, and as he pass roun' grinnin', jist when de Maja get on, de mar, she rar, and she run, and she jump, and de Maja he bob, and he cuss, and de girt broke, and de saddle turn, and de Maja tumble spraulin' in de mud-puddle, not lookin' like de proud sodja who cum so splendid down Massa's lane. Ha! ha! ha!" roared Jumbo. "Dar, Massa Preese, I see him, dar. How he look—one patch of mud on de nose—his mouf stuff full—his eyelids a drippin'—his white bosom spattered wid dat vile clay—his uniform tore, and spoiled, and dirtied. He look like de roosta in de rain, or old Massa's peacock, when young Massa Chals, fore he went to college, wid all de young niggas, pluck out his fedders, and he slunk away to hide himself in de swamp." And Jumbo laughed until the big tears rolled down his black cheeks, while the skiff shook as if in a spirit of sympathetic fun. The Priest roared until his powerful voice came echoing back from the hills across the astonished waters.

"Well Jumbo," he said, "that is funny enough. I will have a good laugh at Worstal. But did it cure him of his passion?"

"Lor, Massa Preese, nuffin do dat, 'till Missus Anna put out de flame wid a flat no, like my old Nell, by trowin' her dish water 'stinguish de fire on Jim a scream-in' and a twistin' in de blaze. No, no, dis nigga no sing 'bout Missus Ausson after she gib de Maja de mitten."

While the skiff glided down the star-lit stream, Jumbo began in that clear, melodious mournful voice peculiar to the Southern negro, and poured forth an old plantation-strain slightly modified by his own genius to suit circum-stances. Softened by the waters, the lingering notes returned from cave and rock, to fill night with their sweetness.

Does yer lub yer banjo, Joe,
  When day's work am done,
And de soun' cum' sweet and low
  In de settin' sun?

Does yer lub de mock-bird's note
  Pourin' soft and loud
Dat sweet music from him troat
  Like light from de cloud?

Does yer lub de Sunday song
  When de week is o'er,
Mountin' up so high and long
  To de hebbenly shore?

Dar no banjo, dar no bird,
  Dar no meetin' hymn,
Sound as dis yer nigga heard
  When his Missus sing.

"Well might the Major pay for such a song. I will be generous, and give you double price, and as much more for your story," said the Priest, handing a dollar to the delighted negro. Jumbo had evidently expected some such result, and pocketed the money with that characteristic laugh, and grin only exhibited by the African. Of course he became a fast friend of the Priest, on whose part the donation was as much a calculation as had been the music on the part of the negro.

But just at this point of the journey a blaze of lights was seen on a hill, arising suddenly from the very edge of the water. Behind dark trees the dim crescent of the moon hung like a fairy-chariot, waiting for some beautiful queen of night to glide into its graceful curve, and drive with beamy reins her translucent steeds through the realms of universal air. Also the music of a military band broke in mingling sounds upon the ear. Soon in the distance were heard merry voices, and before the bright windows were seen the forms of flying dancers.

While the Priest is leaving the boat, and climbing

9*

the hill, we will **take a nearer** survey of the apartment. Crossing the threshold we stand in the large dining-room of the Magnolia House.   The chairs and tables have been **removed, and** piled without, close along the wall on the broad verandah stretching around three sides **of the** building.   **Every tree** on the sloping lawn is hung with lamps, whose beams sparkle in the fountain jets, while the collected radiance, streaming far through the midnight, **can be seen for miles.   Even the dark peaks of** the sur- **rounding** mountains are faintly revealed **and** gilded **before** the brilliance expends **itself in** space.   **The ex- hausting heats of a** sultry summer day have been **suc- ceeded by** a delicious breeze, waving in the light the **branches of the grove, and** imparting such coolness to the air, that even the flutter **of a fan is not visible, or** neces- sary.   We behold in our view the beauty and chivalry of the South.   **A** temporary suspension of hostilities has **col-** lected together, from every part of the Confederacy, **men** and women **who seek** forgetfulness and relief **from the** strain and **intensity of** their feelings, amid the **gay scenes** of a fashionable watering-place.

Thus between the blood and roar of battles do mortals sport, regardless **of the carnage which** has preceded, and **reckless of the** slaughter which **may** follow.   **Here** are congregated, in somewhat worn and faded uniforms, yet with bright scarfs and epaulettes, officers of every grade, interspersed with distinguished civilians in grave attire, and elegant ladies dressed splendidly for the occasion. The faces of the men are usually seamed with care, and bronzed with war, and the women often exhibit passing shadows from heavy hearts, while here and there a scar on the cheek, an arm in its sling, or a limp in the gait, show that sword and bullet have left behind their traces.

Still, for the moment, the strains of the music, and the brilliance of the lamps, and the exhilaration of the dance show that joy will soon reign supreme.

We can only now pause to notice especially two persons in the gay, moving, buzzing crowd. At one end of the hall, and towering above all, we at once recognize Major Worstal. While not too closely scrutinized we admire him for his striking manly majesty. His erect form, and huge proportions, in contrast with the inferior group, display him to the utmost advantage. His shoulder-straps direct our attention to his Herculean shoulders, and his brilliant flowing scarf tightly drawn around his waist, gives fullness to his broad chest. His limbs, powerful yet tapering, are equally suited for the saddle or the dance. When we approach, the thickness of his lips, a certain animalism of the cheeks, chin, and neck, and a sinister expression in two unbecomingly small, and deeply imbedded eyes, detract from the pleasure excited by a more remote view. On his arm in all the glow of her rich Southern beauty is Miss Anna Austin. Since we last saw her she has developed into the maturity of her womanhood. But lovely as she is in form and feature, her chief attraction is that expression of her dark eye, and that light around her sweet countenance, which denote a cultivated mind, and a refined heart. She moves in an atmosphere of love. Not a baby-negro on the plantation who does not smile as she passes through the cabin on her errand of kindness. Not a black mother who does not brighten as she stops to notice a sick child, or inquire about a son, or husband out in the blaze of the cotton-field. Not a soldier in the hospital who does not bless her as she glides among the wards, like an angel, to cheer, and relieve the suffering. Not an officer who does not take off his hat with quick salute as she rides along the road, or through the encampment. As she now stands, in simple white, with a diamond on her breast, and a rose in her hair, hanging on the arm of her cousin, it seems as if womanly beauty was leaning on manly strength to gain attraction from the contrast. While the pair stand waiting for the music to begin the dance, they unconsciously draw to themselves all eyes in every part of the vast room. Worstal is evidently flushed with an unusual excitement. When we observe him closely we remark that he often, and ungracefully shifts from one foot to the other, as if he were not at ease. Indeed he beholds in every officer a dreaded rival, and his fear has again made him desperate. Miss Anna is there, a tempting, admired, brilliant prize in the very midst of numbers who utterly eclipse him in talents, and rank, and reputation, and everything but his grand physical proportions. The vast body appears almost conscious that it is not inhabited by a corresponding soul, and the whole man, flesh and spirit, exhibits a state of nervous desperation. The Major has determined to make one more, possibly a last effort. He has failed in seclusion! he may succeed amid the multitude. He will seize some opportunity in the noise of the crowd, to make real the visions which for years have been floating before him like painted morning clouds. Owing to some delay in the arrangements of the band a moment is afforded for conversation.

Bringing his steaming face near the soft cheek of his cousin, the hair on either lip was seen to move, as he whispered in the gentlest tone he could command, "Anna, you always look best on horse-back, or in the ball-room. To-night you are particularly splendid."

"Thank you, cousin Henry," she replied looking from

behind her fan with a twinkling eye, and a gurgling laugh, "I cannot say that you have always appeared to the best advantage on your horse, superbly as you ride. One instance I think I remember when your equestrian costume was rendered not specially becoming. But now you are magnificent, and I am proud to be by your side."

The Major grew more deeply red at the beginning of these words, and smiled faintly at their conclusion. Something in his tone, and manner had revealed to Anna the purposes of his heart, and given shape to her answer. She now resolved to terminate a relation becoming constantly more embarrassing. Before the Major could improve his opportunity the music burst in sudden strains over the hall, and soon the cousins were whirling amid multitudinous circling forms through the mazes of the dance. Notwithstanding the allusion to the discomfiture our friend Jumbo so graphically described to the Priest, Worstal moved with the beautiful girl in all the conscious pride of splendid appearance, and certain triumph. What precisely transpired between him, and Miss Austin can never certainly be known, but he understood during that evening she would never be his wife. His pride would have prevented an exhibition of his disappointment, had not some other circumstances occurred to wound him in a place even more sensitive than his heart. He is suddenly abashed, and confounded. His confidence vanishes. His words are smothered on his lips. His cheeks burn beneath their hair. His very form droops, and sinks. While the dance continues the immediate cause of the confusion does not appear. But when the music ceases suddenly, leaving the Major and his cousin in a part of the hall further from the verandah door, the difficulty discloses itself.

The Major, spurred by his jealousy, had come hurriedly

to the springs on his horse, and not suitably provided for the occasion, so that he was compelled to wear his enormous military boots. He had discovered that one of the high heels was hanging loosely, and must soon give way; and the anticipation of passing through the hall on a limping leg, with the woman on his arm who had just rejected his advances, stung him more deeply than even her unuttered, but unmistakable refusal. Indeed, as he moved blushing and halting along, the contrast between the pride and majesty of his entrance, and the dejection and awkwardness of his withdrawal, was sufficiently amusing. Nor did the winks, and nods, and nudges of his companions in arms diminish his pain and desperation. While Miss Austin had expressed herself by her acts rather than her words, he still imagined that all eyes in the assembly had read his rejection. The mortification of that hour marked his character for life. He retired from the scene at the earliest opportunity, disappointed, chagrined, disgusted—a volcano of burning passions.

As he stood alone in his room he ground his teeth, and tore his beard, and swore vengeance against any man who should ever dare marry Anna Austin. While thus transported by rage, a knock was heard, and the Priest, whom Jumbo had amused in his skiff, entered the apartment.

"Father John," Worstal exclaimed, in surprise, "what in the name of all the saints has brought you here?"

Nothing could present a greater contrast than the jolly Priest and the grim Major. After roughly, but cordially shaking hands, Father John stepped backward, and said playfully to his old friend, "Henry, I have just been studying your countenance, and I infer from certain lines and colors that your dispositions are now not particularly pious. When you invoke me in the name of the saints, I am not at present disposed to rank you among the number."

The Priest then burst into peals of laughter. The fat on his huge cheeks, and about his great neck waved like a river rippling in a breeze. His vast paunch shook with sympathetic merriment, while the tears coursed down his broad face. This still further aggravated Worstal's anger, and he uttered the most startling imprecations.

"Beg your pardon, Henry," at last said Father John, bringing his merriment under control, "but Jumbo rowed me here in his skiff, diverting me on the way by describing that famous ride with cousin Anna. Just afterwards I saw you limping through the room with her on your arm, your *understanding* sadly disordered by the removal of its *sole* support, and your gait not remarkably graceful. The two things together have been too much for me."

"Curse Jumbo!" shouted Worstal, "I will beat the lying nigger to death with his oars, and throw him headlong from his skiff to the fishes. Curse Anna Austin! I will kill the first man who offers her his hand. And curse you for a skulking Priest, Father John," he exclaimed, as he rushed at the merry ecclesiastic, and tried to clutch his beefy neck.

The enfolding fat, however, proved a shield, and prevented strangulation. With a marvellous strength and dexterity, the Priest seized the soldier, and held him as a boa holds an ox, until his passion became exhausted in its utter helplessness. Father John then continued to laugh in safety, as their two bulky bodies were brought into this unexpected contact.

"A warm embrace, Henry," he said, "is bringing our

hearts near after a long separation.   Surely this is ardent friendship."

Worstal now seeing the utter absurdity of the situation, began himself to laugh, and the Priest perceiving he incurred no further danger, relaxed his ponderous arms, and the two men were soon quietly seated.

"Father John," began the Major, "we have not met since you followed my poor father and mother to the grave, and left me a lonely boy on my plantation."

"And yet, Henry," said the Priest with a mischievous laugh, and a peculiar wink of his merry eye. "You have been throttling the very man who said ' dust to dust ' over your parents, and put you in possession of your estate."

"An end to this," replied the Major impatiently, and with some stateliness, and dignity. "Are you not afraid to trust your great carcass over the confederate lines? I heard of you last as a chaplain in an infernal Yankee regiment."

"Oh," replied the Priest with a sudden, and solemn gravity, "My mission is for holy Mother Church. In peace, or war she knows no party. We are after souls, Major, we are after souls. A Priest's gown is the shield of Heaven."

"But the Yankees are after bodies, Father John, and if danger is in proportion to flesh I know of no two men in more peril than you and myself."

The Priest soon disclosed the immediate business to the Major, and received from him a minute account of the history of Charles Austin, with every particular of his family, and estate, and also information of his present rank, locality, and military prospects. A careful record was then made to be speedily transmitted to Arthur Cleveland. Father John communicated his intention to remain within the confederate lines. Soon after he and Worstal retiring were buried in slumber until late the next morning.

How striking the presence of the ecclesiastic, under the circumstances narrated! As the old Rome for centuries, through her history as a kingdom, a republic, an empire, sought by a ubiquitous army to compel the world to her temporal dominion, so does the New Rome, perpetuating an inherited genius for supremacy, endeavor by a ubiquitous Priesthood, to make universal her spiritual dominion. And certainly the spectacle has its sublimity. Here amid all the passions which agitate a Republic torn with civil war, is a silent and pervading agency, regardless of sectional battles, and temporary interests, working to establish on eternal foundations the dynasty of its Pontiff. Thus the artisans of the deep, defying storm and wave, build with unobserved skill, and industry, vast ocean-structures stronger than tempest, or billow, or earthquake.

10

CHAPTER XII.

THE SPY.

"Mr. Cleveland," said Bishop Frances, as he sat in his study, with the gentleman addressed, "I have conceived a capital plan, relating to yourself."

"You are always busy, my friend," he replied, "in instructing my ignorance, and advancing my welfare. May I inquire what your new project is?"

"I have been reflecting," said Frances, "that while your gifts are evidently best suited to influence the more cultivated classes of America, that yet the man who may shape this country for the Church, should understand the masses."

"If I could indeed, aspire to such a work, I should certainly seek the knowledge you suggest. But, that ambition on my part seems absurd."

"My dear President," returned the Bishop, "a scarlet hat must represent St. Peter in this country, and the man who wears it, should be educated for his mission."

Cleveland flushed at these words, into a redness equalling the reward which was to dazzle round his brow. "I entreat you, Bishop, do not return to this subject," he exclaimed hurriedly.

"Rome," resumed Frances, "always studies the populace. The Irish and the Germans in this country, are ours by inheritance, except Orangemen and Turners, whom we consign to mother earth, and father Satan.

"The Chinamen will easily transfer their reverence for

110

their wise Confucius, into adoration of our infallible Pope; and the worship of Boodh and Tau, prepares for the invocation of Michael, and Mary. Even the inherited fetish of the African, will find some point of contact in our system. The Indian will prove more troublesome. His singular devotion to the great Spirit alone, without the mediation of inferior agents, renders him indisposed, like the Jew, and the Turk, to our images, and saints. Even the old Greeks and Romans, through their mythologies, were more accessible. You perceive how our Catholicity embraces the peculiarities of all races, and is broad as humanity. Now you, Mr. Cleveland, to be equipped for your work, must for a period throw yourself among the people. Your associations have been tooo exclusively aristocratic."

"I am willing," replied the disciple, in a glow of young enthusiasm, "to endure any sacrifice, and perform any labor which my superiors deem necessary. But what do you propose?"

"It is my opinion that you had better obtain a chaplaincy in one of the armies; which, of course, to the Church, differs not. She is above party. Father John has just written me that there is a vacancy in the regiment of Colonel Austin. I think I had better apply immediately for the position."

A few weeks after this conversation, two men singularly different in appearance, stood on the left bank of the Potomac, looking earnestly towards the opposite shore. An occasional glance behind showed that they had some apprehension of danger in that direction. In a few minutes a skiff, rowed by a soldier in gray, darted out of a cove beneath the right bank of the river, and came swiftly to the bank from which they were gazing. When the boat reached the shore, both entered in silence, and were rapidly ferried across the stream. The taller, and more slender of the two persons thus transported **was evidently** a gentleman. Guided by the soldier, he proceeded to **a** small and worn hand-trunk, and taking from it a suit **of** Confederate gray, soon appeared in the uniform of an army chaplain. **Arthur Cleveland** was thus commencing the new **duty assigned** by his superior. The soldier who had conducted him **to** the spot, after giving directions for **their** brief journey to the Southern **army,** disappeared, and our old friend was speedily walking along the road with his **new** and singular companion, The **man was in the garb of a peddler.** His entire aspect was puzzling and **ambiguous. His face had some traces** of **a** German origin, but his conversation indicated **a birth in one** of those **provinces where French is** the prevailing language. Nothing could exceed the agility of his small form, the piercing **brightness** of his eye, or the **play of animation** and intelligence on his countenance, **so** that there seemed an incongruity between his pack and his attire.

As they plodded along together **over** an uninteresting road, Cleveland said to his companion, whose name he had ascertained, "I presume, Nathan, that this war has greatly increased the profits of your trade."

"Oui, Monsieur," replied the peddler, "where de 'Merican get de lead de Jew get de gold."

"You must find it dangerous," returned Cleveland smiling at the answer, "to be passing from army to army with your goods."

Nathan turned towards him with a twinkle of the most significant cunning. His face appeared to beam with the very enthusiasm of his craft. He said with a species of mock gravity, "You say de truth, Monsieur Priest. 'Tis von veritie. But de peril make de profit. I visite de confederate camp. I risk dis neck," and here he clutched, dramatically, with his small fingers, that imperilled part of his body, "I see vat dey vant. I advise de partners in de metropolis. Dey bring de goods, and make one soon, vast, huge profite—two, tree, five hundrede per cent."

"Now I perceive," answered Cleveland, "how the Israelites are amassing from this war their rapid wealth."

"Ha, ha, ha," laughed Nathan, "De unyon and de reb, wid dere swords and dere muskets, build our great splendid stores, and de palace, and de synagogue, and de temple for de Jew." Then stretching his hand behind, and striking his pack significantly, he added, "Dis civile war, Monsieur Priest, give us no wounds and scars, but de stocks and de monies."

"However," interrupted Cleveland, "is it right to take advantage of the national necessity? It seems like trading in the blood of our people, and getting fortunes from their graves."

"Ha! Ha! Ha!" responded Nathan with a shrewd leer. "De bisness of de Jew is de monies. De friend of de Jew is de monies. De countrie of de Jew is de monies. De life of de Jew is de monies."

"But how does it now happen that you are buying lots and building houses, while once you had only personal property, so that, bound to no other land, you could at any time return to your own? Have you lost faith in your religion?"

"Ah," replied Nathan, lifting up his eyebrows, and elongating his face, "de monie better dan de prophecie; a house for ourself dan de promise for our cheeldrens; a store on de Broadway dan de hope in Jerusalem."

10*

"Do you then no longer expect restoration to the holy land?"

"By gar," said Nathan, "de monie fulfil de prophecie; de monie buy from de Turk de citie of Daveede; de monie make de meellenneeum."

"Then your creed," rejoined Cleveland, "begins and ends, I believe, in money."

"And vat, Monsieur Priest, is your creede, ven vidout de monie de souls burn in de flame of de purgatorie by de word of de infalleebelle Pope?"

"Ah, Nathan, I discover that you neither believe in an infallible Scripture, an infallible Messiah, or an infallible Pope."

The Jew stopped and laid his hands on Cleveland's arms, gazing piercingly into his face, and said, emphatically shaking his head, "No, no, no,—never in de infalleebelle Pope. Do de Pope eat? Do de Pope drink? Do de Pope sleep? Do de Pope go craze wid de fever? Do de Pope grow old? Do de Pope die? Do de Pope turn to de dust? Do de Pope feed de worm? If de Pope be mortale in dese tings he be mortale to err."

Cleveland winced under the shrewd thrusts of the Jew. They touched him more deeply than a labored argument provoking a studied reply, where the force of his adversary's reasoning would have been lost in his effort to furnish a learned answer. But just at this point of the conversation appeared two persons on horseback, evidently subordinate Confederate officers, and fully armed with sword, pistol, and musket. One was a man of gigantic frame and powerful muscle. The other was pale, attenuated, and diminutive, but wild in his expression and determined in his air. A cloud of dust enveloped the horsemen as they rode furiously toward our travelers.

Both drew the rein as they approached. The smaller equestrian, leaping to the ground, demanded Cleveland's passport, while the larger, dismounting, seized the Jew with the utmost violence, and taking from his pocket a stout rope bound him tightly by the wrists. Nathan submitted to the disagreeable operation with a perfect composure. Cleveland, having satisfied the inquisition of the officer, proceeded to inquire the cause of this strange violence to his companion.

"This cursed dog," exclaimed his captor, "is no Jew, but a Yankee spy. Our order is to escort you, Mr. Priest, to the camp, and hang this rascal on the first tree."

"But certainly," said Cleveland, in a tone and manner of great excitement and alarm, "you will give him an opportunity of trial before execution?"

"I have no discretion," replied the soldier, grimly, and chewing more vigorously the tobacco-cud between his long teeth. "Only last week the villain came to our camp disguised as a nigger. We soon discovered the cheat, tore off his wool, and removed his soot, and were taking him to be shot, when he burst from the guard, ran for the woods, and dashed into the river. A hundred muskets blazed after him as he swam, but he was unstruck. Reaching the opposite shore dripping and nearly naked, he most provokingly applied his thumb to his nose to signify his triumph and contempt."

The officer then turned towards Nathan with a glare of savage vengeance, and said between his teeth, while he shook his huge fist over his victim. "The dog shall die without trial, and without mercy." During the progress of this conversation, Nathan stood calm, scrutinizing the faces of his executioners as he would have examined the countenance of an expected purchaser. Nothing could

have been noticed peculiar in his demeanor except when
the gaze of the officers was for a moment withdrawn,
Cleveland observed him, with a sly wink, and a peculiar
smile, elevate his tied hands, while by their awkward
movements, and a peculiar jerk of his head, he seemed
attempting some adjustment about his neck. The party
then passed on until they came to a wood skirting both
sides of the road. A sapling was deliberately selected by
the officers, and their united strength bent it to the
ground. A rope was then tied around the neck of Nathan
without the slightest remonstrance, or resistance on his
part. Cleveland thought that he noticed again the same
equivocal expression almost of amusement playing over
his face which he had observed before.

The tree having been held by the two confederates
firmly in its bent position was suddenly let loose, and the
spy flew violently upward, dangling, and struggling, high
in the air. One of the officers levelled at the suspended
form his musket to make sure work, when hearing a voice
on the road, he lowered his piece, and turning around did
not resume his purpose, supposing that the bullet was not
necessary to complete the work of the rope. Cleveland
was astounded, and sickened by this first experience of
the cruelties of war, and turning his gaze from the body
of Nathan, now hanging still, with an occasional convulsive quiver shaking the branches, and leaves of the
tree, he perceived that Charles Austin, was seated on his
horse, just behind him, also looking upon this sad spectacle of death. He at once moved towards his former
pupil, while the joy of the meeting banished every shadow
from his face. The Colonel was equally pleased to see his
new Chaplain.

After the most cordial greetings had been exchanged,

Austin, pointing to the body of the spy, said : " Ah, Mr. President," using the old title, " that is worse punishment than our Faculty inflicted on mischievous Freshmen and defiant Sophomores. But the necessities of war are imperative. I had information the rascal was coming, and solemn as is this scene, I must smile to find you traveling to our camp in such company. Please mount this horse, which Jim has led here for you, and the remainder of your journey will be more comfortable, and, I trust, in better society."

Cleveland gladly acceded to the offer, and the two gentlemen were soon riding side by side conversing, as if they had never witnessed the ghastly spectacle they were rapidly leaving behind.

" I hope, my dear Chaplain," said the Colonel, " you will be pleased with your new vocation. If war has its sorrows, it also has its joys. To promote your comfort, and enjoy your company, I have ordered a hammock for you in my own tent, should you choose to share the quarters of your old pupil."

" Thank you, my dear Charles, thank you," replied Cleveland, intensely gratified with so friendly and thoughtful an arrangement. " Nothing could suit better. The pleasure of your company will be a compensation for all my privations."

As these words were concluded, the party reached the summit of a hill, from which the confederate camp burst upon their view. There was an involuntary halt to survey the scene. Austin kindled, while he gazed. His eye flashed. His face glowed. His form dilated. His soul seemed beaming with enthusiasm through his body.

Standing in his stirrups, and lifting himself from his horse, he leaned forward, and pointing, with his gloved hand, he exclaimed: "See! how grandly that banner floats in the setting sun! My heart beats in sympathy with every waving fold. It may pass through storms of bullets and balls, and shells. It may be torn on many a field of carnage. It may be stained with the blood of friend and foe before its day of triumph. But it shall fly victorious over the capital of the Confederacy, even if my body lies ghastly beneath its glory. Pardon me, Mr. Cleveland. I am ashamed of my excitement. I know you have renounced the world for the Church, and cannot feel, as I do, the inspiration of such a spectacle."

"My dear Colonel," replied the chaplain, "I shall never mingle in any discussions in regard to this deplorable controversy. My mission is to relieve suffering and save souls. The Church, and not the country, claims my devotion. Still I can understand the glow of your own consecration, by feeling the ardor of my own."

And certainly the scene beneath their feet was adapted to inspire the emotions we have recorded. The encampment was situated in a cultivated valley, encircled by high hills, through which, between green banks overhung by trees, wandered a mountain stream. Its waters sparkled and purpled in the last beams of day, mirroring beneath the tents the mingled verdure of leaves and whiteness of canvass. In the centre rose an immense pavilion, over which floated the magnificent standard to which Austin had pointed with such enthusiasm. On every side stood rows of tents. Within a large enclosure, were drilling numerous bodies of troops, whose bayonets were glancing in the slanting light, while officers were riding rapidly from point to point, waving their swords, which seemed flashing in circles of fire. The rattling of arms, and the shouts of command, could occasionally be faintly heard, when the breeze blew more strongly. Behind the opposite hill, the sun was apparently poised on the tree-tops, and then sinking and wavering, a crescent of flame gleamed through the branches. Suddenly a peal of music burst from the band, mellowed by the distance. While Austin and Cleveland are riding down the hill, and proceeding leisurely to their tent, we will relate what was transpiring in another part of the country.

CHAPTER XIII.

WOMAN'S SPHERE.

UTTER desolation pervaded the heart of Mrs. Cleveland when the violence of her grief expended itself. Every object in her home recalled a happy past, and became an arrow in her heart. Thus her joys were causes of tears. When she pressed Ada to her bosom each feature of her countenance recalled the image of her father. If she visited the grave of Ella, she always fancied standing over it the form of her husband. Yet amid her trials she retained confidence in Heaven. Indeed, her conviction that Cleveland would be eventually reclaimed constantly strengthened. She was greatly comforted in the midst of her sorrows by receiving a letter from Mary Ellingwood, breathing the most delicate sympathy, and containing a cordial invitation to Willow-Shade. The Judge added a postscript urging, in a paternal manner, an immediate compliance with his daughter's request.

Mrs. Cleveland, having previously returned to her ancestral Presbyterian faith, made her preparations, and in a few days, accompanied by Ada, was most hospitably received by friends, whose kindness increased as trials multiplied. A bright New England May, amid the fragrance of roses, the bloom of orchards, the sparkle of streams, and the song of birds, restored, in some measure, a widowed spirit to its wonted cheerfulness.

Mrs. Cleveland and Mary Ellingwood sat one morning

120

on a bank at the foot of the garden. Above them was a large willow, whose tapering boughs waved dripping in a brook, making the softest music with their gentle motion. We will approach them in the midst of an earnest conversation. The object of Mary had been to draw the mind of her friend from the contemplation of her sorrows, and she had completely succeeded.

Coming near, we hear Mrs. Cleveland exclaim, with the greatest animation and emphasis, "Never, Mary, will I believe, never, that the sphere of our sex was intended to be what many of our female lecturers and writers so violently maintain."

"Miss Humly, for instance," said Mary, with a bright laugh, "who never can get a husband, and Mrs. Stinger, who can never live with her husband. As Ned says, if women are to be wasps or butterflies, he prefers the butterflies."

Mrs. Cleveland smiled, but proceeded in her own graver manner. "The delicate organization of woman indicates that she was intended for retirement. Certain pursuits heretofore restricted to men should certainly be opened to her ambition. While often succeeding as a physician, yet in surgery are necessary operations from which she recoils, and which would roughen her into a disgusting masculinity."

"I was tempted, not long since," rejoined Mary, "to hear one of the strong-minded defend the rights of the sex. In attire she was neither man nor woman, but a mixture of both. She was evidently a male spirit in female flesh. Her face was in bass, perhaps brass, and her tone was in treble. She complained of oppression, and glared defiance. She plead for masculine privileges in a feminine voice, whose squeak was her refutation. Her mistake was in supposing all women like herself,

11

inclined more to fight than love. If she were right, I am sure our sex would soon govern the world, and the men retire in disgust to the kitchen and the nursery."

"Well, Mary," answered Mrs. Cleveland, "your words are graphic as colors, and they lose nothing from your manner. And now suppose woman admitted to the ballot. How repulsive to have her opinions discussed by the town, and her vote made the subject of bets as well as of speculations! The secret ballot is a public wrong, and imagine a lady pushing through a yelling and insulting crowd, to decide some excited political contest. Besides, there are certain periods in the history of the mother when seclusion is essential to delicacy, health, and even life. God Himself has placed between us and many positions and employments His own eternal barrier. The very form of man indicates that he was intended both for the sterner pursuits of peace and the dreadful struggles of war."

"When," added Mary, "the rougher masculine nature requires to be soothed, and refined amid the quiet scenes of home, let our women become Amazons, and where will be the influence of mother, and wife, and sister? Those images of love which soften and elevate, would vanish from the world. Our race would degenerate into vulgar brutality. The touch of womanhood not only beautifies but preserves society."

"Moreover," interposed Mrs. Cleveland, "If we vote, we should fight. We can claim no privileges we cannot defend. The ballot implies the sword. Imagine a company of women marching against a blazing battery, or firing from a ship wrapped in flames and shattered by shells! Conceive a female Farragut before the thunders of Fort Philip!"

"Preposterous!" cried Mary, greatly amused at the picture. Then laughingly holding up the needle and scissors she had been using in work for the soldiers, she said: "Behold the suggestive weapons of our warfare! It's ours to heal and not to wound; to nurse, and not to kill; to be angels of mercy, and not ministers of destruction."

"And I often think," rejoined Mrs. Cleveland, "that a devotion of my whole life to relieve suffering is a duty I owe to my country and my race. The yearning to forget myself by assuaging the miseries of others is almost irrepressible."

These words thrilled the heart of Mary Ellingwood. She arose from the grass, and stood before her friend, glowing in the beautiful light of her young womanhood. A tear trembled in her blue eye. Her voice melted into tender tones of sympathy. A halo appeared to encircle her white brow.

"Mrs. Cleveland," she exclaimed, "you have touched a responsive chord. While my noble brother, and thousands of our soldiers are enduring privation, and braving death for our flag, I reproach my indolence, contented amid the winter blaze, or beneath the summer shade, to scrape lint and cut bandages. Let us go with our sisters! Let us seek the wounded and the dying! Let us labor in the hospital and on the battle-field! Pardon me if I have transgressed delicacy by suggesting what should have proceeded from yourself as the older, and the wiser, and attribute my boldness to the excitement caused by your own words."

Mrs. Cleveland had, however, caught the enthusiam. Arising also from the bank where she reclined, she clasped Mary in her arms, and bathed her in her tears;

and then and there, beneath that willow-shade, and on the margin of that bright stream, these Christian women resolved, in their appointed sphere, to devote themselves to the relief of their countrymen. Heaven approved their vows, and prepared their way to scenes of organized usefulness, amid which they were to feel themselves parts of a vast system of benevolence, reflecting glory on the nation and the age. They had scarcely concluded the conversation we have narrated, when the venerable form of Judge Ellingwood was seen approaching.

"Why, Mrs. Cleveland," he exclaimed, playfully, "Willow-shade is no spot for tears. If I find you here with such a sad face I will cut down these trees, and call my place Vine-side. The grape is the emblem of joy, and you know I love cheerfulness."

"Dear father," responded Mary, "Mrs. Cleveland and myself have been conversing on serious subjects."

"You astonish me, Mary," replied the Judge, with a smile of playful incredulity. "You too sober! Impossible! My grave willows will turn themselves into vines with as much ease as you will get the mischief out of your eyes, and the smile away from your lips. What does all this mean?"

"Your daughter," answered Mrs. Cleveland, "and myself have been talking about our suffering soldiers. We wish to give our efforts as well as our prayers to their relief."

Judge Ellingwood started at this suggestion, and was greatly affected. He stood a moment absorbed in reflection. Then stooping down he took the hand of Mary, and affectionately kissed her cheek.

"My child," he replied, looking down upon her with mingled love and admiration, "I shrink from the desolation my age will experience in your absence. My home will indeed be lonely and my heart oppressed. Yet I cannot withhold my assent. I have laid my son on the altar of his country, and I am willing to place my daughter by his side."

" Oh, dear father," exclaimed Mary, kneeling and bowing reverently her graceful head, "let me have your blessing !"

Mrs. Cleveland was instantly in the same posture by the side of her friend. The Judge, placing a hand on the brow of each, looked up to Heaven, and silently commended their plans and their persons to Almighty God.

11*

CHAPTER XIV

"Mr. Gordon," said Edward Ellingwood to an immense man standing by his side on the deck of a steamer, "what can be the explanation of these movements? We have digged across an island, and cut through a swamp, and our work is all to be abandoned. We are ordered on to-morrow to turn our boats in the opposite direction."

"General," replied the stalwart Chaplain, "trust Grant and the Almighty. Old Fort Donaldson has been in his furnace since he came to Mississippi."

"Furnace! Parson, furnace!" replied Ellingwood, laughing, "he has seen more water than fire. He has been rather in bayous than flames."

"Beg your pardon, General," said the Parson, with a majestic air, and a lofty wave of the hand. "Moral furnace, I meant, moral furnace!"

"Well, Gordon," answered Ellingwood, greatly diverted, "we are tired with a long day's labor, in forcing our way through vines, and trees, and over logs, and alligators. Let us improve the silence and coolness of the evening, by a further discussion of your views."

The Parson looked pleased. As the full southern moon is pouring over him her light, through waving limbs, and festooning vines, in her bright beam, we may observe his person. His proportions are strikingly grand; his height exceeding six feet by several inches. He is bony, and sturdy, although with a slight stoop, and a sunken chest. His eye is blue, and his voice has a marvellous and powerful penetration. His hands are in perpetual motion, and, indeed, the whole man overflows with an excess of nervous influence, magnetizing with an infectious restlessness all who approach him, so that you lose your ease the moment you are in his presence. While gifted with a vigorous intellect, and a vivid fancy, and a true heart, a defect of early education has not lessened his natural vanity. He walks and talks as if he thought the zenith was always particularly over the head of the Rev. Granite Gordon, while the creation was circling round him in obeisance.

"General Ellingwood," he began, after a short silence, "Grant is iron. The age is iron. We have iron railways, iron locomotives, iron telegraphs, iron cannon, iron ships, iron houses. Iron will knock over nobles, kings, the pope himself. Iron will usher in the world's millenium of liberty."

"I thought," replied Ellingwood, smiling, at the incongruity between the Parson's vocation and opinions, "that the Gospel was to achieve this mighty work for humanity."

"Iron," answered Gordon, with an imposing shake of the finger and emphatic nod of his huge head, "is the John the Baptist crying in the wilderness to prepare the way. The yell of the locomotive, and the roar of the cannon are heralds of the coming glory."

"But what connection," interrupted Ellingwood, "has these views with General Grant and these miserable bayous?"

"The iron men in this age and nation alone succeed. Even on Wall street iron makes gold. Iron builds our palaces along our Metropolitan avenues. The days of gilded kingship, and silvered aristocracy, and brazen ecclesiasticism have yielded to iron. Now Grant is iron—a man of his age—and Mississippi is his furnace, and he will come out of it like a Parrot-ball and knock this rebellion into fragments."

"Well, Parson, you are an iron prophet," said Ellingwood, laughing so loudly that the guard on the deck stopped his round, and three sleepers from below showed their heads above the stair-hatch, "but your predictions are all golden, and I accept your theory. Inspired by your faith we will turn round our boats with glad hearts. Now grant me one more favor."

"Anything, anything!" he replied, with the most emphatic and affectionate earnestness. "Granite Gordon will oblige General Ellingwood at any sacrifice, as soon as he would preach to a sinner or fight a rebel."

"My brave Chaplain," responded the General, "I owe my life to your courage, and yet have never before had time to learn the particulars from your own lips. Let me have the story."

"Certainly, General, certainly," said Gordon. "Hah! hah! hah!" he roared until his voice rang into the night, startling the silence of the moonlit swamp. "I never could tell since that immortal hour whether I was born to fight sin or fight the rebs."

"Perhaps," interrupted Ellingwood, laughingly, "your vocation is to fight both."

"Very likely," replied the Parson. "My motto is Methodism and the Union against the kingdom of Satan and the hydra of Secession."

"Returning to my request," anxiously exclaimed the General, knowing his Chaplain's grandiloquence on these themes would only terminate with the morning dawn, "I have always been puzzled to know where you obtained the sword and pistol with which you executed such fearful destruction on my enemies, and delivered me from a frightful death."

Gordon drew himself up in the bright light of the moon, saying, "General Ellingwood, I was born among the Penobscot pines. Nature wrote on my soul, Soldier; Grace blotted over the words, and substituted, Parson. But in the battle-blaze, the old inscription comes out effacing the new, as letters made by indelible ink before the chemic heat of a hot iron."

"A most satisfactory theory certainly," answered the General, "equalling your speculations on that metal. Now let me have the facts of the rescue."

"Do you remember, General, when you commanded as Colonel, how your regiment was posted on that illustrious day at Murfreesborough?"

"Perfectly," said Ellingwood. "We stood on the skirt of an orchard with a confederate battery on the crest of an opposite hill."

"Well, sir," returned the Parson with his most magnificent air, "when I saw our splendid boys with their muskets gleaming in the sun, our standard streaming above their heads, and the light of battle sparkling from their eyes, while the cannon of the rebellion were bristling, and bragging in our very faces, it stirred old Penobscot in Granite's breast. The fires of my Puritan ancestors rushed down my limbs, and up into my face. Nature was overcoming grace. Parson faded, and soldier blazed. I retired to my tent for prayer. As I arose from my knees I saw a short sword, and a revolver. My heart ran out after these carnal weapons, and my hands clutched them. The sword was concealed under my chaplain's coat, and the pistol placed in my pocket. These are, I thought, answers to prayer, and instruments of Heaven."

"So," interposed Ellingwood with a laugh, "you were armed for two worlds."

"As I passed from my tent," continued the Parson, "I saw you on your black charger at the head of your regiment, in full uniform, riding amid whizzing balls, and glowing with the inspirations of war. It flashed on me that Providence had armed me for your rescue—perhaps for your salvation."

"I fear," said Ellingwood, with assumed gravity, "the carnal and the spiritual were contending in your breast—always half soldier, half parson."

"When you charged," proceeded Gordon, not noticing the interruption, "I was on the edge of the battle, stooping to pray over a poor fellow lying on the ground, with his head on a stone, and a bullet in his neck, while his blood came gushing about my feet. Just as his eye closed in death, I opened mine, startled by a thundering cannon ball, which lifted my hair, and stunned my brain. I rose with a whirling, burning head. Looking towards the hill, I saw our regiment torn to pieces, and you standing in the blazing jaws of destruction. I rushed for the dead soldier's horse. I mounted him with a leap. I rode straight for the rebel battery, sword and pistol in hand. All I afterward remember is, that you and I had turned the cannon on the flying enemy, while glory burst from my lips like Niagara."

"Well do I remember those words," said Ellingwood, rising, in the utmost excitement, "above the roar, and shout of battle. Heaven seems to have made you both a preaching and a fighting parson, and I shall always feel I owe my life to your prayers and your sword."

The two men grasped each other by the hand with soldierly warmth, and retired to their respective berths for the night. Soon nothing was heard in that dismal place but the tread of the sentinel, the snore of the sleeper, the hoot of the owl, and the occasional plunge of the alligator, who, tired of the moon, slipped from his log into the dark waters of the swamp.

We may infer from the conversation we have just heard, that Edward Ellingwood had been rapidly promoted for brilliant service from his Captaincy, first to be Colonel, and then Brigadier-General. While best fitted for civil life, he had many qualifications for military service. His head and heart were devoted to his country, so that in the line of his duty no privation was too great, and no peril too dreadful. His evident patriotism, his systematic habits, his reliable kindness, his readiness for any service, his calm courage rising, when necessary, to reckless daring, endeared him to his men, and no young officer had brighter prospects.

When the expedition in which we have just left him, terminated, with the faithful Parson at his side, like a gaunt protecting angel, and defended by huge cotton-bales, he dropped down safely on a gunboat, exposed to terrific batteries, whose circling shells, flaming and crashing, were visible in the blaze from the shore, which converted night into day, and made the Mississippi hideous in its glare. General Ellingwood fought nobly, in those marvellous expeditions, from Grand Gulf to Vicksburgh, which showed that Grant's iron soul had been moulded in the furnace for victory. He planted a standard on the ramparts of Jacksonville; was present on the glorious fourth, when the stars of the Republic again floated over Vicksburgh; and he afterwards stood above the clouds on Lookout mountain, beneath our flag waving in the morning sun, and saluted by shouts from the army in the valley, ringing, amid cave and cliff, with prophetic sounds of final triumph.

CHAPTER XV.

A BATTLE FIELD.

WHAT a Pegasus is Fancy! We mount our winged
courser. We turn towards the star of the pole. We sail
through clouds into ethereal regions. Earth, with her
villages and cities, and plains, and rivers, and mountains,
and oceans, gradually diminishes from our view, and
brightens into one of millions of brilliant worlds, shining
and wheeling amid noiseless space. We draw the radiant
rein. We drop down towards our enlarging globe, all
whose faded features crowd back to our gaze in their
original dimensions and relations. Just as the sun blazes
on the hills, flinging over the sky, his purple and his
gold, we hover above the gleaming tents, and illuminated
banners of the northern section of the Confederate army.
The morning reveille comes faintly to the clouds. As we
descend invisibly to a guard-house, the music of fife and
drum, fiercely pierces our ears. We dismount unnoticed,
and leave our airy Pegasus, who instantly dissolves.

Passing the sentinels, who, with loaded muskets, march
solemnly about a rude log building, we enter the door.
A single candle shines dimly over the small apartment,
and reveals the forms of two men. One appears a
German, rather diminutive, but remarkably athletic, and
with a face denoting quick and artful intelligence. He
lies on the straw, having his wrists and ankles tightly
bound by strong cords. Kneeling over him we perceive
Arthur Cleveland.

"Hans," he is saying, "the proof against you is undoubted. You have been detected, tried, and convicted as a spy. In fifteen minutes you will hear the dead march and swing into eternity. Call on the Virgin and the saints for your salvation."

"D'her vimen and d'her sheeldren prays to d'her Marie and d'her Michaels. Vere Hans Christeen, he pray to Him whom d'her Bible call Got, and says ish everywhere to d'her hear and to d'her help."

"But," rejoined the Priest, "You do not believe the Scripture. It is a solemn thing on the threshold of eternity to have no faith in our holy religion **or our holy Church.**"

"Ah! meeshter preest," said Hans, "our fadderland ish now free. D'her Bible ish von myth. D'her Got ish von scare-crow. D'her hereafter ish von priest-lie."

Then turning his eye to the candle which the morning breeze coming through the cracks of the logs had **just extinguished**, leaving a smoking wick without **a single** spark, he continued with a most significant and horrible expression of countenance, "D'her soul when we **dies ish like dat.**"

Cleveland was confounded and amazed. He had never before encountered a reckless Atheism. The stolid look **of the German increased his bewilderment. Hans, having** thoroughly read Cleveland's inexperience, and produced **the** effect he desired, resumed his blasphemies.

"Mine Old Testament ish d'her Sængerfest. Mine New **Testament** ish d'her Gymnaseeum. Mine Sacraments ish d'her Lager and d'her Terbaccer. Mine **heaven wash** dish yer earth."

The Priest **was now horrified and stupefied, while his eyes were closed in despair over such sacrilegious impiety.**

Hans, by a dexterous movement, learned from our modern jugglers, and, by some, ascribed to spirits, slipped his hands and feet through the ropes, snatched up Cleveland's cloak, which was lying near his head, and passed through the door, exclaiming in a low but distinct tone, "Nathan."

The Priest was more confused than ever, when forced, in this wild way, to a recognition of his former traveling companion. Before he recovered from his astonishment, the spy, wrapped in Cleveland's own garment, was beyond the guard. Fortunately for him, the prison stood on the edge of the encampment, and near a wood. When the alarm was given, and his pursuers rallied, he was some yards in advance. His unerring sagacity avoided the sentinels, whom he knew would be more sparsely posted as he dashed further onward. Speedily a hundred soldiers, with muskets cocked and levelled, were running in pursuit. But the boldness of the escape increased their confusion, while the rapid motion of Hans, and the intervening trees, multiplied the chances in his favor.

Emerging from the woods, he was soon climbing like a goat the rocks of the mountain behind the encampment. As he ascended, the soldiers gazed below in hopeless wonder. Hans leaped from cliff to cliff as if nerved and winged by an inspiration of liberty. He rapidly rose to a crag on the very summit of the ridge. Standing there against the sky, with a defiant shout, he waved his hand in contemptuous triumph. He then made a significant sign showing that Hans on the mountain-top, and Nathan on the Potomac-shore were the same individual. After swinging a few moments on the tree where we left him after our first acquaintance, he deliberately took a knife from his pocket, cut the rope by which he was suspended, dropped to the ground, and placing his hands to his neck readjusted the concealed brass collar which saved his life. A few moments subsequently to his present escape, he went to a cave on the opposite side of a cliff, removed his German attire, and dragging from a cleft the dress of a woman, on that very night he re-appeared in the Confederate camp. Before a week he had reported to a General in the army of the Republic every particular of the intended movements of the enemy. Once afterwards he ventured the disguise of a Chinaman, and made a narrow escape with the loss of his pig-tail. We will again meet him in the course of our story. Here we may, however, state that the close of the war revealed him a graduate of a College. Afterwards he acquired a lucrative practice as a lawyer, and has a hopeful prospect of a seat in Congress.

Arthur Cleveland was greatly confused at the singular escape of Nathan, Hans, or Ling Wau, as we may choose to name the dexterous and versatile spy. Colonel Austin met him with a pleasant smile, and a cheerful morning salute, to relieve his embarrassment.

"Do you know, my dear Chaplain," he said, "that we have received orders to break camp? In a few hours, we will resume our northward march and cross the Pennsylvania line."

"As a servant, Colonel, of both the Church and the State, it is mine only to obey," returned Cleveland.

"I cannot repress," said Austin, "my unusual interest in this movement. Hitherto, I have fought on southern soil. The next shock of battle will be on the territory of our invaders. All circumstances indicate that we approach the crisis of the war."

"Of course," rejoined the Chaplain, "I express no political opinions. My business is with souls, not parties.

Yet I cannot conceal a weight of anxiety on my heart, for our regiment and yourself."

"I have no care whatever," answered Austin. "My whole soul is in our cause. Whatever the incidental evils of slavery it is the corner-stone of rational liberty. Manual labor must degrade, and it is only in a class placed above its necessity and surrounded by wealth, that society can find either its refinement, or its security. Besides, the African is never so happy as when under a suitable master. The slave-whip, the slave-pen, and the slave-tyrant, are indeed inevitable and horrible, but not greater evils than are found in every northern city."

"My dear Charles," replied Cleveland, "I must not participate in the discussion of these questions. May I not call you from such themes to the claims of the Church?"

"No! no! Mr. Cleveland," said the Colonel with a smile, and an emphatic gesture of the head. "Hitherto this subject has been avoided. Now I have neither leisure, or inclination for its consideration. See! See there!" he added, pointing with a kindling face to the encampment already in the buzz, and bustle of removal. "Those preparations will decide the future of this continent. Shall we have two governments, the one based on slavery, and the other on freedom? Or will a single Republic maintain its undivided stars? The question Ned, and I debated on your platform is now to be settled on the battle-field. God bless the old fellow, I should be sorry to find him with a confederate bullet in his heart."

A tear hung on the Colonel's eyelid as he recalled Ellingwood's image, and the frightful contingencies of war.

"Alas," he continued sadly, directing his hand to-

12*

wards the camp. "How many of those poor fellows before our final triumph, will be pierced with bullets, and torn with shells, and wasted with diseases! How many will languish in hospitals, or die on the field amid corpses and vultures! What widows, what orphans, what sufferings, what graves along the path of war!"

"Excuse my interruption, Colonel," interposed the Chaplain, "but I perceive our regiment is in motion."

"Yes," said Austin, "I am silly to indulge in such thoughts. Sometimes a shadow comes upon me cast back, perhaps, from my own doom. Pardon me, my friend, I must hasten to my men."

Very speedily after this conversation the tents were all struck, and the army in marching order. Thousands of troops were soon wearily tramping in dust and sun under their drooping regimental standards, while long lines of horses, and waggons, and ambulances, and caissons and cannon wound over the hills, and along the valleys. The Potomac was crossed partly by fording and partly on hasty bridges. Before many days the confederate army lay in the blaze of July, on Seminary Ridge, just behind Gettysburgh, confronted by the forces of the Republic under General Meade on Cemetery Hill. On the first day of the memorable battle Colonel Austin mingled in the fierce fight to secure Round Top, the true key to the entire situation. He escaped unhurt, although greatly complimented for his bravery. On the second day he was ordered to lead his regiment in one of the most perilous, and important assaults in the history of the war.

As he sat on his white charger in advance of his men, Cleveland stood viewing him with the deepest interest and affection. Austin appeared in his young manly beauty, the ideal of an officer. Dark curls waved beneath his military cap. His black eye shot fire. His scarlet sash displayed splendidly his slight but elegant person, while his hand held his rein with an inexpressible grace, and his limbs from thigh to stirrup would have charmed a sculptor.

But what invested the man with his chief fascination was a glow expanding into an almost visible halo about his face and brow, imparted by the consecration of his genius to a cause he deemed right. Yet Cleveland imagined that he perceived an occasional prophetic cloud across the countenance of his friend. While Austin was sitting on his horse, now pawing with warlike impatience, as his nostril snuffed the battle and his neck curved with its thunders, there was a pause in the cannon-roar which for hours shook the air and stunned the ear. A scorching sun was pouring from the brazen heavens his blaze of beams. Not a breeze now lifted a plume. Suddenly came an order to advance.

Colonel Austin dashed amid assailing thousands against the batteries of the opposite hill. Flame, smoke, yells, thunders burst over earth and sky. On every side flew balls and shells hurling round death. The confederate columns were quickly hid beneath dust and smoke. When the cloud lifted, they were seen reeling, breaking, flying before the triumphant soldiers of the Republic, on whose banners smiled victory at last and forever.

Cleveland now noticed Austin's horse, spotted with blood and snorting with terror, rushing riderless over the field. A weight fell on his heart. His brain seemed whirling round in flame. He ran forward in a delirium, heedless of danger, and was trampled to the ground. How long he lay he could never tell. When consciousness returned the stars were shining peacefully over his head, while from every direction came the shrieks of horses and the screams of men. He was alone amid the horrors with which night invests a field of battle after the carnage of the day. Rising and stumbling through the darkness, he saw a man bending over a prostrate officer, and pressing a canteen to his lips. He heard the words:

"Massa Chals! Oh, Massa Chals! Don't die, or Missus Anna's heart will break. Take, take dis wata, Cunnel Ausson."

The Chaplain at once recognized the voice and form of Jim, as he knelt frantically by the body of his master, and tried to recall the fading sparks of his life. Cleveland eagerly joined in the work of love.

Pressing his face, wet with tears, close to that of his friend, he exclaimed in a low passionate whisper, "Charles, dear Charles, my pupil, my friend; give, oh, give me some token that you live!"

A feeble pressure of the hand indicated both life and consciousness, and as the evening star from her golden urn shed down a ray of peace, Cleveland discerned a languid smile of satisfaction on the countenance of the wounded man. Perceiving now the lips move, and the eye open, he stooped again and heard just breathed in broken whispers, the words, "Take me from this dreadful place to the Convent I saw this morning, while observing the enemy. Jim was with me, and can show the way."

The building to which he alluded had been almost deserted before the approach of the two hostile armies, between which it was exposed to double peril. It stood a few miles from the spot where they were, in a deep solitude of the mountains. Cleveland explained Colonel Austin's request to Jim, and asked him to act as guide. The affectionate creature could restrain himself no longer.

He burst into sobs and tears. He threw himself on the ground. He kissed frantically his master's hand, exclaiming, "De Cunnel Jim's best friend. Jim lub de Cunnel when we boys togedder. Jim help de Cunnel. Jim die for de Cunnel."

The Chaplain deemed it best to let the negro's grief expend its own honest violence. Proceeding then to examine Austin more carefully, he discovered that his wound was from a bullet in his breast. He next gently washed away the clotted blood with water from his canteen, and tied over it a temporary bandage. He and Jim united their efforts in lifting the exhausted and suffering soldier, and carrying him tenderly from the scene of death. For some distance they stumbled over the slain, and often almost fell in the slippery blood. Reaching the edge of the battle-field, their path lay over a narrow log crossing a dashing torrent, and then wound amid rocks up a steep ridge. The horrid sounds of death were fast fading in the distance, when a rising moon began to assist their way. They frequently halted for breath, and to rest Austin, whose suppressed groans told his terrible agony. After a slow and weary journey, whose minutes seemed hours, they saw with irrepressible joy, the white Convent gleaming through the night. Placing the wounded man on the grass before the door, a quick pull of the bell was answered by the noise of an opening window.

A head, enveloped in white, was soon thrust out, and a silvery voice, issuing from a sleek, smooth, shaven face, was heard inquiring: "Who comes below, at this unseasonable hour, to disturb our slumbers? Our Convent should be exempt from attack and intrusion."

The Chaplain, looking upward, at once replied: "I am the Rev. Arthur Cleveland, a Roman Catholic Priest, in a Confederate regiment. I have brought here, with the assistance of a negro servant, our Colonel, Mr. Austin, who is wounded, and, I fear, dying. I know too well the charities of the Church to suppose you will refuse admission to the suffering."

"I recognize your voice, Father Cleveland," was the quick and kind reply, "and can assure you we will be delighted to afford relief to so distinguished an officer. Indeed, it is the business of our Order to assuage all misery."

Soon the bolts were withdrawn, and the party entered. A venerable Monk had charge of the building, from which the Sisters had withdrawn, like frightened doves, before the tempests of battle. As every thing possible was provided for the comfort of Charles Austin, we can leave him among friends, and pursue another thread of our narrative.

CHAPTER XVI.

BEFORE the fall of Atlanta, Edward Ellingwood was placed on the staff of General Sherman, who was already meditating his marvellous march towards the sea. He was delegated to a special service in advance, and took temporary command of a small mounted party. For some unexplained reason, he was accompanied by the Rev. Granite Gordon and the Rev. Peter Ledaway. Having ridden rapidly for a few hours along hidden paths, the company reached a lofty hill, and were making observations of the country. Ellingwood ordered a halt, and stood a little apart with his glass anxiously at his eye, having near him the two Parsons. Suddenly emerging from a wood, a body of Confederate cavalry appeared in such force as to cut them off from their party. The Republican soldiers escaped, while the General and the Chaplains, surrounded by overwhelming numbers, were compelled to surrender, without resistance. They were at once placed in the midst of their captors, and made to ride towards the hills of northern Georgia. After the march of a few hours, in clouds of dust, and under a burning sun, they were embosomed in mountains. While ascending a steep ridge, General Ellingwood and Parson Gordon found they could converse in low tones.

"Chaplain," said Edward, smiling, "this is rather worse than Murfreesborough batteries, Mississippi bayous, or Vicksburgh gunboats."

"General," answered Gordon, with a face greatly elongated, and in a most doleful tone. "I feel sad, ominously sad."

"What, Parson," replied Ellingwood. "You despond! The American eagle may as well fold his wings, and make himself a mark for rebel bullets."

"You may laugh, General, you may laugh; but I know you will never doubt Granite Gordon's grit."

"Never, Chaplain, never," quickly returned Ellingwood. "Your parents well named you for our New England hills."

"As you will not question my courage," resumed the Parson, "I may tell you a dream I had on last night. The light was burning dimly in my tent, and I seemed to doze rather than sleep. Suddenly I was transported to the pines of Penobscot. On a mountain cliff I saw sitting a gray eagle. It was the very bird I shot when a boy. I knew him in a moment. As he poised himself on the rock, I dreamed I saw a gigantic serpent crawl and encircle him in fatal folds. The eagle screamed, beat his wings, struck his enemy with his beak, rose with him in the air. Frightful the snake's eye, and crest, and lambent tongue, as he hissed, and wound more tightly about his victim. The bird carried his foe into the clouds, and the serpent soon dropped through the air dead upon the earth. A load was taken from my breast, until I saw the eagle stop, flutter, and then fall, like a thunderbolt, from the heavens. Afterwards I ran and found his mangled body, and read in his doom my own. As the snake killed the eagle, Granite Gordon will soon perish in the coils of the rebellion."

While the Parson, in his grandiloquent, but impressive manner, narrated his strange dream, Ellingwood experienced an ominous tremor creeping, and chilling through every vein. He endeavored to answer laughingly. His unconcern was only too evidently forced and assumed.

"Parson," he said, "this will never do. We are not men to be scared by dreams. Leave signs and wonders to women and children. The greatest marvel I can conceive would be to see you sink beneath misfortunes."

"General Ellingwood," replied the Chaplain, "mine is no coward's fear." Then checking his horse for a moment, and turning his great blue eye, in which stood a single tear, full upon the face of his commandant, he resumed. "I shall never see James, and Sarah more. I am soon to pay the penalty of my own carnal courage. 'They who take the sword shall perish by the sword.' I now see ministers should be men of peace, not of battle. Our weapons are not swords, and revolvers, and cannon, but prayer, and faith, and love. How terrible for us to send into perdition souls we were called to save! My courage was of earth and not of Heaven, and soon I must suffer for my sin. General, when I saved your life I lost my own."

Ellingwood was so affected by these words that he with difficulty remained in his saddle. Yet attempting again to make light of his own apprehensions, and the Chaplain's forebodings, he said with a smile, "I would not like to trust your meekness, Parson, if you were sure you could fight your way through these fellows." These words seemed to strike a momentary flame from the eye of Gordon. The blood rushed to his cheeks. As he raised himself in his stirrups to make a survey of his enemies, his chest heaved out, his lower jaw assumed the rigidity of iron, his teeth became clinched, his form

13

towered gigantically, his face exhibited an unearthly grimness. He seemed calculating the possibilities of success in an attempt against such odds. In a moment, however, he looked as if satisfied that his day of carnal struggle was over, and he sank back into his saddle an altered man. The last sparks of his earthly nature had faded forever in this final conflict. The subsidence of his pugilistic emotions was followed by a heavenly peace which breathed from every lineament of his great, rough, noble face, until it seemed impressed with that beauty of meekness so remarkable in Leonardo's picture of our Lord. Ellingwood recognized that light as a beam from above, resembling the sun-rays streaming down through clouds from the calm vistas of the evening.

"General," began Gordon solemnly, "I seem all my life to have been a great, bullying, blustering, egotistical Parson. I see myself as never before. This too is a prophecy of my fate. I magnified myself, and misjudged you. Your book-prayers seemed a formal mockery. Religion I now understand may be like the still light as well as the shouting tempest. Forgive me, General, I did not intend to be uncharitable."

Here the Parson extended his huge hand, which Ellingwood grasped almost convulsively, and shook with the greatest warmth. The two men now completely understood each other.

"My own dear Commander," resumed the Chaplain, with a tone and look of inexpressible tenderness, "Granite Gordon draws near his Jordan. Beyond are the celestial fields. Heaven is opening to my vision. I am not like you, a College-man, but I have read much, and thought much, and prayed much. Mark my words! This war which began to determine the question of secession, will terminate in giving not only freedom, but the ballot, to the negro. Parson Gordon exhorts you, with his dying breath, to never cease until political equality is established firm as these mountains, and lasting as yon heavens."

Ellingwood turned on the Chaplain with amazement. Although his style was somewhat stilted, his manner had the solemn eloquence of a Prophet. While the General was gazing at the face of the Parson, he was startled by repeated cries of "Glory! Glory! Glory!" Nothing could exceed the thrilling power of his tones, while Gordon's great frame heaved, and trembled with emotion, and his countenance became lustrous with enthusiasm. The guard paused, and stared in amusing astonishment. The Rev. Peter Ledaway started from his horse reddening in a guilty confusion.

While the party thus stopped in a way so strange, and unexpected, a cloud of dust appeared on the road near the top of the mountain. The confederates instantly cocked, and leveled their muskets. Their Captain shouted, "Hold! who comes there? Stop, or we fire!" Heedless of powder or command, on rushed the riders, and soon were discerned the immense face and form of Major Worstal.

"Halt!" he cried in a tone whose loudness corresponded to his size, while rage seemed working in every feature. The guard, perceiving their commander, shouldered their guns. "March!" he yelled with the utmost vehemence, and he and his party turning their horses, were followed by the capturing company and their pursuers. After riding some distance in silence, a dense forest was reached lining one side of the road. Worstal again cried, "Halt!" The order was at once obeyed. "March these infernal Yankees into the woods!" roared the Major. After proceeding a few minutes the party was again stopped. "Dismount!" yelled Worstal, with the look and gesture of a demon.

When Ellingwood got down from his horse, he was seized and searched from his stockings to his necktie. Nothing was discovered on his person but some federal money, several inoffensive letters, and a photograph. Gordon and Ledaway had also every part of their clothing rudely examined. In the saddlebags of each, Worstal found a paper, which increased his rage. Holding up the fatal documents, he burst forth with an expression of savage triumph, "Look! look! here are the commissions of these infernal Parsons, signed and sealed by their cursed government, as chaplains in nigger regiments!" As the Major, glaring like a tiger, shook the papers before his men, they gnashed their teeth in rage, and looking on their victims, shouted, "Death, death." From peak to peak the solemn mountain echoed, "Death, death!" In the midst of this tempest, Gordon stood erect in his gigantic height, with his arms folded across his heart, and a look of calm, and commanding majesty. Ledaway fell in terror on his knees. He appeared to shrink away into himself. His cheeks grew hollow, and his hair almost like the snow lingering still on the mountains, rising above in the serenity of a mocking sublimity. He embraced the knees of Worstal, who spurned away the abject wretch with a kick. He then clasped the feet of Gordon, and kissed them in his frenzy, and begged for help.

"Look not to a doomed mortal like me," tenderly said the Parson, "but to the compassion of Heaven in the Cross of Jesus Christ."

"Heaven," burst forth the coward, "there is no heaven for me. I have abused its commission, to do the work of hell. Seeming an angel of light I was a devil of dark‧ness. With the same lips I urged temperance, and drank to intoxication. I preached the gospel, and cursed in His name who gave it. I denounced theft, and stole from my country. While pointing others the way of salvation I was myself rushing down to my own damnation. Lost, lost, lost," he shrieked, and the rocks replied, "lost, lost, lost."

Just then, a confederate soldier holding up the saddle-bags of the apostate, took from one end, a pack of cards and a bottle of whisky. This caused the villain's shrieks to be answered by bursts of insulting laughter. Ledaway was one of those fallen ministers, who, unable to withstand the temptations of war, had brought disgrace on himself and his religion. Now caught in his sins he found no place of repentance.

Ellingwood viewed the tragic scene with the deepest emotion, and remarked, how exactly in accord were the very aspects of nature. The party stood on a bold ledge of rock, covered with laurel and hemlock, rising hundreds of feet above the valley, and projecting over a torrent, which dashed, and roared down its gorge, enveloped in spray, and sending up sounds subdued by distance. Immediately behind, towered a dark, lofty, craggy peak, piercing the heavens. On all sides, were circling summits, of every size and shape, thrown up by some ancient convulsion, in such a way, as to perpetuate the wild irregularities of its extinct powers. However, the shrieks of Ledaway draw us from the contemplation of the landscape. His frantic importunities increased his own terror, and the contempt of his enemies. A rope was now produced. The sight of this instrument of death brought forth fresh screams from the wretch. It was placed about his neck, and tied by firm knots. He was then roughly seized by

13*

two soldiers, and forced to the brink of the precipice. A third followed, holding the cord, which, ascending a tree, he made fast to a limb projecting above the torrent, tumbling, and foaming below. The miserable victim was soon hurled with violence over the edge of the rock, and arrested by the cord, he swung, jerking and dangling above the dizzying abyss. After a few spasms, the blackened face, and glazed eye, showed that a doomed spirit had exchanged its place of sin for its place of punishment. A soldier now levelled his musket, and before the echoes of its report came back from the mountains, the ball had cut the cord which was swinging in the wind, and the Rev. Peter Ledaway dropped, resting a moment on an overhanging branch, and then fell crashing into the wild waters far beneath, and was borne toward the vain baptistery of the boundless sea.

Gordon beheld the execution of his unworthy companion with awe, but not with fear. Propitiated by his manly courage, Worstal resolved that he should be shot, esteeming the bullet more honorable than the rope. The Parson asked for his saddle-bags, and they were soon brought. He took from them a Bible and a hymn-book, and placed in each a lock of his hair. Turning to Ellingwood, he held the volumes in his hands, and addressed him with the most calm and impressive solemnity:

' General," he began, giving him the Bible, " this is for my dear wife Sarah, with her husband's blessing."

Ellingwood took the book, but was so agitated it almost dropped from his grasp.

The Parson then held towards him the hymn-book, saying, " This is my gift to James. Tell him his father's last wish was, that he might live and die a faithful Methodist preacher." The Chaplain and the General affectionately embraced, and shook hands in a final farewell. Gordon was conducted unbound, and placed a short distance from the soldiers. He looked unmoved on the leveled guns. A heavenly smile played over his rugged face. While the men were taking their aim, burst again from his lips in thundering tones, "glory! glory! glory!" and from a hundred peaks, mellowed like the voices of angels, echoed, "glory, glory, glory," followed by a mingled volley whose reverberations were in strange contrast. Gordon fell, pierced by a dozen bullets, and his spirit rose exulting to that Saviour whom he had followed and preached with a love so eccentric, and yet so sincere. His friend obtained permission to bury his body.

The confederate soldiers, touched by his bravery, prepared his resting-place on a hillock beneath a pine, which towered a fitting emblem of his own tall person. General Ellingwood read from his pocket prayer-book the service of his Church, and dropping tears on his grave, planted over it a flowering laurel.

CHAPTER XVII.

A MOUNTAIN CONVENT.

THE Convent of St. Mary is remarkable for the beauty of its location. It stands on a height adorned with noble trees, and lifting itself from the middle of a valley encircled by mountains, except where they recede to form vistas narrowing with a gentle ascent until they terminate in the blue sky. Meadows, grain-fields, orchards, with here and there a grove of oak, and beech, and maple, are scattered below in pleasing variety. A clear stream winds along the base of the hills, sparkling and flashing through the leaves when the beams of a western sun fall slanting on its surface. Occasionally on the banks an elm lifts its stately foliage, or the gigantic sycamore exposes its white, bare, unsightly limbs. On the left a few gleaming houses of a village are scattered along the mountain, and far above them a spire rears calmly its cross to heaven. The Convent had been erected by an Italian nobleman, who, tired of the world, had fled from the exhausted civilizations of Europe, and devoted his life to charitable works in our own land of hope and promise. He had taken orders, and spent years in traveling on foot among the mountains, and preaching to the poor. He lavished his fortune in relieving suffering and encouraging art. Indeed, he was one of those lovely characters the Roman Church has sometimes produced, and the memory of his piety is still a lingering fragrance in many a home of that wild and secluded region. St. Mary's had been imitated from a beautiful convent on an Alpine summit which reflects itself in a sunny lake. Everywhere over its walls, and through its rooms, and along its halls, are casts and copies from the ancient masters. The chapel is an exquisite conception, especially admired for its chancel-windows. Our Lord's grand figure rising majestically into heaven forms its central attraction, and imparts a unity so often painfully wanting in such pictures. On Him gaze prostrate disciples. On Him look kneeling apostles. On Him are turned the eyes of angels pausing in adoring awe as they fly above the earth.

The situation and arrangements of the Convent were precisely suited to the purposes of Cleveland, and he thought he discerned in them a Providential assistance. He had eaten, and conversed, and slept in the same tent with Colonel Austin, and yet found not one opportunity to make a direct impression. Now, that gentleman, wounded and dependent, and under obligation to him as a saviour from a lonely death on a dreadful battle-field, is wholly in his power. So suddenly did the scene shift as if to reward his persevering labor. Not, however, relying entirely on his own skill, he summoned to his assistance Bishop Frances, and a whole company of returning nuns and priests.

"Mr. Cleveland," said that Episcopal dignitary shortly after his arrival, "I have been studying the face of your interesting patient in the light of Father John's communications. I am more and more persuaded of the importance of his conversion. Should the South succeed, he will exert a great influence in the new confederacy."

"Austin is indeed a lovely character," replied Cleveland. "He possesses that oratorical facility peculiar to the Gulf States, and, with a thorough culture, has high blood and graceful **manners.** His devotion to his cause is heroic."

"Has he wealth?" **returned the** Bishop, **with an** equivocal expression about his lip, and in his eye. Then pressing the **massive** ring flashing on the little finger of his left hand, he added: "**I mean,** of course, large wealth, which **may** be useful to the Church."

"**You observed,** doubtless," responded Cleveland, looking embarrassed, and out of his **element,** "with minute care the statement sent by Father John. The Colonel is not only rich **in his own** right, but, with his sister, will inherit the ample estate of General Brompton when that staunch Presbyterian departs."

"Of course," said the Bishop, musingly, "those Southern plantations will be sadly injured by the **war. Sherman's** bummers **will not be** too delicate in their consideration. Indeed it is impossible to control an invading **army.** Many a barn and mansion must blaze along its **march.** But cotton will again be king, and his white majesty will soon build ruined fences, cultivate desolate fields, and repair burned houses. England, after the war, will **be** possibly willing to cultivate her old friends, unless they **are** hopelessly bankrupt." Frances here pursued his **own thoughts** farther than **was** politic with Cleveland, who began to **feel** certain uneasy suspicions.

He replied in an entirely different strain from **the** Bishop, whose words found no answer in his own unsordid heart, **saying:** "The intellect and integrity of Colonel Austin will always command respect, without regard **to** his wealth. So pure is his heart, so sincere **his** purpose, and so winning his address, that his **enemies** will forgive his faults, and restore his property."

"Above all things," answered **the** Bishop, in a low

voice, and with a look of wisdom, "avoid argument. He is too weak for discussion, and it will only provoke resistance. Win him by kindness and by prayer. St. Mary, the patroness of our Convent, will assist our holy work. The Colonel is under great obligation to you, and this may be turned to advantage. Be certain that his conversion will not retard your elevation to the Episcopate—an honor, I hope, now near at hand." Cleveland blushed, but did not repel a suggestion, implying he was willing to make the soul of his friend a step to ecclesiastical preferment.

We must now, however, return to Austin. Since his arrival in the North he had suffered from the climate. Even the summer night-dews, to which he had been often exposed on the mountains, affected him injuriously. His system was not, therefore, in a condition to resist the effects of a wound in his lungs, and the consequence was a rapid consumption. He lay day, and night on a lounge, which Jim could wheel to the chapel, and through the lower story of the Convent, sometimes indeed taking his master into the garden, and beneath the trees of the lawn. The hectic of death already glowed on his cheek. A strange fire gleamed from his large dark eye. The veins on his forehead stood out from his skin. A slight, but constant and convulsive cough was exhausting his system. He never spoke except by signs, and only to Jim. His soul was pervaded by a dreamy and delicious languor, while before his gaze rose visions of Heaven. Everywhere his eye was delighted with beauty. The Holy virgin, and her Divine Son smiled on him ineffably from the walls. Venerable Apostles turned toward him eyes of love. Saints mounting through flames into the sky stimulated his devotion. Angels floating before his enraptured soul pointed him aloft. Marble forms, into which pious genius had breathed life and beauty, stood around him the silent emblems of purity. From window, and lawn and grove a lovely landscape, in aspects ever-varying, was pleasing him with quiet scenes, where stream, and tree, and mountain contributed their mingling charms. Morning, and evening, the chimes of musical bells, with their silvery sounds, diffused sweetness through his being, and female voices, solitary, and in chorus, were constantly wafting his spirit to the Gates of Heaven, while the solemn organ with its thunderous peal transported to a height of calm sublimity. His existence thus passed painless into dreamy rapture. Austin had in health despised the puerile mummeries of our Modern Ritualism, which admires Rome as a silken lap-dog admires a splendid lion, and is only fit for silly school girls and foppish theologues. Yet with an intellect perfectly clear he suffered himself to be wheeled into the chapel where in the midst of candles and censers and images, he partook without scruple the bread administered by a Roman Priest, and allowed owing to the peculiarities of a dying man's situation. The simplicity of his faith was its security. He looked for substance, and disregarded form. Still his compliance was construed into proof of his conversion, and Rome had the benefit of its public proclamation, and Cleveland the benefit as its successful instrument.

While events were thus progressing at St. Mary's, Jim rode one morning to a distant village to procure some medicine for his master. Seeing there some Union scouts, he galloped home in the utmost alarm, and throwing himself from his horse, and rushing across the lawn and up the steps and through the hall, he cried, "De Sodgers!

Sodgers! Dey cummin! Dey cummin! Oh! massa Chals, what become of massa Chals?"

The poor fellow wrung his hands in an anguish of apprehension. As the report was confirmed, the whole Convent was soon in a buzz of alarm. The nuns, who had returned after their previous exile, were hurried away to the house of a Roman Catholic gentleman on the mountain, and all things were prepared for the arrival of the dreaded troops. Horsemen soon appeared riding armed towards the building, and it was evident, from the numerous nurses, and surgeons, and ambulances, that the Christian Commission was about to appropriate the Convent as a hospital.

Cleveland retired to an upper room, and resolved to report himself to the federal officer as chaplain of the place. As he stood gazing from a window fronting a lawn, he saw approaching two ladies, on foot, dressed in simple white. Color deserted his cheeks. His eye stared. His form shook. He fell to the floor. Rising with a great effort, he stole into the hall, and went painfully down the stairs, and passed stumblingly through the garden-gate. With sweat-drops bursting from his face, and remorse crushing his heart, he climbed the mountain like a palsied old man, and flung himself headlong with his face on the earth. He had seen Mrs. Cleveland.

That lady, and her friend Mary Ellingwood, came smiling over the lawn breathing from their faces that angelic peace bestowed on those who purely practice works of mercy. The scenery without had prepared for the beauty within, and after entering the Convent, they wandered through its halls, and stood in its chapel in a maze of pleasing wonder. As Mary passed the opened door of a large apartment, there burst from her lips a low cry of astonishment.

14

"'Surely," she exclaimed, pale with agitation, "we are in a land of dreams. We have been gazing at painted and sculptured images until fancy is imposing on our very eyes."

"What can so excite your surprise, Mary," replied Mrs. Cleveland, smiling at her friend's expression of astonishment. "Your practical nature is not easily bewildered by visions."

"It is a reality. There! see there!" she answered, while tone and feature quivered with excitement.

"I only perceive," replied Mrs. Cleveland, with a most provoking want of interest, "a pale, sickly, interesting gentleman, who, from his uniform, I take to be a wounded confederate officer, thrown by the recent battle, on the well-known charities of St. Mary's."

"But, do you not remark the resemblance?" said Mary, in a quick earnest whisper, and with cheeks now white as her dress bosom.

"Resemblance!" returned her friend, "resemblance to whom?"

Mary could not reply, but stood gazing in silent tears. She had never before this moment, confessed to herself, that she loved Charles Austin. Indeed, she seemed too cold, and too bright, for a deep affection. But in her breast was a hidden fire. There had never been between Mary and Charles any pledge, although there always existed preference and sympathy. Still, unconsciously his image had lingered in her heart, and blended itself with all her thoughts and plans. She now knew her love was a reality, like invisible mists kindling into view in the dying glory of the sun. She now realized he had been the light of her earthly being. She now perceived, with a woman's intuition, that in his grave would be buried the future, which, during years, her heart had been tracing on her imagination. Her emotions became overpowering.

Mrs. Cleveland, yet wondering at her inexplicable agitation, exclaimed, "What can this mean, Mary? That you should thus be suddenly affected, in this strange place, is most surprising. That face seems to have cast over you some marvellous spell. Yet I have never seen it before."

As the eyes of the invalid remained closed, she ventured to look longer and more scrutinizingly, and at last began to share something of the feelings of her friend. "And yet," she resumed, still gazing, "and yet, the countenance comes before me like something floating from the past years, and which ought to be remembered."

Mary silently stepping aside, and coloring with embarrassment, took from her satchel a photograph, and gave it to her friend, who eagerly examined the picture, and turning once more to Austin, that she might venture another glance, exclaimed, "My dear Mary, I for the first time read your heart. You are indeed right. That is undoubtedly Charles Austin. The face has assumed manliness since we saw him a bright youth at college, and been roughened by exposure, and wasted by disease. Yet I perceive there the old features, with heightened traces of goodness and of genius." Mrs. Cleveland now became deeply affected. Indeed, so great was the agitation of the ladies that they were compelled to seek their apartment.

What transpired between Charles Austin and Mary Ellingwood we will not record. Indeed, their relations were too sacred and too delicate for a public exposure. We can only say that a few faint whispers from Charles filled the eyes of Mary, and traced themselves forever on her heart, so that a grave soon to be dug in St. Mary's cemetery was to rise a perpetual barrier between her and the married state.

His old friends read to the invalid from his own Bible. Kneeling at his side they said the old familiar prayers. Mingling their voices they sang the old hymns of his childhood. Dr. Elton administered to him the Holy Communion after the old forms, so simple, so unctuous, so venerable, and exciting purer, deeper, and more powerful emotion than the most gorgeous pageant of St. Peter's. At last Austin fell asleep. His life simply exhaled itself into heaven like the fragrance of a flower. Mary Ellingwood closed his eyes. Mrs. Cleveland folded his hands across his breast. Jim fell weeping on the cold clay in touching agony. Dr. Elton preceded the funeral procession to the mountain, and said at the grave the service of his Church. Here, peaceful as were the scenes of grief, and calm as were the tones of the aged clergyman, a tempest was stirred in the heart of an unseen spectator.

Cleveland, held by an invisible spell, had lingered round the Convent. He remained during the day in a cave, sustained by leaves and berries. Stalking forth at night, he wandered about the building like a ghost. Often he was on the very point of rushing through the door, and recalling his wife to his bosom. The old affection returned with a violence almost irresistible. He now realized his situation. He felt that he might have been a victim of impulse and of ambition. He saw that he had flung away a happy past, with no comfort in the present, and no hope in the future. He was near the very person of his Emily, and yet separated from her by an impassable abyss. A temporary, but most powerful yearning, rushed back upon him for his old faith, and his old ways, and his old friends. As Dr. Elton's voice penetrated his concealment, recalling other years, and he saw the form of his wife mocking him over the grave of his proselyte, a night of remorse, despair, and anguish, began for a moment to settle on his soul. Still self was stronger than truth. Suffering had not yet produced humility. Ambition triumphed. Hitherto he had imposed on himself. If not arrested soon, he will hereafter impose on others. As the sad procession wound down the road, and crossed the lawn, a storm was gathering on the mountains. Soon lightnings leaped from peak to peak. Thunders shook earth and air. The sky became a single cloud. But no war of elements could equal the tempest in the soul of Arthur Cleveland, as he shivered amid those midnight crags.

14*

CHAPTER XVIII.

IMPRISONMENT.

THE shadows of evening were stealing over Major Worstal's company before they left the spot which witnessed the execution of Gordon and Ledaway. They rode a few miles further and halting, their camp-fires soon blazed through the night. Edward Ellingwood threw himself on the ground near some burning logs, but strove to sleep for many hours in vain. The tragic scenes of the day would continually repeat themselves. Even in his dreams he would see the commanding form of the faithful Gordon, and hear the despairing shrieks of the apostate Ledaway. He was profoundly impressed with the triumphs of a Christian hero whose words, breathing peace, would forever linger in his ear. A solemn and purifying influence had been left on his spirit for life. With morning-dawn, after a hasty breakfast, the party resumed its march. Ellingwood soon found that he was to be blind-folded during the rest of the journey. For five days he traveled rapidly, enveloped in darkness, until the clang of horse-hoofs to his intense ear became a perpetual pain. He seemed transported from a world of vision to a world of sound. The eye deprived of light wraps the soul in gloom. Shut out from those objects whose form, and color, and relations continually occupy attention, it becomes acutely alive to innumerable sensations, awakened by vibrations in the boundless air before unnoticed. When Ellingwood recalled this strange period of his history, in after years, he described his impressions as resembling those produced when the mind conceives two continents of light separated by an ocean of darkness.

On the evening of the fifth day, the party reached a mansion near the ocean-shore of eastern Georgia. Immediately after his arrival, Ellingwood was conducted to his apartment, and the bandage was removed from his eyes. After a sound sleep, in a comfortable bed, the guard in the hall, opened his door early in the morning, and a negro entered to assist his toilet, and arrange his room. Soon afterwards, his servant brought him an excellent breakfast. While he is engaged with his meal, we will repair to the room of Major Worstal. That officer had slept beneath the roof which sheltered Edward Ellingwood. He had spent many hours during the night recalling the past and planning for the future. While Anna Austin, either at the ocean-seat or the military ball, had spoken no word of rejection, yet her intention could not be misconstrued. Worstal had accepted his failure as a fact, and the result had been disastrous to his character. He was stung to frenzy by every recollection of his defeat. The image of himself limping through the hall, was peculiarly irritating. Mortification had now broken down that pride of self-respect, which had been the only conserving power of his nature. Anna Austin no longer smiled on his path a guardian angel. To forget himself, he plunged into the wildest debaucheries. As a consequence, his baser appetites were constantly increasing their ascendency. He had become more profane, more sensual, more brutal, more repulsive. Animalism was now inscribed on his whole being. His very manners changed from the refinement of a gentleman, to the swagger of a bully. He shrank from his own headlong tendencies to ruin, and resolved to make a last effort to reform, by one more desperate proposal to his cousin, whom he regarded as the only angel who could arrest his course. He had received intelligence of the death of Charles Austin, and had meditated long during the night, how to communicate the fact to his sister. At breakfast he proposed to her in an unusually sober manner, another walk to the ocean-seat. She shrank from a compliance with his wishes, but afraid to decline, she accepted his proffered arm, and they proceeded across the lawn.

"Cousin Anna," said Worstal in a tone designed to be tender, "do you know you have a union officer under your roof?"

"I of course inferred," replied Anna with an assumed indifference, "that your prisoner must have had a commission, or he would not have been brought to our house."

"Ah!" returned Worstal, stirred in his lower nature, so that evidently his violence would soon surpass the gentle influence of his cousin. "I doubt whether I should not have hung the thieving Yankee, or at least given him a bullet. Why I did not treat him like his nigger-preaching Parsons I cannot tell."

"What were the particulars of his capture?" anxiously inquired Anna, alarmed at the gathering passion of her Herculean cousin.

"A company of infernal spies were riding into our territory to make observations. This officer and two chaplains were cut off from their party by a detachment of my men, and made prisoners. A messenger was sent to inform me of the circumstances. Ascertaining the names of the preachers, I knew from the papers they were the rascals who had just received commissions in nigger regiments. I rode back like perdition to the

Yankee crew. I searched the villains, found the documents, hung one miserable, cowardly, shrieking cur above a precipice, and then tumbled him down to the crows five hundred feet below; and shot the other parson, who died like a Christian, and a soldier. We bandaged the eyes of this sneaking General, and for five days he saw no more of the sun than old blind Sallie."

During this rough recital, interspersed with blasphemies we cannot record, the delicate, and sensitive nature of Anna Austin shrank with recoil, and loathing from her savage cousin. She said with suppressed disgust, "And may I ask, Henry, the name of the officer you have conducted to our house in darkness?"

Worstal, without a suspicion that the prisoner had ever been known to Anna, answered, "He is General Edward Ellingwood—formerly a Colonel,—recently promoted for his pluck, and success—as clever a fellow as any cursed Yankee can be, born within a hundred miles of Boston."

Miss Austin commenced to tremble violently, when her cruel cousin pronounced the name of a man she knew he would soon hate, and who was wholly within his power. She perceived, however, instantly the necessity of concealing her interest and alarm, and was successful, by a strong effort.

The Major now saw that the unexpected direction of the conversation rendered it impossible, at this time, to communicate the fact of Austin's death.

After tea he proposed another walk, and the cousins were soon in the seat they occupied in the morning. Anna, during the day, had been deeply excited by the knowledge that she and Edward Ellingwood were under the same roof, and yet forbidden recognition. She was now in a subdued mood, suitable for the sad information in reserve for her spirit.

Twilight was settling over the ocean. Not a wave kissed a murmur from the shore. The sea gave back to the sky a single star. Solemn night would soon project shadows like that about to fall on Anna's soul. Even Worstal was softened by the scene.

After some preliminary conversation, he said, with all the sympathy which his vices had left in his debased nature: "I exceedingly regret that General Brompton is in Richmond, and that as your only surviving relative, I have to tell you some bad news."

Anna started from her seat. She asked hurriedly: "Did you say my *only* surviving relative? Surely, surely, you do not mean that Charles is dead. Speak! oh, speak, and relieve the dread you have excited."

"Dear cousin," he answered, taking her delicate white hand, and sinking his voice into its utmost possible softness. "Your fears are too well founded. I received, several days before reaching Sea-Side, a telegram from Richmond, announcing his death, and have not before had courage to tell you." Anna's cheek became white and cold as winter. Her hollow eye refused a tear. She clasped her hands, and uttering a low cry of anguish, she sank into the arms of her cousin. Her head, resting on his bosom, sent fire to his heart. His blood rushed wildly along his veins. His soul became a tempest.

Forgetting the meanness of the action, he impressed a kiss on the lips of the unconscious girl. He then laid her gently on the grass, and taking a huge magnolia leaf and folding it into a suitable shape, he brought water from a neighboring rivulet, and sprinkled her face and bathed her hands and brow. Anna soon recovered, and rising slowly, placed her arm in that of her cousin, signifying her desire to return. This action made Worstal's heart again beat violently, and put flame into his blood. His undisciplined nature knew no restraints. Bending down, he said with passionate earnestness, " You have no relatives left but General Brompton and myself. He is now an 'aged man, and will not live many years. The South is disturbed by war. Our niggers are becoming ugly since this Yankee proclamation. I have property and position. I have loved you since our childhood. I can give you protection and a home. Become my wife, Anna, and save me from the devil."

Here the poor wretch stopped. He knew that he was passing the crisis of his fate, and the quivering magnolia leaf in his hand shook, until the water-drops, still on its surface, fell to the ground. There indeed seemed no other angel in the universe, who could beckon him towards virtue, but his lovely cousin. She herself felt that she was deciding Worstal's future, for perhaps time and eternity. Indeed, one reason why she had never given, in words, a negative, was her fear of hastening his ruin. While indignant and disgusted with a proposal made amid the agonies of such a moment, the thought of Edward Ellingwood, and a consideration for Worstal himself, constrained to self-control. However dreadful the effect of her words, she now perceived, that the time had come for an express and final refusal.

" Cousin Henry," she said, with a painful effort, " this is not the hour for you to speak, or me to hear anything touching this subject. My heart has been smitten by a blow such as it can never again receive. This, however, I had better now say, once and forever—what you propose is impossible. I will always love you, as a cousin, but never as a husband."

This reply stirred all the demon in Worstal, and shaped

his whole future character and history. Nothing but the dignity of Miss Austin's grief shielded her from his rage. He walked with her to the house in silence, but his soul resembled a volcano, whose flames are only more violent from suppression.

Ellingwood, from his window, had seen Anna pass over the lawn in the morning, leaning on Worstal's arm. He could not keep his eye from the cousins as they conversed on the ocean-seat. He had observed their return to the same place in the evening. Not wishing to be a spy on their actions, he had withdrawn to his lounge, and coming to the window, after he supposed they had retired, he perceived Anna in the arms of the Major. While they were walking slowly back to the house, the conclusion was forced on him that they were married, and that he was either under the roof of General Brompton, or of his successful rival, in whose hands he was a helpless prisoner.

The blow was sudden and dreadful. The photograph of Anna was at that moment next his heart, folded in the flag so solemnly given him by his father. She had been to him the ideal of every thing true, and pure, and beautiful in woman. She had been for years his thought and dream. She had been to him, in expectation, his wife. Shall she be taken from his love and hope? Nay, is she not even now married to a debauched, loathsome, blasphemous wretch, who had searched his person, bandaged his eyes, and for days made his ears witnesses of the most repulsive vulgarity and profanity?

Ellingwood could no longer endure such reflections. He tore open his bosom. He unwound the silken folds which wrapped, in hallowed stars, the image he once adored. He dashed it on the floor, and exhausted by fatigue and suffering, fell on his bed in a wild delirium.

CHAPTER XIX.

REMORSE.

“CLEVELAND, I have more work for you,” said Bishop Frances, during a conversation which occurred in the drawing-room of St. Mary’s.

“My dear Bishop,” was the quick reply, “Speak, and I obey. Submission to my superiors is the rule of my life.”

“Your conversion,” said Frances, in a most complacent tone, “I regard as the great work of my Priesthood. The moment when you vowed yourself to Pio Nino, while kneeling before his picture, and that in which you took the irrevocable oath of our order, can never be forgotten. The conversion of Austin has more than realized all my expectations. Let me inform you that a mitre has already rewarded your previous successes, and a Cardinal’s hat will now certainly follow.”

Cleveland was at once delighted and confounded. An elevation so sudden and dazzling had not been expected. Frances, warmly grasping his convert’s hand, added: “I am the first to salute Bishop Arthur Cleveland.”

“And I,” replied the new dignitary, “can only regard myself as utterly unworthy—a weak, faithless, stumbling, unprofitable servant.”

“Humility,” rejoined the Bishop, “is the root of piety. The Monk of Cluny was, in his own eyes, a vile sinner. The halo of sanctity lingers in the valley, and cannot crown the hill.”

“But I know, that to your own persistent partiality

and influence at the Vatican, I owe this undeserved elevation."

"Reserve your sackcloth for your cell. Our infallible Father at Rome has heard of your numerous American triumphs, and sees your future availability. St. Peter and Loyola, neither on earth nor in heaven, ever forget their faithful servants."

Not many days after this interview, Cleveland was consecrated in the chapel of St. Mary's with quiet, yet imposing splendor. When the ceremony was concluded, and he was walking over the lawn, with his arm familiarly in that of Frances, the latter suddenly pausing, and turning towards the new Bishop, said: "I told you I had work for you, and you have not yet inquired its character. You then promised me obedience as a superior! Will you now engage to please me as an equal?"

"Nothing," responded Cleveland, "can afford me greater gratification, than to comply with your wishes."

"Your marvellous success with Austin, inspires a hope that you may win Ellingwood. Of course, the circumstanes are not so peculiarly favorable. It strikes me, however, before you settle in your Diocese, you had better begin your episcopal career, by a direct effort to convert your former pupil, now a General in the Federal army. Father John has informed me by a telegram, shrewdly sent, that he is a prisoner of Major Worstal, at Sea-Side. That officer is an hereditary Catholic, and will materially aid your plans." The face of Cleveland glowed with pleasure.

"Thank you, thank you a thousand times for this suggestion. Heaven has indeed honored my labors. Gladly will I undertake this mission, and pray the Virgin to bless my efforts."

"When this work is achieved," said Frances, "you must see Rome. No man's ecclesiastical education can be complete, until he has breathed the atmosphere of the eternal city. At her altars you will kindle with new inspiration. I wish you also to know his Holiness, to participate in the grand service of St. Peter, and study for yourself our system, extending from the Propaganda as its centre, to the remotest limits of the earth."

Bishop Cleveland speedily made arrangements to visit Sea-Side. Having been passed over the lines, attended by Jim as his servant, after a fatiguing and perilous journey, he received a warm welcome from General Brompton and his family, and was charmed to occupy an apartment looking over the expanse of the ocean. Yet we must not be misled into inferring that his experience, previous to his consecration, had been without struggle and suffering. We may remember him on the mountain, and perhaps it may be well even here to narrate, what transpired immediately after the funeral of Charles Austin.

He had watched from his concealment, with the deepest emotion, the form of his wife, fading in the distance, as she removed with the members of the Commission, from the Convent of St. Mary. He returned to the deserted building, and wandered about its silent apartments, solitary, desolate, miserable, seeming, even to himself, a hollow ghost. Pictures, statues, images, looked on him reprovingly. Saints seemed to shrink away from his gaze, as if he were a contamination. Angels, had in their eyes, the sadness of pity and rebuke. Demons glared in flame from their canvass. The face of our Saviour turned on St. Peter, in his tears, almost overwhelmed the heart of Cleveland, when he remembered how nearly he had forgotten his vows, and rushed to the embraces of his wife.

Passing a large mirror, he imagined he saw in his hair the prophetic blight of age, already crowning him prematurely with its winter-snow. His face was furrowed with his sufferings. He moved almost like a lost spirit through the tenantless building, and was tempted again to break away from a position he began to fear was false. But then his future would lie on either hand between men whom he had betrayed. His situation reminded him of a decaying bridge in a mad torrent with both ends shattered from the shore. He had no faith in himself; he had no faith in Protestantism; he had no faith in Romanism; he had no faith in man; he had no faith in God.

The return of the inmates of the Convent, and especially the society of Bishop Frances, terminated these solitary sufferings. Then followed the excitements of his appointment and his consecration. Now he is at Sea-Side absorbed in his new mission, and with only occasional mutterings of those former tempests.

CHAPTER XX.

JIM AND JUMBO.

Major Worstal suddenly received an unexpected order to join a distant expedition. He was in command of a prison not far from Sea-Side, and was not prepared for such a commission. However, the order was imperative, and he was compelled to obey. He preceded Jumbo to the stable to superintend the operation of grooming Minerva, to prepare her for a long and hard ride.

As the African was meekly following his great dimensions, a low chuckle arrested his attention, and caused him to turn his head. He observed a broad grin overspreading the negro's face, and when Jim made his appearance, the father and the son were plainly in a spirit of sympathetic laughter, subdued, however, by fear of the dreaded Major. With an energy, inspired by his presence, each knelt, rubbing vigorously a front leg of Minerva, while Worstal stood observing the operation, with his hands in his pockets, and rolling his tobacco in his cheek. As Jumbo and Jim plied their black hands, their thick red lips, stretched from ear to ear, showed shining rows of ivory. Grin now answered to grin, and chuckle to chuckle. Sometimes the filial, sometimes the paternal merriment was evinced by a quick poke from the offspring to the parent, and from the parent to the offspring. Their amusement became contagious. Even the countenance of the Major gleamed into a smile, as he said, "Why, Jumbo, you laughing nigger, what ails you this morning? I suppose when General Brompton arrived he gave you a quarter for stealing his chickens during his absence ?"

"No, no, massa Maja," replied Jumbo, with a sobered face, and laying his straw-whisp on the floor, as he looked up with an air of injured innocence, "Jumbo want no quata to 'munerate de compensashun ob de service he gib de Gineral."

"Oh, I understand," interrupted Worstal, "My uncle has given Jim that old hat for running away and leaving Colonel Charles to the mercies of the Yankees."

This speech brought Jim to a pause, and made him take from his wool an immense rimless hat, with the top knocked in, which came down nearly to his eyes, and which once, in a more hopeful condition, had covered the honored head of the Lord of Sea-Side. Holding up the remnant in his left hand, and pointing at it with the straw-whisp in his right, he answered, with a touching protest, "No, massa Maja, no, no. Jim nebber do dat. He played wid massa Charles by him cradle. He foller massa Charles to de roarin fiel of battle; he nuss massa Charles till him die; he stand ober massa Charles' grave, and he want no dispensashun from de Gineral's head for dat dar servis."

"What in the mischief then made you niggers grin like two monkies over a pea-nut ?" asked Worstal impatiently. The father, and son instantly resumed their rubbing, forgot their gravity, and were soon repeating another series of grins, and chuckles and pokes. The Major was getting furious. Taking his hands from his pockets, and snugging his quid into his right cheek, he seized his riding-whip, and roared forth.

"You impudent black villains tell me at once what you are laughing at ?"

"Massa Maja," answered Jumbo, again suspending his labors, and assuming the air of a patriarch, and scratching his head with a significant wisdom,

"Dis Nigga's gray wool hab learnt in sixty years dar be some t'ings by 'speriens had bess be kep in de basement ob de soul like de Virginny apples in de cellar ob de house."

These words were followed by an emphatic application of the straw-whisp to the region of the stomach as if that was the deep seat of wisdom.

"But it is dangerous in these times for you niggers to have secrets. Tell me everything," said Worstal, whose curiosity was thoroughly aroused.

"Massa Maja," "rejoined Jumbo, "if me tell what de unyon ofica say in his 'lirium, me might rais de 'citement ob dat housol, and Jumbo displore de sconsesquences of his observashuns down to de time he shut de whites of him eyes on dat hebbenly light," pointing to the brilliant sun pouring his rays into the stable, and showing long dancing lines of illuminated motes.

"You blasted nigger," cried the angry Major. "Out with it, or I'll bring this whip about your wool."

As the instrument of punishment was threateningly raised, and Jumbo began to fear its sharp sting around his ears, he saw that he had gotten himself into trouble. Jim enjoyed his sire's dilemma, and with a nudge uttered a low chuckling laugh. Jumbo resumed:

"What dat ofica speak war not 'bout de bisness of de gubberment, but 'bout de 'fections of him heart."

This still more inflamed the impatient curiosity of the violent Worstal.

"I don't care," he exclaimed, lifting the whip, and shaking it over the negro's head. "Speak, or I strike."

"Will Massa Maja take all de 'sponsibility?" asked Jumbo, thoroughly frightened.

"I tell you, speak, you black dog," thundered the Major, vigorously applying the whip.

Resistance, or delay were evidently in vain. Jumbo began with a solemn, and deliberate air of mystery.

"Do de Maja know; could de Maja tink; could de Maja conceib de comprenshun of the idee dat de Yank ofica lub his cousin, Missus Anna Ausson?"

"What do you mean, you old monkey? How dare you talk about such a thing?" shouted Worstal.

"Me do dat," said Jumbo slowly, "'spressly by de comman of Maja Henry Wossal hiself. By dat dar same comman, me now stop my observashuns."

Here the provoking fellow deliberately took up his straw-whisp, and resumed his task of rubbing Minerva's leg with a most tantalizing energy.

Worstal stamped with rage. He yelled:

"Tell me the story without stopping, or I will tear the tongue from your black carcass."

Jumbo now put down his straw-whisp, and began in earnest.

"Massa Maja den take de 'sponsibilitie of dis nigga's 'munications. He go dis mornin to de room of de unyon ofica—he opun de winder to let in de light ob hebben—de ofica lay dar a tossin, and groanin in de bed—he start up wid his eyes a rollin, and a starin like de ghost—he trow 'bout his arms like Massa suga-press—he cry wild as de hurt hoss Jim tell me 'bout flying on the battle-fiel—he say, Oh, Missus Anna, why, why you 'ceive dis heart, why you break dis heart, why you tear dis heart, why you marry dat?"

"Marry!" burst forth Worstal, pale with rage, "Marry! Marry who?"

"Shall dis nigga tell," said Jumbo, hesitatingly and imploringly, and evidently fearing the consequences of his words.

"Out, out, out with it, you dog, you monkey, you devil," shrieked Worstal, inflicting some sharp blows on Jumbo which made him rub his arms as energetically as he had rubbed Minerva's legs. But even yet the negro was afraid to speak. The Major, however, seized him by the shoulders and shaking his whole body, said, "Marry who?"

"Marry," cried Jumbo, with the utmost haste, as if he wished the offensive sentence delivered, and the danger over, "de unyon ofica say, 'why you marry dat coas, vulga', swearin', drinkin', bullyin', blasphemin', murderin' Maja' Wossal?"

It was done. Henry Worstal saw his own picture before him, painted by his prisoner, Edward Ellingwood, whom he now knew was his rival and his enemy. He presented a spectacle of terrible passion. A demon glared in his eye. Jumbo was terrified; and in his fear, told what he had not intended.

"Me see," he added, "de pictur of Missus Anna lyin' on de ofica's floor, and it be dar dis minnit."

Worstal turned around instantly without a word, and stalked fearfully over the yard. He crossed rapidly the piazza. He entered the hall door, and rushed swiftly up the stairs, and burst into Ellingwood's room. There lay his prisoner on his bed in a soft slumber, and there on the floor lay the very photograph thrown aside unexamined by himself during the search on the mountain. He picked up the hated image, and gnashing his teeth, threw it violently down, and with his heel ground it into pieces, until the fragments were imbedded in the carpet.

He then stood scowling down on the sleeping Ellingwood, with his hand clutching his sword-hilt. Nothing but General Brompton's presence in the house shielded Edward's life. As it was, it can hardly be comprehended why his heart-blood did not stain his pillow. However, Worstal had that dread of his uncle which men powerful in muscle often feel towards their intellectual superiors. He therefore turned reluctantly away, and as his order was peremptory, he saw himself compelled to leave in Eden the very serpent he had introduced. He hurried to the stable, flung himself on Minerva, and was soon flying over the country like a devil just let loose from hell to work ruin on the earth.

CHAPTER XXI.

"Bishop Cleveland, we are indeed happy to welcome you to Sea-Side. We owe you eternal gratitude," said General Brompton after breakfast one morning in the parlor.

"Yes, truly," added his niece, "we can never repay your kindness to Charles," and her eye filled, and her voice softened as she spoke. A tear also quivered on her uncle's lid, and rolled over his cheek, and dropped to the floor.

"Oh, it was one of the highest privileges of my life," replied the Bishop in a tender, winning tone, "to bear my dear friend from the field of death, to nurse him during his sickness, and administer the consolations of the Church."

There was an almost painful contrast between the sadness of the group and the brilliance of the hour. A fresh breeze blew through the opened window from the sea. The morning sun had wheeled his circle of fire high above the ocean, yet was still tracing a long path of rippling flame over the waves, which danced, and flashed through the pines. Birds sang inspiringly on the branches, and flowers glowed brightly over the lawn. The uncle sat on a lounge with his niece by his side, and Cleveland on a chair opposite the window, occasionally turning an admiring eye upon the scene.

"How magnificent this prospect!" ejaculated the

Bishop, wishing for a moment to divert the attention of his friends.

"How well your trees are arranged to display that blue expanse! How rich and splendid your Southern landscape! That sky rivals Italy."

"We would be happy to forget our sad thoughts in admiring this familiar beauty, but you will not think it strange if our minds are reverting to other topics than the charms of nature," said the General mournfully.

"Pardon me, I pray you," interposed the Bishop somewhat anxiously, "if my remarks have produced in your hearts a needless jar."

"It is our own gloom, my right reverend sir, which requires apology. I fear you will not have a particularly sunny visit at Sea-Side. War spreads a cloud over everything, and it seems impossible for us to escape the recollection of our great loss. Will you not describe to us the circumstances of my nephew's wound, and death?"

"I will most willingly comply with your request," answered Cleveland. "I only regret that I am not the bearer of joy instead of woe."

"We are prepared for the recital," said General Brompton. "I have given orders that only Doctor Bainbridge and Father John be admitted to the house, so you need fear no interruption. I believe you joined the regiment of Charles, on the Potomac, as Chaplain."

"Yes, I have borne the commission of your confederacy. Your nephew and myself, shared for weeks the same tent, and often the same bed."

"Did he seem to have any presentiment of his death?" inquired the General.

"We observed nothing peculiar in him, unless, perhaps, if possible, a more earnest attention to his duties, and an increased grace and sweetness in his manners, which, you know, were always charming. Not a soldier or a drummer-boy in the regiment, who did not love and esteem him as a friend."

"Will you inform us, Bishop," said Anna, touchingly, "how our dear Charles looked on the day of his wound? I have in my mind, a vivid picture, and I wish to see how it accords with the facts."

"We had a hot, dusty, weary, march from the Potomac. Then occurred the hurried preparations for battle, and the intensity of mind, incident to such a scene. Fatigue and anxiety had exhausted your brother, aggravating his cough, and increasing his emaciation. On the first day of the engagement, he was stationed in a grove, and near a mountain-spring, as a reserve, and had time to recruit himself and his men. On the terrible fourth, as he sat on his noble white horse in full uniform, he seemed a model of soldierly beauty. His slender person towered almost into majesty, and his eye and face, shone in the mingled light of genius, courage and devotion. He charged, at the head of his regiment, like a thunderbolt. When the roar subsided and the smoke lifted, I saw his frenzied steed flying over the field with an emptied saddle and snorting in his terror. I can only remember that I rushed forward, was trampled on the ground, and when consciousness returned, found myself stumbling beneath the stars, and over the slain. The horrors of that night, scare me even in my dreams." And as he uttered these words, he placed his hands before his eyes as if he would shut from his view some vision of terror.

Anna suppressed a cry bursting from her lips, and relieved by tears, said:

"Pardon my agitation, and I will endeavor not again to disturb your thrilling narrative."

16

"Surely," returned the Bishop, smiling benignantly, and in his peculiarly musical voice, which resembled the silver notes of the flute, " a sister's grief over a brother's wound, needs no apology.   Shall I proceed?"

"By all means," exclaimed the uncle and niece in the same breath.

"I and faithful Jim," resumed Cleveland, "then raised the Colonel, carried him over the field, and bore him to the Convent of St. Mary's, as he himself had suggested in a faint whisper before relapsing into his swoon.   Here he was tenderly nursed for many days.   The place, from its beauty, and associations, and advantages, was all that could be desired for a dying Christian soldier.   My friend, during the last periods of his life, reclined on his lounge, and was wheeled through the Convent, and over the lawn, and into the chapel.   He never spoke, communicating only with Jim and by signs.   A heavenly beauty diffused itself over his face, which seemed encircled with a light from the eternal world.   His image will linger in my memory forever.   I suppose you know, sir, that he partook of the Holy Communion in our Church?"

"Yes," replied the General, "I am truly thankful you admitted him to that sacrament.   As a speechless and dying man, I presume you extended the privilege as an extraordinary favor."

"We regarded his participation," returned the Bishop, "of course, as a proof that he considered himself a Roman Catholic."

General Brompton started, and Anna looked surprised. The former then asked:

"Was my nephew buried according to the rites of your Church?"

This question brought scarlet to the cheek of Cleveland,

bright as his anticipated hat. He was, for a moment, entirely discomfited. The recollection of his wife's appearance on the scene, and of his own keen pangs and mortifying disappointments, rushed over him, and he was almost unable to reply. With a desperate effort for composure, he at last answered: "Just before the Colonel expired, the Christian Commission came swarming like locusts into our Convent, took possession of your nephew, and he was committed to the earth by an Episcopal clergyman in unconsecrated ground, and according to the Protestant form." The uncle and the niece were evidently gratified at this conclusion. With the utmost warmth, the General then grasped the hand of Cleveland, saying: "We are under inconceivable obligation to you for your kindness. Ever consider ourselves, and our home, at your disposal, and accept thanks from our grateful hearts." Anna's silent tears told more impressively than words how deeply her heart was moved.

Dr. Bainbridge and Father John were now announced, and soon entered the room. After the customary morning salutations, the Physician said: "General Brompton, I have just been visiting your prisoner. He is a most interesting and striking person, even in the wildness of his fever. But I fear his condition is extremely critical."

"It gives me great pain to learn this," answered the kind old lawyer. "Edward Ellingwood is rather my guest than my prisoner. He was the intimate friend of Charles before the war. His sister and Anna love each other warmly, and for the Judge, his father, I entertain a profound esteem. Although a Union officer in arms against the Confederacy, he shall receive, under my roof, every attention I could give a son."

The opinion of Dr. Bainbridge had darted a pang

through the heart of Anna Austin. Her blood appeared
to be on fire, and to burn through her very cheeks. She
was soon compelled to recline on a pillow of the old-
fashioned sofa. Edward Ellingwood was in the same
house—wildly delirious—perhaps about to expire in a few
hours—yet she had not exchanged with him a single
word. She had not even seen him in his sufferings.
These reflections, preceded by the account of her brother's
wound, and death and burial, produced a tumult in her
breast, and robed her life in gloom.

The gentlemen were too much occupied to notice her
emotion, and soon withdrew to visit the prisoner, leaving
her alone in her sorrow. When they entered the chamber
of Ellingwood, they found him in the height of his fever-
frenzy. He was sitting on his bed. His eyes stood out
glaring from his head. His face worked with terror.
His hands now clutched his pillow, and now were flung
out wildly about his person. The veins of his forehead
were swelled almost to bursting with the hot rushing
blood. Every sinew of his body was strained like a cord.
His imagination was evidently picturing some frightful
vision. Turning the backs of his hands before his eyes,
while his fingers twisted fearfully and his face was half
averted, he exclaimed, in the most penetrating and terrified tones:

"Stop! stop! Don't shoot that man! Don't! don't!
don't! Take away that rope! Don't hang that poor fellow! Hear his screams! See his body! How he twists,
twists, twists! Poor Gordon! Save him, my God, save
him! He is dead, dead, dead, dead!" Here burst from
his lips dreadful shrieks, and Ellingwood fell back on his
bed helpless and exhausted.

Anna attracted by his yells stood at his door the image

of grief and despair. Dr. Bainbridge felt the pulse of his patient, and pronounced him at the crisis of his disease. He remarked, "Medicine is of no possible avail. Only good nursing and heaven's blessing can effect his recovery."

The Bishop, regarding Edward with the greatest tenderness, turned to the physician, and proffered his services, saying, "Doctor, General Ellingwood was my former beloved pupil, and I must claim the privilege of attending him during his sickness. Permit me to have a lounge brought into his room and to nurse him day and night."

"Certainly," replied Dr. Bainbridge, "nothing could be better. In his situation he needs the sympathetic care of friends more than my prescriptions."

"And I," interposed Father John, "will be pleased to relieve the Bishop when he is exhausted by watching, and fatigue."

"I too," said Miss Austin, stepping forward from the door, "must claim some part in promoting the restoration of my friend's brother, and my brother's friend."

"I regret exceedingly," added General Brompton, "that my necessary absence at Richmond will remove me from the scene of these pleasing labors. However, it will afford me an opportunity of procuring from the government an order which will keep General Ellingwood at my house, and from the prison, until his health is sufficiently restored to justify his removal."

All the arrangements were made according to these suggestions. Bishop Cleveland, and Father John slept in Ellingwood's bed-room, and were ceaseless in their care. Dr. Bainbridge visited him constantly, and contributed his long experience and famous skill to promote the

16*

recovery of the suffering stranger. There was only one other return of the delirium. Ellingwood then seemed to see Worstal and his bride before the marriage-altar. He plead frantically that the ceremony should stop, and poured on the head of his enemy the most withering curses. Anna started in terror when she heard her name wildly uttered. Then followed days of stupor. The patient lay balancing between life and death. His chamber was darkened. The tick of his watch over the mantle had a sympathetic emphasis. Every voice was subdued, and every step was muffled, and every face was intense with anxiety. When Dr. Bainbridge examined Edward's pulse the spectators stood around silent as if eternity was suspended on his announcement. Finally the crisis passed. Ellingwood lay for hours during which his life appeared to pass before him like a panorama.

He was a boy at Willow-Shade; he was on the commencement-platform, with Charles Austin, delivering his valedictory; he was dashing amid balls and shells, against the enemy; he was steaming through a Mississippi bayou; he was floating before the blaze of Vicksburgh batteries; he was leading an assault on Lookout Mountain; he was on the rock where Ledaway was hanged, and Gordon was shot; he was in deadly fight with Worstal; life-histories crossed his vision like processions of clouds. Amid all were the faces of his father and sister, while Anna Austin, smiled an angel from heaven. Once she came into his room and pressed to his lips a glass of water. Her touch thrilled through his veins like electric sparks. At last, careful nursing, medical skill and a good constitution, with the blessing from above, triumphed, and Edward Ellingwood began to exhibit proofs of a certain recovery.

CHAPTER XXII.

PERHAPS there is no period of life when sensation is so acute and vigorous, as that which marks the transition from disease to health. The simple relief from pain is itself a pleasure. Our exile from nature invests every object with novelty, and it is saluted as a friend from which we have been long separated. Besides the body itself, through protracted confinement, becomes more delicate and sensitive in its organs, and the nerves rested and relieved, return to their ordinary functions, prepared to experience fresh and intenser delights. If the heart of Edward Ellingwood had not been oppressed, his system, with advancing health, would have attuned every scene to joy. He dreaded the hour which would compel a conversation with Anna Austin, whom he still believed was Mrs. Major Worstal.

Passing one day through the hall, after a long ride, she stood at the door of the parlor where Jim was fanning him as he reclined on the sofa.

"Good morning, General! Excuse my absence on some necessary matters, and let me congratulate you on your improved appearance."

There she was with the glow of the morning in her cheek. Her eye sparkled beneath her graceful hat, with the light of her peculiar beauty, while her riding-habit added to the charms of her person.

"Thank you, madam, for your kind sympathies," replied—or rather stammered—Edward as he felt the crimson in his face.

"Madam, madam!" she repeated with a mock gravity, and emphasis. "General Ellingwood must certainly discern in me some marks of premature dignity, or possibly of premature decay. Perhaps," she added elevating her head, and with a quiver of scorn on her lip, and in her voice, "the war he wages against the daughters of the South has brought the wrinkles to their faces, and the snow into their hair."

"Madam, pardon whatever fault I have committed," cried Ellingwood utterly overwhelmed with surprise and confusion.

"Madam!" resumed Anna, now completely indignant, and retiring with a stately bow, she kept saying as she passed down the hall: "Madam, indeed! what can he mean? are we changing vocabularies as well as governments? or does my appearance indicate an age which requires a matronly title?"

One glance at her image as she passed a mirror assured her that youth and beauty had never touched her face with more winning charms, and she was left in a state of complete bewilderment, from which her reflections during the day did not relieve her.

Ellingwood himself was overcome with mingled embarrassment and despair. So firmly had the hateful thought of Anna's marriage to Worstal become imbedded in his mind that he never asked a question even of Jim in regard to the repulsive subject. The terrible suffering of his delirium had been chiefly caused by the belief that such purity and beauty had been wrested from him, and consigned to a savage like the abandoned Major. His recoil from inquiry was therefore entirely natural.

After the circumstances narrated, Miss Austin scarcely met Ellingwood even in the presence of others, and always with an evident chill in her manner.

Thus, while frequently together during brief intervals, there was between them an ever-widening chasm.

After arising one morning from an unusually stiff and awkward breakfast, where they once more were alone, Ellingwood stepped for a moment to the window, and gazing towards the ocean, was transported with the prospect. In the exuberance of his excited pleasure, he exclaimed :

" Mrs. Worstal, what could exceed such a view ?" For a moment Anna was transfixed. The blood rushed like a torrent to her face, and then she was struck with the absurdity of the mistake. Ripples of laughter came gushing from her lips, and her face beamed with fun.

" Madam ! Mrs. Worstal !" she cried, " General Ellingwood supposes that my sudden antiquity of appearance carries with it the supposition of marriage ; or else he believes that is which ought to be, and he, therefore, consigns me in wedlock to the most probable person he imagines, who happens to be my transcendent cousin. Surely, I must have played well the part of Mrs. Hercules. Know then, sir, that I am still Anna Austin, and that I call no man master."

It is difficult to tell, whether delight, astonishment, or confusion preponderated in the mind of Ellingwood. He poured forth a torrent of untimely apologies, and concluded the whole with a blunder :

" From what I myself observed," he said, " I could but infer that Miss Austin was the wife of Major Worstal."

" What you *observed*, sir !" she replied with a flush of anger, while indignation flashed from her eye, and curled on her lip, and thrilled in her tone, giving her beauty a stateliness and elevation which showed a woman's fire beneath a woman's gentleness. "What you *observed*, sir!" she repeated slowly, "and under what title, may I ask, am I to be *observed* by General Edward Ellingwood? I do not choose to be the subject of his scrutinies. Surely, it is not the part of a soldier to pry into the conduct of ladies." These words brought the embarrassment to its crisis.

Ellingwood saw the time had come for explanation. He was at once himself. With recovered dignity, he replied: "I perceive that I have been guilty of extreme folly. I was standing at my window when you and Major Worstal passed, arm-in-arm, over the lawn. I was admiring your own matchless grace, and his grand proportions, without conceiving there was the slightest impropriety in my conduct. You will forgive me if my glance was prolonged by my interest further than delicacy permitted. But as I gazed, I saw your earnest conversation. I saw you reclining on his breast. I saw you supported in his arms. Pardon my offence! It was punished by days of agony."

The last sentence went to the heart of Anna. It revealed the cause of all the delirious anguish she had witnessed, and showed, that after years of separation, the conversation on the college lawn had not been misinterpreted. She was gratified to know that a cloud over her own image could cause so much darkness. She quickly exclaimed, with a sense of relief equal to that experienced by Edward himself: "Mr. Ellingwood, under the circumstances, not even delicacy could criticise your conduct. All is forgiven and forgotten. When you remember that Henry Worstal is my cousin, and was supporting me under an overwhelming sorrow, occasioned by his sudden communication of my dear brother's death, you will understand my relations and **my conduct.** Let us thank Heaven that an explanation has been made which will relieve our present and our future from so much suffering." She held out her hand while she spoke.

Edward could **not resist** the impulse to stoop, and imprint on it a kiss; **nor** will we deem him unmanly if his eye left on it the moisture of **a tear. That** pressure of his lip changed the course of his life. **It melted away** the barriers of years. **It** thrilled **responsively in a** true woman's heart, on which his image **had** been ineffaceably inscribed **by a true woman's love.**

The recovery of Ellingwood **was now rapid and com-** plete.

On the evening of the very next day he proposed a sail on the ocean. As he and Anna passed along the shore there was stirring the softest breeze of evening just suffi- cient to ripple the water into waves, and wake its **music** on the beach. **They soon sat down together** behind **the** white sail **on the same seat, while** the blue sea and the blue sky enclosed them in a **world of the** affections. From its urn of gold the star of love shed down its light of beauty.

Ellingwood, turning to Anna, said, "I need scarcely ask Miss Austin if she recollects our conversation before parting, after the scenes of the commencement, which, read in the glare of war, now seem prophecies."

"Never," she replied, "can those memorable days be forgotten. The four happy persons," she added, with a tear and a heaving bosom, "who then stood together be- neath yon moon will never meet more on this earth."

While speaking she pointed to a circle of glory just rising in cloudless brilliance from the ocean, and casting along the waves from its bright edge to their boat a dancing breadth of radiance.

"My lips did not then dare express," resumed Ellingwood, "what was felt in my heart. Our approaching separation and the tokens of war forbade what would otherwise have been proper. Possibly even now political differences may rise as a barrier between us."

"I have always esteemed," answered Anna, with a blush just visible in the moon, "the heart of woman a province never to be disturbed by such strifes. If not cold like yon night-queen it should be equally free from the tempests which sweep over the hearts of men. I have never yet yielded to the bitter feelings which, North and South, sway so many ladies of our land."

"It is enough," cried Ellingwood with the eagerness of delight. "I was certain I could not have been mistaken. In that hour I considered our spirits pledged without words, firmly, and forever."

He then imprinted a kiss, not as before on Anna's hand, but on Anna's lips. Out on that calm ocean, and beneath that pure sky, a true man and a true woman experienced that mysterious commingling of being by which two souls remain separate, and yet become one. All nature beneath, around, above expressed sympathetic approval. The waves laughed love. The breeze breathed love. The stars smiled love. The angel of love himself sprang upward to make his record of hearts never to be divided by the trials of life, the gloom of death, or the years of eternity. Such a love alone makes happy marriages, blissful homes, prosperous nations. Such a love, next to piety, is the want of the world. Until our age learns to reverence the affections, divorce will continue to lacerate hearts, rend families, disgrace tribunals, cloud the country, and outrage human nature.

Edward and Anna, absorbed in each other, did not notice a vessel approaching from behind. Suddenly they heard her noise upon the waters. Turning in the direction of the sound, they perceived her vast, dark, gliding hulk, and on the sky, the black smoke which rolled in clouds from her chimney. When she came near, the beauty of her figure and the grace of her motion were inexpressible. While her main-mast was passing across the moon, Ellingwood discerned clearly the stars of the Republic once more in glory over his head. His soul was transported. He rose in an ecstasy. He waved his hat wildly. Forgetful of Anna, he repeated with a thrilling pathos inspired by his patriotic emotions, some lines sent him by a friend in manuscript, and since made public.

> Flag of Beauty! wide and high,
> Earth saw thee given to the sky
>   In Freedom's night;
> Then through revolution-fires
> Flashing borne by patriot-sires
> While a gazing world admires
>   To Freedom's light.
>
> Flag of Freedom! where a spot
> Darkening did thy beauty blot,
>   No stain we see.
> Glad to God our song we raise;
> Nations swell the voice of praise!
> Every star floats in the blaze
>   Of Liberty.
>
> Flag of Promise! let a world
> Wide thy glories view unfurl'd
>   O'er land and sea!
> Float, since God has purged thy stains;
> Float, till earth has burst her chains;
> Float, while Heaven bends o'er our plains,
>   Pure, bright and free!

> Flag of Glory! **let no more**
> On war-clouds thine eagle soar
>   Where death-fires play!
> Glow soon love where **now** glares ire!
> Never may a star expire,
> **Till the Heavens in final fire**
>   Have passed away!

While Ellingwood stood reciting these lines, Anna was so impressed with the nobility of his appearance, and the ardor of his sincerity, that she was herself almost carried away by the enthusiasm of the moment. Where the heart of woman is engaged, her head is easily persuaded.

After the excursion was over, the General began to fear that the inspirations of his patriotism might have hurried him beyond the limits of delicacy, and he said to Miss Austin, as he sat with her by the window in the parlor: "Pardon me, Anna, if the sight of the old flag made me forget not even myself, but you. I now almost smile at my own frenzy, and quite reproach myself for not considering your presence."

"Oh, Edward," she replied, "I remember that you are a soldier and a prisoner. You are excusable for disregarding a little rebel like myself, when you saw the stars you defend before your eyes. The vessel had evidently some unusual motive for speed, or our boat would have been overhauled. In that case our relations would probably have been inverted, and I then been the captive, and you the keeper. I fear the temptation to carry me away beneath the old flag would have been irresistible."

"Ah, Anna," answered Edward, with a gratified countenance, "whether north or south, I expect no more liberty. When a woman makes a slave, she never looses his chain. And now, will you sing for me some lines, which were intended to express the spirit of our national unity? They were sent me for correction by the same friend who wrote 'Our Flag.' You know the creative and the critical talent are seldom united, so that while he sings I am expected to snarl. Here, look at the verses, and see if a 'little rebel,' as you call yourself, can have the courage, or the magnanimity to sing them."

Anna took the paper, and glancing her eye rapidly over it, went to her piano, which Edward had already opened. A single touch showed her mistress of the instrument. Soon her graceful fingers were flying, as if inspired, over the white keys. As she played, her soul kindled, and all the power and pathos of her voice awaked to thrill Elling-wood with love and admiration. Far across the lawn, and even over the sea, floated the melody as she sang:

> North, South, East, West unite
> Beneath our Flag of Light,
>   Be one, be true!
> Ours is the furnace-blast;
> Ours is the old-world-past;
> 'Ours is to melt, recast,
>   And shape the new.

> Over the Orient first
> The star of Empire burst
>   In morning-ray;
> It soon o'er Europe gleams;
> See! o'er our West it beams—
> A sun of glory streams
>   To make Earth's day.

> Men of each clime, speech, race,
> Under our Flag find place,
>   And Freedom's rest;
> Your blood with ours must flow,
> Your life with ours must grow,
> Till we a Manhood show,
>   Earth's last and best.

> Let States and sects no more
> Hurl hate from shore to shore !
>   Let all be one !
> Here smiles the hope of man ;
> Here Time's last act began ;
> Here closes God's world-plan,
>   And sets His sun.
>
> It sets, to burst more bright
> O'er man, a son of light,
>   Immortal now.
> See Earth, from fire arise !
> Her beauty death defies,
> While 'neath eternal skies
>   To Christ all bow.

Anna arose from her piano in the utmost agitation. She seemed pale with alarm. Trembling, she exclaimed, with excited fear:

"Edward, I seem to have sung your death-note. I am amazed at our imprudence. Those words may not only involve you, but myself. I dreaded lest you might even be overheard reciting the stanzas to the Flag, and am astonished at my own folly, which has so exposed you in this parlor."

Ellingwood began himself to be frightened. However, he endeavored to quiet Anna's apprehensions, and said jocosely, "I am sure, besides ourselves, there are only negroes about Sea-Side, and they certainly will not object to the sentiments we have uttered. I promise you before long something on a more tender topic."

They then parted for the night. Just after Miss Austin retired, a tender, manly, thrilling voice was heard to sing beneath her window :

> Open, Love, thy lattice wide !
>   Let the moon-beam pass !
> See it through these branches glide !
>   See it on the grass !

Open, Love, thy lattice now!
　Let the breeze come through!
Let it play around thy brow,
　And thy bosom woo!

Open, Love, thy lattice while
　I gaze up on thee!
Let yon star-beam kiss a smile
　From thy lip to me!

Love, thy lattice wide, wide fling!
　Be like yon bright sky;
While the sea is murmuring
　It bends lovingly.

17*

CHAPTER XXIII.

A BISHOP FOILED.

"General Ellingwood, I am rejoiced to see your health so greatly improved," said Cleveland, as he met Edward one evening at the ocean-seat. "I suppose," he continued, smiling, "that not only air and exercise, but also good company promote your restoration."

"Yes," said Edward, laughing, and unable to resist the temptation, "you know, Bishop, it is not good for man to be alone." Instantly observing and regretting the confusion produced by his words, he added in a kind tone, "Certainly nothing could be more favorable to an invalid than this charming spot. To me the sea is an inspiration, and what can exceed that expanse, with its gleaming sails, stretching away to meet the sky, and mingle with its blue ?"

"It is indeed lovely," replied the Bishop, "scarcely surpassed on the shores of the Mediterranean. I am delighted to find my old pupil after many hardships and perils placed in a situation where so much conspires to his recovery and his pleasure. May I hope that in the joy of the fleeting hour he is not forgetting those deeper questions which touch our mortal state ?"

"Nothing like war," returned Ellingwood, "solemnizes a thoughtful mind ; while it may make the trifling reckless, on those who reflect the effect is opposite. I have often heard eternity in a cannon-roar."

"Have you, my dear sir, permit me to inquire, ever

passed from the general claims of Christianity to the particular claims of the Roman Catholic Church?" said Cleveland, in a voice musical as an evening silver-chime.

Looking steadily into the face of Edward, he continued with designed deliberation, so as to note the effect of his words, "I am certain you have heard that your friend Charles received the communion at my hands."

"Yes, Miss Austin gave me *all* the particulars of her brother's death and *burial*," answered Edward, returning the Bishop's gaze, and emphasizing the words *all* and *burial.*

"But," he resumed, remarking a blush excited by this fact, "perhaps we had better avoid the exciting topics you suggest."

"General Ellingwood," replied Cleveland, tenderly and impressively, "I am about departing for Europe on a perilous voyage, and I must express my great solicitude in regard to your ecclesiastical relations."

"You are aware how fixed are my opinions," said Ellingwood. "My father is a rigid Congregationalist, and from him I have inherited an enthusiasm for the Protestant faith, equal to the Presbyterian ardor of General Brompton, while from my mother, I derive an equal reverence for the Order and Liturgy of her ancestral Church. Dr. Elton, my maternal uncle, has, from childhood, directed my theological, as my father directed my legal studies. I fear, if we commence an argument, I may be tempted to show the sharpness of the lawyer, and the hardness of the soldier."

"I, who have known General Ellingwood from his youth, am assured, however, that he *can* say nothing inconsistent with the delicacy of a gentleman," interposed Cleveland.

"As I am certain," answered Edward, "that, although I may differ in opinion from my former President, I shall always admire his talents, and respect his sincerity. He will, of course, pardon me, if I borrow from his own brilliant lectures to maintain the principles I now advocate."

The Bishop felt the thrust, but concealed its pain. He replied, "If Heaven has poured over my mind a sudden illumination, it is not strange that I should wish to guide a beloved pupil to the light. More especially am I anxious, since pointing your dying friend to the Church, and giving him spiritual nourishment from her bosom."

"My dear Bishop," said Ellingwood, "my clerical uncle, hoping to secure me for the ministry, early instructed me in the Primitive and Anglican Fathers. Nothing can shake my belief, that the English Reformation restored the Faith and Order of the Apostolic Church. I tell you in the beginning, that, while I regard the Order, I reverence the Faith, and that my sympathies are infinitely more with Protestantism, which has repudiated the Order, than with Romanism, which, I sincerely think, has corrupted the Faith. Pardon my plainness, and let me say, that we had better avoid argument."

"My dear Edward," replied the Bishop, with his peculiar grace of manner, "I perceive that your heart and head are fully and pleasantly occupied at Sea-Side. As I will not, however, have another opportunity for years, we may at least exchange views."

Ellingwood, perceiving the contest inevitable, resolved with the tact of a soldier, to assume the offensive.

"May I ask," he inquired, "if the Roman system can be constructed simply from the Scripture and the Apostolic fathers?"

"Certainly not!" at once answered the Bishop.

"Then all that the Council of Trent added to the Council of Nice depends on the authority of the Church?" pursued the General.

"Indubitably!" responded the Bishop.

"And the infallibility of the Church, presumes the infallibility of the Head?" continued the soldier-lawyer.

"That necessary consequence, is the glory of Rome, and will, hereafter, be proclaimed by a General Council."

"Then you resolve all that separates Anglicanism and Protestantism from Romanism into the Papal Infallibility?"

"Unquestionably," returned Cleveland, "that doctrine is both the foundation and the key-stone of the eternal Arch."

"Allow me then, to urge," said Ellingwood, "that as I must employ my reason before I accept either Scriptural infallibility or Papal infallibility, I am, in any case, thrown on my individual responsibility; and that I prefer the words of my Lord attested by supernatural evidence, to the declarations of His vicar who utters no prophecy and performs no miracle to sustain his claim."

"General Ellingwood, we will defer until another interview that branch of the subject," quickly interrupted Cleveland, surprised and embarrassed by the force and fluency of his pupil.

"As the whole question between us, by your admission, turns on Papal Infallibility," pressed Edward, "my reason rejects the dogma, because it would place the sanction of eternal truth on heresy, and superstition, and crime, and subject the world to the sway and worship of a mortal, who, claiming an attribute of God, exhibits every weakness of man. No system could, with me, involve difficulties so monstrous. If hair-cloth mortifies the flesh, human infallibility certainly mortifies the spirit."

Feeling his soul kindle with his theme, and fearing his zeal had carried him too far, he added, with a most respectful air and tone, "Excuse me, I pray you, excuse me, my dear Bishop, if I have assumed the theologian, and spoken with a boldness made improper, both by my own ignorance, and your office."

Cleveland was evidently disappointed. His numerous converts had been among dreamy girls and fashionable ladies.

Charles Austin had been too weak to offer resistance, and had indeed never even thought of accepting his conclusions. In Ellingwood he found a manly intellect he had himself furnished with arguments, and disciplined into strength, and which, to much of the learning of the divine, united the vigor of the soldier, and the shrewdness of the lawyer. He was himself also more remarkable for erudition than logic, and had been won to Rome rather through feeling than reason. Now conscious of his own weakness, and his adversary's power, he declined the contest he had excited. Nay! truth had made an impression on his soul, which was destined to shake the very foundations of his life. The pupil had indeed become the teacher, and the teacher the pupil.

Seeing Miss Anna Austin approach, he was greatly relieved, and taking the hands of Ellingwood in his own, and pressing them with cordial warmth, he said blandly: "Your words would embark us on an ocean more stormy and dangerous than that I soon expect to cross. When the mariner perceives the tempest, he steers for the harbor. Let us, then, for the present, take refuge in our mutual friendship. Perhaps at some future time I may write to you fully, and answer your objections. And there," he said, pointing with a beaming face, "before the elements can marshal for battle, comes an angel to smile away our clouds, and calm our tempests. You, I am certain, will be the last to resist the magic of her presence."

As these words were completed, Anna reached the ocean-seat, and stood before the gentlemen in the brightest glow of her loveliness.

"Good evening," she exclaimed, while a western cloud painted the rose upon her cheek. "Good evening, gentlemen. I hope I am not interrupting important discussions which may shape the future of our country, and the world. If my presence will prevent the progress of humanity I will withdraw at once. I perceive in the solemnity of your faces, the gravity of your topic."

The Bishop, and the General smiled. "Nay, Miss Austin, Nay," began the former. "We rather welcome you as a celestial visitant sent down in that evening-cloud to breathe peace into two hostile warriors, and stop the rising clash of battle. Had you come later bandages would have been needed for our wounds." Thus the presence of a pure woman subdues into gentleness the sterner nature of man. Distant be the day when her refining image marred by an unnatural and repulsive masculinity shall abandon our world to grossness, and bestiality!

The Bishop now took occasion to part with Edward and Anna, and they were soon again drinking the nectar which distils, but during one brief period of any human history. He believed that his work at Sea-Side, and indeed in America, was for the present completed. A brilliant reward he knew was awaiting him at Rome. He soon embarked for Liverpool, at Savannah, in the confederate steamer, Britain. As he stood on the deck in the shadow of the evening, with his hands folded across his breast, the sad conviction was forced on his soul that he was bidding adieu forever to the land of his birth.

He gazed through the gathering gloom on the fading shore with inexpressible pain. Night soon veiled it from his view. Raising his hand to his face he felt his finger touched by an unconscious tear. Looking upward to a cloud revealed by a sudden lightning-flash his Emily seemed smiling through its illuminated folds. The unstable sea below, and the darkening sky above, oft gleaming in momentary glare, gave evidence of a speedy elemental war, and were exact emblems of his own disturbed heart and uncertain future.

CHAPTER XXIV.

AFTER the battle of Gettysburg Mrs. Cleveland and
Mary Ellingwood were indefatigable in their hospital
labors. Exhausted by fatigue and exposure they had
come to Willow-Shade for recuperation, and were meditating a European tour.

As they were sitting on the piazza discussing plans, the
Judge approached in that bright, gay manner which sheds
such grace and beauty over age.

"Ah! ladies," he exclaimed, holding a letter in his right
hand, and glancing over it through his spectacles, "this
era of iron is realizing the fairy-tales of the nursery. Here
is news to make your hearts flutter. Edward is a prisoner
in the hands of a giant."

"What can you mean, papa?" cried Mary, in alarm.

"I mean just what I say," replied the Judge. "Your
brother was captured by his rival, cousin Hercules, and is
now on his parole at Sea-Side."

"Sea-Side!" exclaimed the ladies in a breath, with lifted
hands and wondering faces.

"At all events," said Mary, "he will have an angel in
his prison to smile on him in his chains—possibly to loose
his limbs and open the door."

"I have heard," continued Mrs. Cleveland, "that
Major Worstal is a man whose passions correspond to his
bulk, and I fear he will regard General Ellingwood with
no particular favor. Civil war and private hate are like

the tiger and the leopard let loose on the same victim. Can we leave the country knowing that your son is in such hands?"

"My dear Madam," replied the Judge, "if our movements were to be regulated by the ebb and flow of war, they would resemble an oarless and sailless skiff on the ocean-tide. We can never, at any moment, ascertain or control Edward's situation. Sword and bullet are remorseless executioners. Any hour may telegraph his fate. When I placed my son on the nation's altar, I surrendered him without reservation to that Power which can shield him, whether we are in Europe or America. The arrangements of our voyage have been already made."

"Made! you astonish me, papa! You forget that we ladies need some time for preparations. We thought it doubtful whether you would expose us on the sea to the polite visits of confederate officers."

"The expectation of such gallant attentions," answered the Judge, with a gay laugh, "removes the necessity of an extensive wardrobe, and therefore, of long delay. I believe half a lady's life is stitched by her needle into lace and ribbons."

"And yet," interposed Mrs. Cleveland, "when book and pen absorb that same valuable portion of our feminine existence, gentlemen are first to notice our diminished charms, and grumble at us, as blue stockings, or masculinities."

"And I know," said Mary, raising her eye archly to her father's face, "no more critical glance, than that gleaming beneath the sober brow of a certain venerable New England Judge, whose neatness always suggests a looking-glass."

"A truce, a truce," answered the old gentleman, with a beseeching tone and gesture. "I would rather encounter a Parrot and a Rodman than the batteries now opening on me. I fly. I submit. Your prisoner, ladies! only let me add for your satisfaction, if the Britain, or any other confederate ship captures you on your voyage, it will be by silencing the guns of the America. That I think about as difficult as to stop the artillery of the clouds. I have obtained permission of the government to sail with my nephew, Captain Dick Ingraham. So much for the privilege of being government officials—you nurses and I Judge." The ladies laughed, and expressed their great satisfaction with the arrangement.

Now follows all the bustle of preparation. However absurd and extravagant to incur expense, and increase luggage, by American purchases for a European tour, even the most experienced travelers cannot always take the next train for New York, and the next ship for Liverpool. Perhaps, as our ladies had never been abroad, they did not wisely economize time, and money, and labor. Certain it is, that for the next few days the coachman and the seamstress were in constant requisition at Willow-Shade. Purchases were made. Fashions were selected. Dresses were cut, fitted, discussed. Trunks were procured, packed, checked, expressed. Needle and tongue and the last "Bazar" reigned supreme. Yet beneath the confusion and the energy, was an unexpressed sorrow weighing on every spirit, caused by the recollection of Edward Ellingwood, and the state of the country. When all humiliating preliminaries—so needful for the transportation of the human body, and such painful satires on the difficulties of our mortal locomotion—were completed, Willow-Shade was abandoned to silence and desolation, under the care of faithful servants. The Judge and his daughter, and their friend, were soon whirled, by rail, to our national metropolis, and rattled over its streets to the pier of the stately America. Entering the cabin, our party received a warm welcome from Captain Richard Ingraham. When gliding, through the evening, over the bay to the ocean, they admired the islands, bathed in light, reposing on their green inverted shadows, and the graceful outlines of circling shores, with their smooth slopes and bold heights. There was a glow of inspiration in the prospect, followed by that rush of the emotions awakened in those about to be transferred, for the first time, from the young civilization of America to the old civilization of Europe.

On the fourth day of the voyage, the ladies stood on the deck of the swift ship conversing with the Judge and the gallant Captain.

" Dick," said the former gentleman familiarly to his nephew, " do you really think that steam is so great an improvement over the sail?"

" Let me reply, uncle," answered Ingraham, " by another question. Would you go back from the rail-car to the stage-coach, and from the telegraph to the mail-bag?"

" Aye, aye, that settles all paternal objections," cried Mary, clapping her hands with glee. " A Wall street broker would not be more restless if he did not study the market by steam and lightning, than my own dear papa without the telegraphic column of his morning paper rushed in three hours from New York to Willow-shade."

" I grant we are perverted by excessive civilization," answered the Judge, smiling at the truthfulness of his daughter's picture. " I admit, too, that without steam and electricity this country could neither subdue rebellion nor preserve its existence. I concede that Stephenson and Morse are as much our saviours as Grant and Sherman. Yet I sigh for the old days when instead of that puffing funnel, and yon black-smoke cloud, the silent vessel with her stately masts, tall and tapering, glided gracefully over the sea."

"Sentiment! uncle, sentiment!" cried Ingraham, laughing. Then pointing to a distant speck on the sky, he added: "If that should prove the Britain, you may thank Heaven for a steam-screw, and a Rodman."

All looked intently in the direction indicated. The Captain lifted his glass to his eye, but unable to make out anything clearly, soon lowered it, and held it in his hand.

"Why, Judge," began Mrs. Cleveland, "I did not know that a gentleman of your age so preferred the beautiful to the practical. You will be wanting back the gods of Greece. This age of iron, steam, and lightning, will never make an Agora, a Jupiter Olympus, or a Parthenon."

"No, no! I am not quite prepared to restore heathenism. But I must say I would rather behold ten old wooden ships, with their old stately grace, go into battle in the old sailor-like way, than to see two steam-rams butting each other like the horned patriarchs of the flock; or a low monitor gliding snakily over the sea like the fabulous serpent; or even a dozen such ships as Dick's, driving against each other like fire-fiends. Imagine Nelson, or Perry, fighting under that smoke-stack, or in the roar of battle, stopping their ears to keep out the scream of a villainous steam-whistle. Why, nephew, you have taken away all the poetry of war. Nothing remains but iron, and powder, and blood."

18*

"Well, uncle, before many hours you will praise Heaven for the iron and powder, if not for the blood." Then raising his glass, and gazing intently, while all stood around in silent suspense, he added, still looking: "That ship is the Britain. No other vessel on the sea could show such grace and speed."

The ladies turned pale at this announcement, and even the Judge appeared grave. "Here, Dick," said the latter, "let me have your glass. I have been used to the ocean since a boy—indeed I served two years as a midshipman, and the law sharpens a man's wit, even if the bench dulls his brain."

Ingraham gave his telescope to the Judge, who adjusted it to his eye. Lifting it, and turning it towards the enlarging vessel, he looked long, and eagerly. Completing his observation, he turned to the Captain, saying: "Dick, you are mistaken. Confess that an old lawyer, of seventy, has better eyes than a sailor of forty. Beg your pardon, I forgot you were a bachelor. That is the British flag."

These last words made fire flash from the glance of Ingraham. He was no longer the gallant, but the commander. Snatching the glass he gazed an instant, and then burst out:

"That ship is the Britain—built by British capital—constructed by British workmen—owned by British subjects—launched in British waters—manned by British seamen, and plundering our merchantmen for British pockets. See! she is hauling down the lion; up goes the confederate flag! Judge! ladies! clear the decks! Go below. We must prepare for action! The America shall never run away from the Britain."

"God bless you Dick," exclaimed the Judge, hastily grasping his nephew's hand.

"God bless you! God bless you!" ejaculated the ladies, somewhat colorless with feminine alarm, as under the escort of Judge Ellingwood, they passed into the cabin to go below. We need not think it strange if the party knelt solemnly in prayer. Indeed, again and again the calm voice of the brave and venerable Judge was heard amid the thunders of battle, beseeching heaven to grant the America victory.

Above was the noise of hasty preparation. Then came down the hurried tramp of men. Voices of command rang over the waters. As the wind was rising rapidly, and the sea already rolling heavily, the sails were furled. Captain Ingraham resolved to obtain, if possible, a raking fire from the top of the wave, and made all his arrangements accordingly. Nothing could exceed the graceful majesty of the Britain approaching with her masts and arms on the sky, and leaving behind far along the deep, a trail of smoke rising in clouds from the ocean to the heavens. Above her could be distinctly seen a confederate flag waving its defiance against the stars floating from the America. Now there was a sudden flash followed by a lifting smoke-wreath, and a thundering roar; and then a gigantic ball came crashing across the federal ship, tearing away her bulwarks, and killing an officer and wounding seven men. The groans of the dying mingled with the winds, and blood-spots were on the deck. Broadside after broadside roared and blazed from the confederate, carrying down fore-mast, and mizzen-mast of her foe, and on every hand scattering death.

The ship of Ingraham was noiseless as a cloud. Her purpose now became evident, and speed was essential to achieve it. Hence the furnaces of the America were blazing, and her boilers hissing, while unfortunately for the Britain her fires had been neglected. The two vessels now dashed over the sea in huge eccentric circles. They rush; they turn; they gyrate. It becomes the whole effort of the America to obtain a broadside against her adversary from stem to stern, and the whole effort of the Britain to prevent such an advantage. Nothing could exceed the sublimity of the spectacle. The ships appeared like two circling sea-monsters breathing flames, and instinct with life. They puffed; they panted; they palpitated—each propelled and animated by a heart of fire. But in this contest the steam of the America gave her the superiority. While her foe has been firing, she has not discharged a shot. Now her end is attained. She is to windward. She is on the crest of a wave. She has the Britain lying below her visible from rudder-head to figure-head. The glance of Ingraham interprets the moment. His trumpet rings—" fire." The America is in a blaze. Thunders burst from her ports. A tempest of balls is hurled against the Britain, raking her decks, crashing into her engine, shattering her boiler. One huge missive passing through her hatch pierces her hull, and lets in the ocean. A shell falls into her magazine. It bursts as the vessel goes down enveloped in smoke and steam. Flames for an instant reveal her outlines, and glare across the sea and flash into the sky until the waves and the clouds seem mountains of mingling fire.

CHAPTER XXV.

AGONY.

"SPLENDIDLY done, Dick, splendidly," said Judge Ellingwood, warmly embracing his nephew on the deck of the America. "Yesterday made you an Admiral."

"I thank Heaven for victory," replied Ingraham. "Such an hour occurs but once in a sailor's lifetime. But some of my poor fellows have paid dearly for our triumph," and tears chased each other down the bronze of his manly cheek.

"Ah! Mary and Mrs. Cleveland have given me a sad account of the havoc. They say the mutilations are fearful. The Britain made many a widow and orphan before she sank down in the sea. These stains of blood on your deck tell a tale of death. Is your ship injured?"

"Battered, and pounded, and bruised," answered Ingraham, "but not at all disabled."

"The Spanish ambassador recently remarked to me, in the White House, that there is a special Providence over children, drunkards, and the United States. Perhaps he meant satirically that we were young and intoxicated. But certainly the peculiar favor has been extended to the America. Have you heard anything more from the Britain?"

"Some of her spars and masts, and rigging, were seen this morning on the waves, and a lion, with the head knocked off, floating meekly beneath our stars. We knew that animal was her figure-head. The Britain is on the bottom of the Atlantic, and will remain there until the sea gives up its dead."

"Did none of her officers or crew escape?" inquired the Judge, anxiously.

"Oh, yes, uncle," answered the Captain. "Just before the magazine exploded, a yawl pushed off, with twenty men. We saw it pull towards us in the light of the flames, when that glare and thunder burst from the sea into the sky."

While this conversation was occurring on the deck, Mary Ellingwood and Mrs. Cleveland were sitting together in the cabin. The latter seemed fearfully agitated. A tempest had evidently rushed over the calm of her life. Mary said to her, in a most tender and earnest tone: "It seems impossible, absolutely impossible. Surely you must have been mistaken. Your nerves have been shocked by the battle, and made your imagination sensitive to impressions."

"You know, Mary," replied Mrs. Cleveland, with a sad expression, and an emphatic shake of the head, "I am not liable to practice deceptions on myself. Not all the artillery of earth could startle my soul like that one glance at his person. A wife does not easily mistake her husband."

"Pardon me, my dear friend, if I ask the particulars, that I may judge for myself," interposed Mary.

"I was dressing a sailor's shattered arm when the terrific explosion occurred which sank the Britain. Looking over the sea, I perceived a loaded yawl in the brilliant light. Not long after, it reached our ship, when I was attracted by the plash of its oars. Then your cousin hailed the boat, inquiring the number and names of those aboard. Conceive my agitation, as I heard a familiar voice respond, and soon after repeat—Bishop Arthur Cleveland."

She could utter no more, but fell back, almost lifeless, on the sofa. Mary hastily snatched a glass, and sprinkled some water on the face of her friend, and she was soon restored to consciousness. Mrs. Cleveland then resumed— "Suppressing my emotion, I retired to my state-room, and flung myself on my berth, immediately in front of the cabin-lamp. The door was open, and not long after a form passed I recognized instantly. It was Mr. Cleveland." That name again aroused feelings in the bosom of the wife she had supposed buried forever.

When her agitation was once more subdued, Mary ventured to inquire: "Do you suppose he saw, and knew you?"

"I am certain of the fact," said Mrs. Cleveland. "The light shone brightly on my face. As he passed, he turned through the door a casual glance. He started, threw up his hands, stumbled over the floor, and fell heavily. Afterwards I heard a groan from his state-room, which will haunt my ear forever."

The recital of Mrs. Cleveland was here interrupted by the mournful toll of a bell, whose deep voice rang far over the ocean. The ladies knew the signal, and hastened above. A sad spectacle met their gaze. On the deck were the bodies of ten sailors, ghastly, and mutilated, lying side by side. Their wounds were concealed as much as possible beneath their shirts, and their manly faces were composed in death. Even to the inevitable neck-tie they were clothed in their nautical attire. After a brief service, solemnly said beneath the stars of the flag floating gaily in the morning, there was heard plunge after plunge, and soon the waters settled calmly over their bodies to hide them until they hear **the trump of the** Judge. Retiring from the scene, both ladies sought in slumber, relief and rest from excitement and fatigue.

That Bishop Cleveland saw, and recognized his wife, will **be evident** from his diary, long afterward found by Captain Ingraham in a crevice of his state-room. Although **stained** with tears, and showing plain proofs of a mind fevered by suffering into insanity, **we** will conclude our chapter with an extract from its wild, and often incoherent pages:

"I see my Emily. Heavens! what serene, holy, suffering **beauty.** I gaze at her, while I write, through **a** crevice of my state-room. In her face—melancholy, agony! That hand I have clasped. That bosom I have pressed. **That lip,** oh how often, have **I kissed!** My brain whirls. Shall **I rush to her?** Shall **I fall** at her feet? Shall I beg her forgiveness? Emily, oh my Emily, let us **build** again our home. Nay! too late! too late! too late! **Gone** that bliss forever! Last night a thin board was between our bodies. I heard her breathing. **I felt her heart-beats.** Our child! **My Ada! Is** she cold in her grave? Her **father knows not. I see** her! There! there! there! **Her** blue eyes! **Her** sunny smile! It burns my heart! Her little fingers are in my hair. Worms! worms! they **creep, worms.** Her breath scorches my cheek! **Her** curls are snakes—hissing, twisting, glaring. Stop, Ada, stop! I am your father! father! ghost! skeleton! devil! Nay! I am Bishop—the Right—Reverend—Arthur—Cleveland! A mitre! a cardinal's hat! a tiara! St. Peter's! The Vatican! **An American** Pope! Infallible! **Sovereign!** Adored! God!"

CHAPTER XXVI.

Major Worstal having executed the commission which took him from Sea-Side, was returning thither, through Richmond. He resolved to obtain from the confederate authorities, a revocation of the order that had removed Edward Ellingwood more immediately from his power. Indeed, his object was to have his rival conveyed to the prison he himself commanded. A strong Southern feeling, occasioned by the national policy in arming the negro, greatly assisted his plans. General Brompton had used all his influence to defeat his nephew's vengeance, and had hitherto succeeded. He now perceived that the Richmond Cabinet was wavering; and fearing to press Ellingwood's cause too far, he resolved to employ personal solicitation. While he and the Major were sitting in the room of the Capitol Hotel, he said:

"Henry, you have always been disposed to oblige me, and I want now to ask a particular favor." Worstal reddened to the forehead, and scowled frightfully. Anticipating what was to come, he replied, abruptly, and almost rudely:

"Uncle, I know what you want. You are trying to keep Ellingwood at Sea-Side, and have used every means to thwart my plans. Now you would persuade me to yield,—it is no use—I'll have my way."

"But you forget," urged the General, "that your

prisoner is a son of my old friend, and that Charles loved him as a brother. Besides he and Anna "—

"Don't talk to me about Anna!" cried Worstal, rising, and blackening with rage. Stamping on the floor until the dust flew from the carpet in clouds, and danced in the morning sun-beams, he exclaimed, "She has treated me like a dog. This thieving Yankee has stole her heart. Yet you uncle would have him stay at Sea-Side, and woo and win your niece. My obligations to you are now gone. You have turned my enemy. Never," he added with a frightful oath, "shall you change my purpose."

General Brompton was surprised and indignant at the brutal violence of his nephew. He too arose, and. confronting him, looked steadily into his face. Placing his hand on his shoulder he said in a deep, low, firm voice, "Henry, beware! I read your heart. You wish General Ellingwood in your prison to take his life, and gratify your vengeance. You may obtain your order, but his blood I require at your hand."

Conscience-smitten Worstal cowered, and trembled before his uncle's burning gaze. Recovering instantly his effrontery he returned glance for glance, and said defiantly, and fiendishly, "And you have a care General Brompton! Too great an interest in a Yankee officer may cost you your position, and bring a mob down on Sea-Side." Then turning away abruptly he left the room.

General Brompton was startled and alarmed at his nephew's threat and tone, and saw that he must abandon Ellingwood to his fate.

Worstal in a few hours had the coveted order in his pocket. Again and again he took it out, and unfolded it, and read it with demoniacal joy, and replaced it with the glad consciousness he had achieved a victory which placed his hated rival wholly in his power. He at once took the train for Sea-Side. The fiery speed of the cars increased the flame in his breast. He felt towards Ellingwood as Satan had long before towards Adam, when he leered on him in the midst of Paradise, and resolved to turn his heaven into hell.

Nothing in the meantime could surpass the pure and intense joys of Edward and Anna. The former had greatly reproached himself for his imprudence. Even in his sleep the words Miss Austin had sung came floating on his soul until he waked in alarm. Visions of captivity crowded on his fears. He once dreamed of a dark prison, a manacled captive, and an angel entering with a smile to unloose his fetters. Still on the next day was a renewal of the spell. The young soldier was suddenly transported from the rude and bloody scenes of war to the uninterrupted society of her whose image had lived in his heart for long separating years. Anna and Edward walked, and talked, and rode, and sailed, and sang, and lost themselves in each other with all the cloudless raptures of a true love. Even Nature smiled on them sympathetically. The bloom of the orange shed down its fragrance. Around, and beneath, and above them waved and flashed brilliant southern flowers. The dreamy languor of the air dissolved them into greater tenderness. Earth, sea, sky were uniting to complete their bliss. But no spot had such a charm as the ocean-seat. Reclining there one evening, Edward said,

" I have been laughing, Anna, at my absurd mistake in supposing you Mrs. Major Worstal. What a fool I was! I could more readily believe Diana would marry Vulcan. My idiocy cost me dear. Pardon me if, after all I suffered, I have no particular love for your mighty cousin."

"I can assure you, Edward," replied Anna, smiling, "he has not the highest affection for you. I shudder when I think of you in his power."

"Sometimes I have an awful fear," responded Edward, "that he will come a shadow between our lives. Here we are, side by side, and heart to heart, and yet a whole war-history is to be written before you can be my wife."

"Stop, Edward, stop," she cried, with a ringing laugh, "no clouds over Eden! Let us now pluck flowers in our sunlight—thorns and gloom will come of themselves, and soon enough."

"Anna, your words are like a morning when the birds sing," he replied, taking her hand, and turning on her a face full of manly love. "Now let me paint you a picture. The war is over. Peace smiles over the country. A vessel comes into yon harbor. A happy company pass over the beach, and cross the lawn, and enter the house. When night approaches lamps flash and blaze from tree and window. Merry voices are heard. Before the altar of that Church stands a happy pair. The service is over and then come kisses, congratulations, presents, music, dancing—shall I finish my sketch, Anna?"

"No, Edward, no," she answered. The deep tranquility of love, breathing from her heart to her face, was converted into the most violent alarm, as she cried, pointing to a wood immediately in their rear: "There come, I fear, messengers of danger."

Looking in the direction indicated by her delicate finger, we perceive two men emerging from the trees, and running over the field. Jumbo and Jim are in eager haste. The father held in his hand a fragmentary hat, crumpled out of all shape, by his agitated fingers, while the son, in his rush, had torn a pantaloon, whose tatters streamed shabbily in the winds. On Jumbo's smooth shining head, dotted over with clumps of white wool, stood big sweat-drops, which rolled down his cheeks, and scattered as he ran along the grass. Being somewhat rotund in body and stiff in limb, his efforts at haste made him resemble a fat, unwieldy, antiquated ox, driven to provoking haste by pelting boy, or barking cur, and not specially graceful in its movements. Jim followed close behind, looking very much like a black, fleshy, farm colt, fitted for the cart or plough, but forced into the awkward violence of the race. The son was evidently gaining on the sire, whose paternal dignity, with panting chest, and puffing lips, interposed to check the disrespect-ful speed.

"Dar, young nigga, dar," he cried, in a tone of fatherly command, "stop you'se shins! you'se bess keep 'zactly in dat place which suit the gosslin who always hab de man-ners to run behin' de goose."

"De goose! de goose!" replied Jim, with all the chuckle his breathlessness permitted.

"Dat am de truf. But 'spose de waddlin' goose hab big fat and short leg, and de gosslin' am in hurry?"

"Nebber, Jim, nebber," panted Jumbo, holding out his arm before his advancing offspring, and turning his black palm with a restraining push, "forget de respec' due de venerashun of dat bein' who brot you on dis yer yearth. Your fadda will tell de news to dat angel ob light and ob lub." Jim, not entirely heeding the admonition, Jumbo continued, "De Scripta say, 'git up before de hoary head.'"

At this point, the son tumbling, fell at the feet of his dignified progenitor, and the father, with all his hurry,

19*

could not resist the temptation for one word of parental reproof.

"Dar," he exclaimed, with evident satisfaction, as Jim arose, rubbing his bruised shins, "Dat be judgmen' ob Hebben on you for forgettin' de comman'."

Just at this moment, however, Jumbo himself struck his great foot against a stone, and, like many others, falsified his unauthorized application of Scriptural inflictions.

"Yes," cried Jim, stopping and laughing from ear to ear, "judgmen' ob Hebben not from fadda to son, but from son to fadda."

The fallen patriarch rising slowly, and scratching his thin wool, with a bewildered look, started forward, side by side, with his sole male heir and representative, saying, while he ran:

"I'se tell you, Jim, de truf of de 'terpretation ob de word can nebber get unda a young nigga's wool, till it 'spand to greater comprehenshun ob de ideas."

By this time the black pair had approached the ocean-seat. Jumbo was in advance, still clutching in his hand the injured hat, while Jim, instructed by the rebukes he had just received, followed behind at a reverential distance. Both drew near, bowing and scraping in their African way, and equally conspicuous for the African heel, and the African lip.

Miss Austin, who had observed their curious progress over the field, and imagined what transpired, smiled in spite of her alarm. She exclaimed hastily, "Jumbo, you seem to be the bearer of important news. Tell me at once!"

The voice of his mistress made the faithful creature forgetful of himself, and recalled all his fears. He replied with trembling eagerness, "Missus Anna, we'se 'fraid de Ginral's in danga ob de prisun, and dat dar not nice as de Sea-Side."

"What is your reason for thinking this?" asked Anna, now fearfully anxious.

"Mysel, and dat dar young nigga war pickin berries in de wood, and Massa Wossal, he pass 'long wid six sodgas, and he not see us, and he ride a cursin', and a swearin', and a sayin' he had odas to take de Gin'ral to de prisun, and he sware he see how, how "—here Jumbo hesitated.

"Speak, speak, quickly," said Anna.

"Shall Jumbo tell 'zackly what de Maja say?"

"Exactly," answered Anna emphatically, and hastily.

"De berry words?" answered Jumbo looking inquiringly into the face of Ellingwood, who cried in a loud and decided tone,

"The very words!"

"Well," resumed Jumbo, "he say,—he say—he say, he see,—he see—he see how de Yank ofica cum' Souf to —to—to be a courtin', and a marryin' and a carryin' 'way de Soudern gals."

Edward, and Anna colored, and smiled. The latter then said sadly, "I fear it is too true. My uncle has written to me informing me that Henry has employed every possible means to thwart his efforts, and to have your parole revoked by an order for your removal from Sea-Side, and confinement in the prison he commands. He has undoubtedly succeeded. We must prepare for the worst, and trust in Heaven."

Here Jim showed a manifest desire to interpose his advice. Rolling his eyes first towards his parent, and then towards General Ellingwood, running his finger through his wool, and shifting from foot to foot, he at last ventured to say. "May'se Jim 'spress his 'pinion afore de Gin'ral and de Missus?"

"Certainly, certainly," answered Edward.

"Is'e then 'spectfully say, dat Massa Brompton's Tiga stan' in de stall, jist rubbed and saddled. He beat Massa Henra's mar as de lightnin' beat de wind."

"No, no, Jim," replied Ellingwood, "I am on my parole, and if my imprisonment means death, my honor cannot be violated. Besides, there come the Major and his troop."

Anna, overcome by these words, fell into the arm of Edward, who, supporting her, brushed away her tears, and snatched from her lips a rightful farewell. Just at this moment Worstal and his band appeared.

He saw his cousin in the arms of his rival, in the very place he had been himself rejected. It is not wonderful such a spectacle should wake the tiger in his heart. Spurring Minerva he galloped towards the ocean-seat followed by his troop. The clang of hoofs aroused Anna to a consciousness of her position and her peril. She read at once the demon in the eye of Worstal, who had, during his journey, been revolving the reports he had heard from Sea-Side. Before his eyes he had demonstration of their truth. Here was a man—a union officer—a Yankee invader—his prisoner—introduced by himself into the house of his uncle—whom he had just seen unclasp his arms from the person of the girl he had loved in boyhood, and always expected to make his wife.

He was too much infuriated for words. Black and silent as a cloud, he rode to the place where Edward and Anna were now standing. He pointed to two of his men, and then to the General. He remained on Minerva while the soldiers hand-cuffed Ellingwood, and lifted him on his horse. While the troop were riding away, with Edward in their midst, the Major lingered behind, near his cousin. She came, and standing near Minerva, looked up into his face with an agony of entreaty. "Henry, cousin Henry," she exclaimed, clasping her arms over her swelling bosom, "Show the kindness and generosity which marked your boyhood when we played as children around this very seat!"

"Kindness!" he replied, with the mock and taunt of a fiend. "Generosity! Anna Austin, *Cousin* Anna Austin, who jilted him at Magnolia Hall, and twice refused him on this spot, begs favor of Henry Worstal towards a Yankee officer, who has just removed from her person his loving arms—an infernal General, who has come to free our slaves, to burn our homes, to pillage our plantations, to kill our people! Rather shoot, or hang the villain like a dog." Then taking his order from his pocket, he shook it over Anna's head.

"Here, look here, dear cousin! Here is proof I triumphed over *kind*, *generous*, Uncle Brompton, who would have saved Ellingwood to marry his niece. Here is proof I will be avenged." Then striking his spurs in Minerva, she leaped forward with frantic power, and occasionally waving the fatal paper, and looking back with the leer of Satan on his cousin, he galloped out of view.

CHAPTER XXVII.

ANNA AUSTIN required for the development of her latent power the very trial to which she was now exposed. Heretofore she had resembled the rose blooming in the window, and shielded from sun-blaze and tempest. Now, disciplined into solitary strength, she would prove a plant loving indeed watchful attentions, yet capable of independent growth and endurance. Losing none of that aroma which is the charm of her sex, her noble womanhood will develop into sympathetic congeniality with a manly nature trained to sturdiness by early lessons at home, and stern struggles in war.

Anna had slept many hours profoundly, overcome by her fatigue, when she was awakened by a gentle rap upon her door.

Having waited her response a negro maid said, " Missus Anna, Jumbo and Jim is here."

She replied, " Tell them to come into the parlor in ten minutes."

She arose, made a hasty toilet, knelt an instant in devotion, and hurrying down stairs, and entering the appointed apartment, seated herself on the sofa.

Jumbo and Jim soon after presented themselves, bowing respectfully, and looking affectionately, yet evidently jaded by a long ride, and loss of sleep.

Turning to them with the utmost anxiety, their mistress

exclaimed, " Quick, quick, tell me what has happened! Jumbo begin !"

The old negro, hitching his shoulder and shaking his head, obeyed.

" Missus Anna, we saddle de hosses as you auda. Is'e mounts Tiga and Jim mounts Nell, and wes'e fly like de clouds. Soon wes'e cotch de soun' of hoss-hoofs, and wes'e sees de Maja's sodga's, and de Gineral tied in de middle, and his mar led by de bridle. De Maja once stop and look ahind as if he cotch de nois' ob de hosses, but wes'e keeps out ob his sight. Den he succeed for'ad, and we follows ahead, till dey come 'bout a mile from de prison. We stops and hitches in de wood, and crawls wid de greatest cumspecshun tow'ad dat sweet-smellin' place." Here Jumbo's black nostril gave a significant twitch with a corresponding upward roll of his eye-whites and expression of his countenance. He then proceeded, " Dey tuk de Gineral to de Maja's quata's near de gate, and we stay dar lyin' in de berry-bushes for obs'rvashun. Now, please, Missus, let dis yer Jim finish dis 'arashun."

" You have done well, and shall have your reward," answered Anna, with a sweet look of approval.

" Our reward," responded Jumbo, " am to serb de Laud, rescue de Gineral, dispint de debbil, and show dat hell can't get de betta ob hebben."

" Now Jim," resumed Anna, smiling at this pious philosophy, " tell me what you have seen and heard."

" 'S'not to be s'posed," said Jim, turning with a dubious glance of mingled respect and satire toward his father, " dat de gosslin will hab de gab of de goose, but I'se say what I'se know from de 'pearance ob de spy. I'se creep near de prisun, and I'se lay a crouchin', and a lookin', and I'se see Fadda John and de Maja, and de Dr. Og'a comin', and I'se shake like de swamp aggers; de Maja's say, wes'e kill de cussed Yank'. 'No, No!' say de Preese, 'spar him life for Missa Anna sake.' De Oga' grin, and look kill, but he say nuffin. Den de Maja' swar and he rave, 'till dis nigga's years shake like de leabs ob de 'nolia in de sea-winds. Soon dey go 'way, de Maja cussin ebbrey step."

"My Missus," here interrupted Jumbo, with a look of paternal condescension, and approval towards his hopeful son, "see dat dis young nigga hab learn' by 'sperience, de way to 'municate idees. Pleas let him disprove hiself, by tellin de rest ob de circumstans'."

"Go on, Jim, go on!" replied Anna, with a slight degree of impatience, yet, well knowing that the only way to obtain the facts, was to let her faithful negroes have their own method of narration.

"As we crawl from de place, a man cum creepin in de shadder ob de trees, made by de risin' moon. We'se sca'd, and tremlin 'till he say: 'Whist! I'se know you niggas, I'se tot I'se heerd de nois.' 'Ha!' hes'e say, 'Jim, I'se know'd you'd be hur.' Den de light ob de moon fell on him face, and I'se see de spy dat cum in Massa Chal's camp on de bank ob de 'Tomac. Wuns he war a nigga, wuns he war a Dutchman, wuns he war a Chinay-man, wuns he war a woman-nuss, and he couldn't be drowned, nor hung, nor shot. Says he, 'They's'e gwine to starb de unyon ofica. I am actin' nuss in de quatas ob de Maja, and de Docta and de Preese. You'se nigga dig tun-nel in dis yer' groun' unda de room ob de Ginral, and under de room ob de Maja. Make hole trough de floor and bring de grub, and I'se sabe his life, and hes'e 'scape when hes'e can. Wes'e spoil deyr cussid plans.' Den he turn 'bout and creep back, and we'se crawl to de hosses, and ride like de furies to disport dese proceedings to our Missus." Anna became pale during this recital. She saw clearly, the peril of Edward Ellingwood. Perceiving the necessity of cultivating a perfect control over her feelings, that she might successfully use her faculties for the work before her, she said calmly:

"You have both nobly performed your task; return now and get all the sleep possible. I shall order you a late and substantial breakfast. Do nothing for the present, but assist me in the rescue of General Ellingwood."

The negroes then withdrew. Anna, after reflection and prayer, resolved to pursue the course indicated by the spy. Indeed, it was an infinite relief to know, that in the very quarters of Major Worstal was a coadjutor, on whose skill, and courage, and fidelity she could perfectly rely.

An unforeseen event, however, occurred, which greatly increased her difficulties, and almost terminated fatally, for that beloved life she had vowed herself to save. We may imagine the terrible transition for Edward Ellingwood from the society of Anna, at Sea-Side, to a captivity under Worstal, in prison. In the face of his foe he read only hate and triumph. He saw himself suddenly turned from Paradise to Pandemonium. As he approached the wooden walls the atmosphere became oppressive, and loathing crept down his very limbs. The presence of Worstal drove him to madness. Ogre's face, scowling in hideous ugliness, intensified his misery, so that even the kind countenance of Father John gave him slight relief. Looking, on the day succeeding his confinement, from his bed through the window, madmen raved and idiots gibbered, amid scenes he never afterwards dared recall. Soon he felt his head throbbing, burning, whirling. His former delirium returned, arming him with preternatural strength. The hiss of the steam from a locomotive, standing near, pierced his brain, and the yell of its whistle increased his frenzy. He dashed through the window. He rushed out a gate. He leaped on the locomotive. He hurled off the engineer. With a scream of wild joy he moved the lever. A shower of balls, from the pursuing guard, fell harmless around his person, and they ran in vain to stop the machine, gliding swiftly backwards. Its speed increased. It passed the encampment. It flew through a field. It thundered over a bridge. It rushed by a forest. It darted through a village. Telegraph-posts almost appeared a colonnade. Fences, trees, houses, flocks, men, bridges, streams, towns, valleys, hills, flashed by like a madman's visions. The delirium of Ellingwood grew with the speed. He became wild with ecstacy. Once he climbed up the support, and out on the cover, and stamped, and danced, and screamed, and then crawled down before the boiler without injury. After his capture, he could only remember, that he looked behind him; that he saw another locomotive in full chase; that he reversed his own engine; that he leaped off at a curve of the road; and that he jumped and shouted in frantic exultation, as he beheld the two fire-monsters dashing towards each other like blazing demons, and, meeting with thundering crash, leap into the air, and driven into each other, fall on the track in helpless, burning, smoking ruin.

CHAPTER XXVIII.

THE feeling that the life of Edward Ellingwood was depending on her courage, and wisdom inspired Anna Austin with a solemn sense of responsibility. Her fancy often pictured him in his prison surrounded by remorseless enemies. A thin face and a sunken eye pursued her night and day.

General Brompton was still absent, and she had no earthly friend to consult. Edward's frenzied effort on the locomotive she knew would excite his foe to greater watchfulness and greater cruelty. Her two faithful negroes appeared animated with superhuman strength, and daring, and in this she recognized the favor of Heaven. She felt also in her own soul born a new power. Jumbo and Jim rode every night to a wood adjoining the prison. Here they fastened their horses, and then proceeded to dig the tunnel, working until nearly day-break.

After their return in the morning Jumbo always appeared in the parlor to report the progress of the night to his anxious mistress.

We will collect together the substance of several conversations, and thus have in one view the state of affairs. The old negro came into the apartment, soiled with dirt and exhausted, and even haggard with his severe and perilous labor.

Anna inquired, "When you tied your horses, Jumbo,

and went near the prison, how did you decide where to begin your tunnel?"

"Ah!" he answered, lifting up both hands with a look of wonder. "Lau, Missus, dat spy, he knows ebberyting —he mus hab 'municashun wid de sperits—he cum a hitchin, and a crawlin, and a dukin, and he say, 'Niggas see dis yer bank! Hur am a cabe Hebben made for yer dirt. Scratch 'way yer darkies, de ole beava, and de young beava, and I'se let yer know what's gwine on inside. Dey be starbin de Ginral, and tell yer Missus he be wastin' 'way to his skin and bone.' Den we's 'gin at de bank, and I'se digs, and Jim's carry 'way de yearth in ou' hats, and piles it in de cabe—tight wuk, Missus."

"Yes, and you and Jim are not remarkably slender," replied Anna, laughing. "Betta's for de Ginral," answered Jumbo, casting his eyes complacently down on his own rotundity, "betta's for de Ginral! He no stick in de place we'se leave, like de fall 'possum in de small gum-hole. He cum trough like dat varment in de spring afta de winta's fast. De Ginral he lean 'possum afore he crawl away from de Maja."

Anna could not repress a smile, although such grave interests were involved. "But were you not afraid of being discovered, and killed?" she again asked.

"Lau, Missus, Hebben help us, and keep up our sperits," exclaimed Jumbo. "We hear de cry ob de gaud, and de groan ob de prisners, and de cussin ob de sodgas, and de peace passin' standin' cum in our hearts while we be lyen' on de groun."

"And how do your lanterns answer, now that you have gotten into the earth?"

"Dey be'se betta, Missus, dan de staus ob de sky, or de lamps 'bout de trone, in dat same cabe."

"Has there been, thus far, any suspicion of your movements?"

"Wuns we'se hear de crack ob de sticks, and a tredin' ober our heads, and de Maja swearin, and de Oga groulin', and we'se squeeze doun, and poke de lantern ahind. At fus we'se shake like de quiverin' leabs. Den we'se nudge, and we'se snigger, and we'se laugh to tink we'se cheat de Maja and de Oga, as de young 'ginny niggas steal de coon-cub in de light ob de shinin' moon."

Having received these communications, Miss Austin dismissed Jumbo to his breakfast, and his slumber.

After several nights of labor, the negroes were sure they were approaching the cabin where Edward Ellingwood was imprisoned. The spy made observations during the day, and stealing to them in the darkness, guided their course. At last they began digging upward, and heard, with mingled joy and fear, the sound of voices above. Just as Jim was removing a handful of earth, a ray of light darted down from the room of the Major, through a crack of the floor.

"Dar be Satan a drinkin' brandy-smash," whispered Jumbo.

"And dar his Doctor a stirrin' de julep," answered Jim, in a low tone, while the two negroes nudged each other with suppressed African snickers, beneath the very feet of their dreaded enemy.

Everything was now managed with the greatest circumspection. A branch tunnel was completed immediately under Ellingwood's room, and a hole made large enough to reach through a hand, and convey food and letters. The spy communicated the scheme to the General, and loosened a board, which could easily be removed from beneath.

20*

After the work was finished, Anna Austin felt a weight lifted from her heart. Yet she trembled, as the crisis of her plans approached. Having written a note and prepared some food, she summoned Jumbo into her presence. She said to him, with the greatest solemnity, " Everything now depends on you and your son. Let Jim be under the room of the Major and the Doctor, to hear what they say. Do you go beneath that of General Ellingwood, and give him this package."

Jumbo replied gravely, " De wish ob Missus Anna be minded like de law of Moses, sayin', ' niggas nebber steal from de massa.' "

Anna was too anxious, to be amused at Jumbo's Scripture, and she proceeded to say : " The spy, you know, informed us the General will be alone at midnight. When the guard cries twelve, push away the board, and give him this as I directed."

The negro took the package, and was dismissed. When Anna heard the clatter of his horse, her heart beat wildly. A slight accident might destroy her plans. That life, dearer than her own, was suspended on the sagacity of two faithful, but untutored negroes. She fell on her knees before the sofa, raised her eyes to Heaven and prayed earnestly and long for strength, and guidance, and success.

While these projects were in progress Ellingwood was passing through experiences which would leave traces on all his future history. After the ride on the locomotive, his delirium soon exhausted its violence, and he lay in a dull, heavy stupor. Reduced diet and close confinement were gradually exhausting the springs of his life.

The spy had continued occasionally to supply a little food, or he would certainly have died. Even now there was danger that his strength would not be sufficient for his escape. On the night so anxiously expected he was making strong efforts to keep awake. The full moon poured from her zenith through his window a flood of mild splendor. All the events of his life were again passing before him, not in the whirl of delirium, but like the slow unfolding of a vast picture. The tramp of the guard could be heard in different directions, and at intervals their monotonous cry. A single dog howled dismally. Every breeze brought to his ear mingled moans and blasphemies. The desolation of his situation was almost insupportable. With the midnight "all's well," he cast his eye over his bed. A board moved visibly. He was for a moment startled to see it pushed slowly aside. A black hand was reached upward. Silently and eagerly he snatched a package from its fingers. It was then drawn down, and the board replaced.

Ellingwood, hastily alleviating nature by a few delicious morsels, tore open the letter, purposely written in large characters, that he might decipher it in the moonbeam. He eagerly read:

"DEAREST EDWARD:

"All is ready. Beneath your room is a tunnel, dug by Jumbo and Jim for your escape. On to-morrow night at twelve raise the board, descend, and be certain to replace it. After leaving the tunnel you will find horses in the wood. Ride for your life, as the blood-hounds will soon be after you. Six miles from the prison you will find a stream. You and Jim ride up it some distance to the right, and Jumbo down to the left in order to confuse the dogs. The latter will return to Sea-Side, and the former act as your guide. Farewell. Trust in Heaven. I will pray constantly. Yours in eternal love,

ANNA."

P. S.—"I will send you three revolvers and a prayer-book."

When Edward had read these lines tears started from his hollow eyes and ran over his sunken cheeks. He kissed the note again and again in rapture. How blissful to know in such an hour that his Anna was to prove his delivering angel! Yet in the midst of his transport he could scarcely refrain a smile when he recalled the incongruities of the Postscript, suggesting a mingled confidence in prayer and powder. He now heard the step of Ogre, and he had just time to place the letter in his breast and turn on his side, and compose himself into the appearance of slumber, when he felt bending over him a horrid face, and glaring down on him a fiendish eye, and touching his wrist-vein a cold finger marking the decays of his life. While the venomous breath was on his cheek, he heard in the next apartment the hoarse voice of Worstal.

When the negroes returned, Jumbo took Jim into the presence of Miss Anna.

She said to the former, "Has every thing happened according to our plans? Tell me at once!"

"Ebbery ting, Missus. Dis ole han' tuk 'way de board, and hole up de bundle, and de Ginral he tuk it from dese finga's, and Is'e shut de place, and den crawl 'way.

"But Jim tell de Missus what you'se he-ard."

Here the worthy son rolling up his eyes, and lifting both his hands in alarm, and horror, exclaimed, "Why, Missus, as Is'e laid scrouchin' down Is'e see de Maja, and de Oga in de light ob de candle. Wuns Is'e tot dey look right down de crack in dis nigga's face. De Maja say he wait no longa—starbin too slow—he pisin—he stab—he shoot—he hang de Yank' cur, aud trow him to de buzzads. De Oga he grin, and he swear, and dey look like two debbils gwiue 'bout in de flame ob de pit, and Is'e shuk woss, dan when de roarin guns kill five hundred Massa Chals' reg'ment."

Miss Anna turned pale at this recital. She perceived that her arrangements were not one moment too, soon. Possibly even now Edward's life has become exhausted by his privations, or Worstal's hate has leaped over every barrier of prudence, and quenched itself in the blood of its victim.

On the appointed night, the horses were tied as near the mouth of the tunnel as appeared safe. Jumbo and Jim entered as usual. They remained for some time in their concealment, awaiting the midnight signal. Worstal and Ogre were sleeping in their room.

Father John having seen that his efforts to save their prisoner's life would be vain, had refused any longer to share their quarters. When the guard cried twelve, Edward arose carefully. Hastily dressing, he took everything he thought he should need, or that would not be too speedily missed. He knelt an instant in prayer. Rising, he threw a hasty glance around his prison and looked anxiously at the rude door which separated him from his murderous enemies. He withdrew the board, and tremblingly letting himself down restored it to its place. Just as his hand thrilled with the touch of the faithful Jumbo, he remembered he had left Anna's letter under his pillow. For an instant he was fearfully agitated, and in doubt what to do, but a moment's reflection showed him

the peril of leaving the precious paper. He drew back
the board, lifted himself into the room, snatched the letter,
thrust it into his bosom, and as he returned to the dark
passage, he heard the terrible voice of Worstal, uttering
curses in his dreams. Greatly exhausted by his effort
and excitement, he crawled slowly after Jumbo, and passing the main tunnel, they were followed by Jim. With
great difficulty they reached the open air, whose pure
breath was an instant invigoration. The party then
crept along the ground and came to the horses without
exciting suspicion. Jumbo handed two revolvers to the
General, and one revolver to Jim, the former having
mounted Tiger, and the latter Nell. The party then rode
slowly through the wood, beneath a moon slightly veiled
by a single passing cloud. Emerging into the broad
road they spurred furiously.

Before many minutes, they heard the ominous boom of
a cannon. Looking behind them as they flew, they saw
glancing lights in the prison yard and windows. Soon
the deep bay of two blood-hounds startled the very stars.
The loud cry stopped the heart of Edward. He shook
in his saddle as he had never done before the batteries of
the enemy. The horses, frightened, ran with increased
speed.

At the stream mentioned in Anna's note they complied
with its directions, but failed to baffle the dogs, who far in
advance of their masters, approached with an ever louden-
ing cry, fortunately not taking the track of Jumbo on his
return to Sea-Side. Ellingwood resolved on his course.
He whirled around Tiger and waited for the brutes. He
soon perceived them bounding and barking in the moon-
beams. Every sinew was distended as they leaped, and
they seemed endued with an infernal power and grace.

Seeing Ellingwood waiting they stood a moment with open jaws. Their eyes gleamed like orbs of blood. Edward seized the opportunity. He was practiced with the pistol. Holding a revolver in each hand he poured a shower of bullets on the majestic beasts, and left them struggling in their blood. Then turning Tiger, he and Jim urged their horses to their utmost speed.

Just after Ellingwood left the prison the spy had entered his room, and hastily arranged his bed to give it the appearance of being occupied. In a few minutes Dr. Ogre came to observe his patient. As he lifted the cover he started back in surprise. His victim was gone. He awoke Worstal, whose rage was demoniacal when he learned the fact of the escape. He rushed to the window and finding the bars firm, he stooped to examine the floor, where the loose board soon exposed the entire plan.

After a hurried examination of the tunnel, an alarm was made. The cannon was fired. The dogs were let loose. The direction of the fugitives was ascertained. A mounted party, led by Worstal, started in pursuit, and soon found the hounds lying dead on the road. Deprived of their assistance, every effort of the company was baffled.

Returning next morning, after a fruitless search, the Major stalked through the encampment like a fiend. He kicked one prisoner until he died. He choked a second, and shot a third through the brain. Indeed his savagery was indiscriminate, and he was equally brutal to his own soldiers. As he passed over the enclosure of the prison, spotted with blood, bearing in one hand a revolver, and in the other a huge knife, blaspheming as if hell's own mouth had been opened, the desperate wretches on every side, by one spontaneous impulse, rushed on him in overpowering numbers, and hurled the giant, disarmed and helpless, to the ground. His own men, goaded by his cruelties, joined the assault, and flung themselves on their commandant.

Against such an infuriated mass, resistance was impossible. They trampled him on the earth. They stamped his face. They tore his hair. One old prisoner beat him with his own pistol. Then went up the cry, "hang him, hang him." They carried the herculean miscreant to the gallows, tied a rope around his immense neck, and soon Major Worstal was swinging lifeless between earth and heaven. But the impulse of vengeance was not yet expended. Fagots were piled beneath the savage. Fire was applied. Soon retributive flames were blazing around the body, while idiots and lunatics gibbered and danced and yelled in their glare. When the rope was burned, the huge carcass, blackened and disfigured, fell heavily on the angry pile below, and maddened winds scattered the ashes of the murderer into every part of that enclosure which had witnessed his cruelties.

CHAPTER XXIX.

Anna Austin spent the night of the escape in fearful suspense. Seldom do such anxieties press themselves on any solitary soul. The breast of this lovely Southern girl resembled a peaceful vale, glowing in its quiet beauty, until suddenly disturbed by the rush of the whirlwind, and the rumble of the earthquake. She paced her apartment in anguish. Sometimes she fell on her knees in prayer. She flung open the lattice, and standing in the moonlight with clasped hands, gazed towards the prison. A waving branch made her give a fearful start. The bark of a plantation-dog struck her ear as an omen of terror. A shrill midnight cock proclaimed to her the crisis of Edward's fate, and a cloud crossed the moon like a shadow over her hope, when the low boom of a cannon made her suspense an agony. She threw herself on her bed, and was scared by dreams of flying horses, and shouting men, and baying hounds. Once across her path was a corpse. She shrieked, supposing it was the body of Edward, and was horrified to discover the ghastly face of Worstal. Then angels hovered over her head on glittering wings, and gliding along slanting sunbeams, vanished smiling into heaven.

Towards morning, gentle slumbers sealed her eyes. She was awakened by the clatter of a horse's hoofs, when she found a noon-sun streaming through her window. There is a rapid step on the stair, and a sharp rap at the door, and regardless of forms, Jumbo stands panting and grinning in her presence.

Starting up, she exclaimed: "Quick! quick! tell me, tell me! Has he escaped?"

"Tank Hebben," answered Jumbo, rolling upward his negro orbs with a look of devout gratitude, "de Ginral be clean gone from de Maja, as de Maja from dis yer earth."

"At once, Jumbo, all! all! tell all that has happened!"

The faithful fellow, in his peculiar and vivid way, then narrated the events of the escape, in their order, until the time he left General Ellingwood and his darling Jim. He then proceeded to state, that he had ventured near the prison, and lingered around in the wood until Worstal and his troop returned in their disappointed rage. Here, however, we must have his own animated African style:

" And now, Missus, we hab something awful to tell."

Miss Austin remembered her dream, and was prepared for the communication. Pale and trembling, she replied, with a great effort to regain her composure:

"Go on, Jumbo, I am ready for the worst."

" Well, Missus," he resumed, "when I'se cum near de prison, I'se tie de mar in de holla, and I'se clumb de hill, and look down on de bad place. De sodgas war wadin' in de mud, and lyin' in de sun, and creepin' in der holes. Some war grinnin', some war jabberin', some war cussin', some war hollerin', some war eatin', some war fightin', some war moanin', some war dyin'. Den cum de Maja, lookin' like Satan howlin' back to his hell. He strike wun sodga, he choke anudder, and den he shoot a fella. Den dey all rush on him, and dey trow him down, and dey tramp him, and dey tar his hair, and dey beat him, and dey look like de little debbils tormentin' de big debbil. An' dey cry, 'hang him,' and dey tuk him and dey tie rope 'bout his neck, and dey string him up, till he hang a workin', and a jurkin', and a danglin', like a sarpent on de swamp-tree. Den dey tuk de limbs and de boads, and put under him, and dey sat de pile on fire, and de flames mount a roarin', and howlin', and curl 'bout Maja, and he fall last on de burnin' wood, and I'se turn 'bout and run and jump on de mar, and I'se fly here as if debbils war 'roun' dis ole head, like de crows a cawin', and a flappin' over massa corn-field."

Here Jumbo stopped, overcome with the horrors of his own narration. Miss Anna sank back fainting before the terrible picture. The iron had pierced her heart. Her own blood had been given for the rescue of Edward. The exultation at his fate was mingled with tears for the wretched, but deserved doom of her cousin, who had from childhood been linked with her history. We must leave her in her grief, and look back after him, whose escape she had so nobly planned and achieved.

General Ellingwood had been guided by Jim along devious ways, which so completely bewildered their pursuers, that the chase was reluctantly abandoned. After riding a few hours, our fugitives found themselves before a cabin. A negro, his wife, and a troop of children stood around the door, with grinning welcome. Anna's thoughtful care had been before, and provided everything possible for comfort. When Edward entered the house, he found a change of linen, a stout undress suit of confederate gray, a pair of strong boots, and a supply of powder and balls. Food had been sent forward, and a nourishing breakfast speedily smoked on the table, and certainly no cup of coffee ever inspired more gratitude, or afforded more refreshment. Then followed a bath in a sparkling mountain stream. Thanks to Heaven and Anna were continually bursting from the lips of Ellingwood. The scenery about the cabin was charming. Behind rose a wooded hill, and stretching for miles in front wound a valley, watered by flashing streams, while, in every direction, were visible the bloom, and brilliance, and glory of the Southern landscape.

Edward Ellingwood remained for several days amid these scenes, until completely refreshed in body and mind. The horses had been sent home soon after their arrival, that their absence might not excite suspicion against Miss Anna. It was likewise deemed safest to accomplish the rest of the journey on foot.

The General and Jim started at last on their perilous way to the Federal camp. They generally traveled by night, and slept by day in barns, and negro cabins. Everywhere the African was their friend. They waded swamps. They swam streams. They slept beneath the sky. On the mountains they suffered from cold, and on the plain panted beneath the sun. Twice they had marvellous escapes. They afterwards found they had kept in a line parallel with Sherman's march. Often in the distance they saw the sky illuminated by burning houses. Once from a summit, far away the eastern heavens seemed a sheet of fire darting and trembling like the coruscations of an aurora. This Ellingwood subsequently ascertained was from the conflagration of Columbia.

After many wearisome and perilous days, exhausted with hunger and fatigue, he, accompanied by the sturdy Jim, came into the lines of General Grant just before the fall of Richmond. We will not undertake to describe the emotions inspired in his own breast by his arrival, or the joy of his surprised friends. While wild flames were blazing over the doomed capital of the confederacy, he soon afterwards entered amid their glare, and saw exultingly waving from the State-House the triumphant stars of the Republic.

21*

CHAPTER XXX.

"We have fought, and we have lost, and we must sincerely accept our situation," said General Brompton to his niece as they sat on the Piazza at Sea-Side a few months after the conclusion of the war.

"Dear Uncle," replied Anna, "I am rejoiced to hear you say this. Your old arguments always brought over my mind a shadow, and excited apprehensions which now seem to have been prophetic of the result. The questions involved in the war are I hope forever at rest."

"What remains of my life shall be devoted to the prosperity of the South under the flag of the nation. Nothing now will restore our influence but the material wealth of the country. Cotton may not be a lordly tyrant, but must be a wealthy citizen."

"How thankful you should be, uncle, that your English investments have rather increased than diminished your income. Thousands of those once rich are now destitute. Mrs. Alston, only last week, sent North her plate for sale. Mr. Haines has placed his pictures in a New York auction-room. Indeed I know a lady who has disposed of all her jewelry, including her wedding-ring."

"And many of our most refined and noble people will be compelled to seek the meanest employments," said General Brompton, with a tear on his manly cheek. "Indeed we do not yet appreciate the terrible reality of our trials. The time will speedily come, when our former

246

slaves will meet us at the ballot-box, and rule us in official positions."

These words brought scarlet into the face of Anna Austin. Turning towards her uncle in the greatest excitement, she exclaimed: "Impossible! What! Jim vote, and Jumbo go to the Georgia Legislature!" The thing thus expressed seemed so amusing, that indignation was turned to laughter.

After a few hearty and refreshing peals, General Brompton resumed: "My dear Anna, I perceive that our mad extremists are bringing on our whole people humiliations a narrow Northern sectionalism will be sure to inflict. Yet I have deliberately resolved nothing shall ever shake my loyalty to the national government. My motto henceforth shall be—THE NEW SOUTH UNDER THE OLD FLAG. Promise me, that after your marriage, you will not forget your own dear native State."

"Never, never; oh, never!" exclaimed Anna, with the deepest pathos of love in her voice. "Whatever the faults of the South may have been, I admire the gallantry and heroism of her sons and daughters." And then suddenly rising, and kneeling before the General, she added: "Here I promise and vow, that my fortune and position shall be devoted to the land of my birth."

The heart of the old gentleman was deeply moved. Stooping down, he tenderly kissed the forehead of his niece. Placing his hands on her head, he said, amid dropping tears: "God bless you, Anna. God bless Edward! God bless the South! God bless the Country!

When Miss Austin arose, General Brompton pointed to a chair, and after they were both seated, he commenced in a gay tone: "Here, here is something you will take an interest in. I found an Ode to 'Our Flag,' and one to 'Our Country,' in Ellingwood's own writing, between the leaves of a book in the library. I have ventured to make a copy, and I presume you will not refuse the originals."

With a playful smile, and a profound bow, he gave the paper to Anna, who took it with the slightest possible embarrassment, and approach to a blush. She remembered how much suffering those songs had probably caused herself, and Edward.

Just here the conversation was interrupted by a servant with a letter. General Brompton hastily opened the envelope, and glancing his eye with a lawyer's rapidity over the neat page, while a gleam of pleasure played over his features, he exclaimed, holding the epistle before Anna's face: "Ellingwood writes urgently, requesting us to join him in New York on the fifteenth, and take passage for Liverpool in the Russia. He proposes proceeding from thence direct to Rome, where the Judge, Mary, and Mrs. Cleveland are still staying. Ada expects to join the party, and Dr. Elton and his son are to follow in a few weeks."

"Oh, that will be delightful, delightful!" burst forth Anna, clapping her hands, and almost dancing with joy.

The arrangements for a voyage to Europe are soon made in this age. A telegraph was flashed from Willow-Shade to Sea-Side at noon. By three o'clock, the trunks were packed. At four, the coach was at the door. Before five, tickets were purchased, and checks arranged, and General Brompton and Anna Austin were sitting in the car with their faces northward. Two negroes occupied the side seat near the door. What nice respectable servants—that father and that son! Jumbo and Jim, are going to Rome with their master and mistress. Five o'clock and five minutes! the steam-whistle shrieks its signal. There is a jerk and a jangle—a slow motion—a rapid increase—a lightning speed. Our party are speedily in New York; they embark on the "Russia;" in ten days they are at Liverpool; in three more they are in Paris, and soon after they have reached Rome.

As we have not described the joy of meeting in our own commercial metropolis, we will not linger to depict it in the eternal city. We will begin with Judge Ellingwood and General Brompton, arm-in-arm, and cigar in mouth puffing to the moon, within the walls of the Coliseum. How suggestive of the age! men of the new world in the mistress of the old world! Clouds of American tobacco-smoke curling lazily and gracefully in the glimmering beams through that vast edifice, where mailed gladiators exchanged their deadly sword-thrusts; where the Christian martyrs stained the jaws of the wild beasts; where Roman Emperors in their purple sat enthroned, while the shouts of a hundred thousand citizens burst from the circling tiers, and shook the velarium, and expended their thunders over the palaces of the Cæsars, or above the majestic capitol, or were borne out by the breeze, even to the luxurious villas of the Campagna! How different the frock-coat of a Yankee Judge and a Georgia Lawyer from the robe of Pompey and the toga of Cicero! Different! Different as an electric telegraph from an ancient courier, or a senatorial chariot from a flashing locomotive! Yet, modern Rome is still of the past. The purple of the Empire, and the scarlet of the Papacy, are symbolic colors of a perpetuated dynasty.

When the conversation had been continued for some minutes between the gentlemen, amid scenes so classic, and so suggestive, as they passed to and fro, Judge

Ellingwood suddenly pausing, and pointing to the arm of
General Brompton resting on his own, said, with impressive emphasis :

"How emblematic this, of our restored political relations! May North and South, like our own hearts, be
united in a common love for a common work under a
common flag !"

The General stopped, and taking both the hands of the
Judge in his own, replied with the most profound feeling,
"I shall stand true to my pledges. The doctrine of
secession has been tried by the sword in battle with the
doctrine of unity. I accept the decision of the war. All
my influence shall be employed with our noble people to
make them loyal to our inseparable stars. Heaven has
decreed that we be one single nationality from the Atlantic to the Pacific—possibly from Darien to Labrador.
Our soil is consecrated by the blood of heroes to universal
Liberty."

The gentlemen then joined arms again, and resuming
their walk, Judge Ellingwood replied—a gleam of satisfaction spreading over his features, followed by a shadow
of distrust, "My greatest fear now is from our own provin-
cial narrowness. Northern sectionalism having achieved
its triumph may be as dangerous as Southern sectionalism.
I pray that our statesmen may rise to the greatness of the
age and of our destiny! Selfishness turned this magnificence around us into ruin, and only the comprehensive
spirit of Washington breathed into our Republic can preserve us from worse than Roman wreck."

"And when these political questions are settled," answered the General, "as you once suggested in our Washington interview, there will arise in our country a religious issue which will shake its foundations. No man

reading history can doubt that the old Roman Imperialism which subdued the world under Emperors is continued in the modern Italian Imperialism which would subject humanity under the Popes. In some respects the latter has the advantage. It so blends ancient mythology and scriptural truth, that heathenism and Christianity unite to sustain the Pontiffs."

"Now mark my prediction," interposed the Judge, somewhat excitedly. "I have most reliable information that before ten years the Jesuits will assemble a pretended Ecumenical Council to proclaim from the Vatican the infallibility of the Pope. They wish for him both the temporal and spiritual sovereignty of the world. He would absorb to himself the whole Episcopal power, and become the judge of doctrine, the channel of grace, and the object of worship for our race—in mortal flesh an immortal God!"

"I had once supposed," returned the General, "that such assumptions could only deceive the ignorant masses whose idolatrous propensities demand a visible deity. How can the intelligence of our age forget Constantine's Dotation, the False Decretals, the murders of the Borgias, or the indulgences of Leo! Yet the defection of cultivated and sincere men in England and America establishes that education may improve a sound mind, but can never supply sound sense. I fear learning often confuses weak heads, and intensifies natural silliness."

"It is indeed a great mistake to conclude," said the Judge thoughtfully and sadly, "that the proclamation of Infallibility will overthrow the Papacy. It may cost it the Vatican, St. Peter's, Rome, the Tiara. It will alienate masculine intellects. It will bind Romanism to a fossilized mediævalism, and separate it from the progress

of the age, and make Rome the see of a liberal Bishop
and the capital of united Italy, and produce another Protestant schism. But it has a charm for dreamy divines,
esthetic ladies, and the simple multitude. How your
southern negroes would delight to kiss the toe of the unerring Pio Nono amid a pageant of St. Peter's! John
Chinaman will find slight difference between the worship
of Tau and the invocation of Peter. Besides, the new
Rome like the old must have a strong central power.
What can equal a Pope, holy, supreme, infallible, ruling
the world without even the annoyance of his Bishops in a
General Council!"

"You have been recently to Moscow and St. Peters-
burgh. Is there no hope in the Greek Church?" inquired
the General.

"None whatever!" answered the Judge. "Observation and study have shown me the same corruptions and
idolatries in Eastern and Western communions. There
is no difference except in repugnance of race, and enmity
to Papal usurpation."

"Then our only reliance," replied the General, "is in a
Reformation in the Greek Church, and in the Latin
Church similar to that which purified the Anglican
Church."

"Permit me to say further while we are on the subject," interrupted the Judge, "that I believe the Greek
race had its mission of culture, and the Latin race its
mission of imperialism, while the Saxon race is exhibiting
a mission of diffusion. It represents vigor, aggression,
progress. It has colonized over the world the English
language, English ideas, English law, English liberty.
The dominion of Britain may contract to her islands, but
her work will be immortal in our great American Re-

public. Prussia will soon by a united Germany add to the Saxon ascendency, and then woe to that power opposing the genius and destiny of a race ordained by Heaven to give our world Political Freedom and Pure Christianity !"

"And I," replied General Brompton, "in the light of our late war, and of the movements of the age in Europe and America, now perceive the work of our Republic. When I return I will aid in organizing every possible social and religious element into compact resistance to the Pope. He relies on immigration, and Jesuitism to possess our land, and thence extend his sway over our humanity. When the infallibility of his Holiness is decided, every minor difference will be absorbed, and the whole struggle concentrate itself into a gigantic contest between the Power of the Pope, and the Power of the People. This will be the grand final battle for our continent, and our world. That decided, Liberty and Christianity may have their universal triumph in both a political, and religious Millenium."

When we hear such conversations beneath smoke-clouds, puffing, and circling, and floating over the broken arches of the Coliseum, we may smile at the theories suggested, as the offspring of American extravagance, excited at once by strong tobacco and classic association. Our skepticism certainly has a right to be amused, and even indignant. Yet, how different the aspirations of the Judge and the General from those immortalized by the ruins around which they stand! That structure, lifting its vast, oval, roofless walls to the stars, is the monument of a power which sought to enslave a world, and by its wrong, wrought its ruin. These Christian Statesmen, representatives of a

22

new race, a new continent, and a new ambition, are projecting schemes to hurl, by the bloodless Press, and peaceful Ballot, a despotism from their country, that all nations, through her, may become in faith, and truth, and love one Universal Brotherhood.

CHAPTER XXXI.

FEW human beings ever experienced greater torture than Arthur Cleveland after the delirium in which we left him on board the America. Visions of the past haunted him like phantoms. His wild agony soon settled into a condition of pitiable melancholy. He stole forth from the vessel at Liverpool, after the other passengers had left, like a wandering ghost. Pale, gaunt, spectral, he resembled a tomb, occupied by a skeleton being, who, finding escape impossible, had resigned himself to his gloom. He had lost faith in Rome, and found faith in nothing. Had he been an Oriental he would have believed dogmas his reason now rejected. Had he been a Latin, he would have inclined to Papal imperialism. But his blood was English. He had a long line of ancestors, whose veins had been filled from the Norseman, and the Saxon, and the Briton. He had, indeed, been a traitor to the genius of his race. Yet he had in him all those latent tendencies which, developed in the Reformation, had hurled-from old England Romish usurpation, Romish idolatry, and Romish corruption. Impulses now revived in his breast, transmitted from sturdy men, who had dared chains and flames in martyrdom for the very Truth he had so impulsively renounced. In an evil hour of excitement, his unconscious ambition had involved his life. But the tendencies of his race, guided by Heaven, could be no longer stifled. Cleveland knew a Cardinal's hat awaited him at Rome, and he was still fascinated by the glittering prize. Ambition, and Truth had a fierce contest in his breast. Starting for the pontifical city, he suddenly took a different direction. He explored London. He flew over England. He visited Scotland. He darted across to Ireland. He went to Paris. He made a rapid survey of the Alhambra. He stood on the Alps. Approaching Rome, he saw in the distance, the dome of St. Peter's. Then lingering for days in view of the eternal city, he capriciously crossed the Mediterranean, ascended the Pyramids, and hastened to Jerusalem, to Constantinople, to Athens, to Venice, to Florence. Finally he darted away to St. Petersburg, and Moscow, and was once just about embarking on a voyage to Calcutta, and Pekin. He resembled a ship in the counter currents of a whirlpool, now nearing the vortex, and on the verge of wreck, then borne in an opposite direction, crossing, and tossing, until at last, drawn within the fatal circle, it sinks in the sea forever.

When Cleveland finally entered the pontifical metropolis, he was graciously received by his Holiness and assigned an apartment in the Vatican. The scarlet hat was soon about his head; a diamond cross flashed over his breast; jewels sparkled from his fingers; his splendid vestments were unusually becoming, and imparted to his person a noble Roman dignity. As he mingled in the magnificent service of St. Peter's, he felt that his ambitious dreams were realized to an extent he had never even conceived. But vain the artistic wealth of heaven to satisfy immortal man. In such a mental state, amid celestial light and angelic worship, he would have found only gloom and discord. Indeed, the Papacy had become in every aspect, hateful to his heart, and the brilliance only increased the disgust. He considered himself in a state of gilded imprisonment, and his aroused Saxon nature, resolved to burst its bonds. To his surprise, he had found Bishop Frances in an adjoining room of the palace, and the old fascination was again casting its spell over Cleveland. They explored together the galleries of the Vatican. They wandered through St. Peter's, from colonnade to dome. They examined the catacombs. Scenes which once would have charmed Cleveland to rapture, now only made his life seem more hollow, and his position more false. But a crisis had arrived in his history. A human spirit cannot long endure a strain so unnatural.

The Cardinal, having been pacing his apartment uneasily, felt he could not refrain from pouring into some mortal ear the struggles of his heart, and obeying a sudden impulse, presented himself at the door of Bishop Frances. Having rapped, and been requested to enter, he took a chair, in great agitation. Abruptly tearing away his robe, and pointing to a hair-shirt next to his skin, he exclaimed: "Here, my friend, you behold what has been concealed from all eyes. This proves my desire to believe the Papal Infallibility. I have fasted. I have prayed. I have scourged my flesh. I have labored ceaselessly. I have sacrificed every earthly prospect. The faith I seek deludes me like a phantom. My life is a deceit, a sham, a lie. Proximity to the Pope has only revealed his mortal frailties, and made belief more difficult. He shows for a supernatural gift no supernatural attestation. Before the altars of Heaven I stand a hypocrite. Rather amid these splendid ceremonies I seem a darkening devil. In the presence of his Holiness my Saxon blood burns in protest against Italian rule. I can

22*

endure my agonies no longer. I make my confession. I beg your mercy."

While Cleveland uttered these words, he held out his hands toward Frances with an expression of supplicating impotence which told his helplessness, and his despair. For a moment the Bishop scowled on his convert in intense disgust. Scorn curled on his lip, and curved in his nostril. His eye gleamed with a snaky lustre, and his countenance was frightful. However, suppressing his passion, his better nature triumphed, and he replied with the most steady calmness: "Your Eminence speaks of impossibilities. Go back to my chapel! Behold yourself prostrate before the image of Saint Loyola! Recall your oath of perpetual allegiance to the order of Jesus, and the person of his Holiness! Remember those awful imprecations on apostacy! Your vow is an impassable chasm between you and secession from the Church to which you are forever consecrated."

"Is there no hope?" burst forth Cleveland. "Have not the miseries of years cancelled the mistake of an hour? Cursed be that fatal impulse! I have sacrificed my wife, my child, my home, myself, in the pursuit of a shadow. After perverting others, I am a dupe myself." Here the sufferer wrung his hands in his anguish, and lifted up to Heaven a face traced with remorse and despair.

Bishop Frances felt his heart touched with sympathy. His craft and severity were rather from his system than his soul. Deep in the iron of his nature was a spring of pity. He answered kindly: "Your Eminence must remember the act and the responsibility are your own. You sent to me requesting an interview. You invited me to your house, and sought me in my own. You im-

portuned for a dispensation. You have received undeserved, and unexampled honor. Your apostacy would
ruin me, shake your converts, disgrace the Church, and
even cloud the infallibility of its Head." Then drawing
nearer the wretched victim of his delusion, and fixing on
him an eye which gleamed through his very soul, he
added in a tone expressing his own imperious will: "I
say once, and forever, no such treason will ever be permitted by our Order."

When Cleveland heard these words he writhed, and
began a shriek which he subdued into a groan. The
horror and peril of his position were revealed. He perceived why his instincts had recoiled from an entrance
into Rome, and that he had entangled himself in a glittering snare from which there seemed no escape. He was in
the Vatican, watched by Jesuit eyes, surrounded by Jesuit
ears, fed by Jesuit hands, guarded by Jesuit power.
Every pass and avenue from Rome was controlled by a
relentless devotee to whom in one excited moment he had
professed faith in the Papacy, and in another moment confessed his renunciation of its claims. He rose from his
seat. He fell on his knees. He stretched out his hands
in entreaty, and cried:

"Beg, oh, beg your Order to have mercy! Ask mercy
from the Pope! Implore of Heaven mercy!"

The abjectness of the tone and posture aroused the contempt of the Bishop. He replied with withering scorn,
"Possibly, your Eminence, these struggles in the Vatican
have the same cause as those in America. You are aware
that Mrs. Cleveland and your daughter are in Rome."

These words transformed the Cardinal. They appeared
to dart fire through his veins. His face seemed glowing
with flame. He started from his knees with a fury utterly

foreign to his gentle nature.   Perhaps indeed for the first time his slumbering manhood was truly awake.   Forgetful of himself and propriety, he flung himself on Frances, and clutched his throat, and cried, " By heavens! Bishop, you lie !   I knew they were in Europe, but had not heard they were in Rome.   You shall never falsify my motives, and stain me with such suspicions."

Frances calmly unloosed the Cardinal's grasp, and replied with the most provoking deliberation, " Violence is unbecoming alike to yourself, and to your office.   There is no escape.   I have one single request.   Promise me that before you disgrace the Church by an attempted apostacy, you will attend her services in the Sistine Chapel during Easter, that in the interval you will not seek to visit your family, and that you will meet me in this apartment within an hour after the illumination of St. Peter's."

Subdued by the tone and manner of Frances, and sincerely ashamed of his rude violence, Cleveland answered mildly, and penitently, " Pardon, Bishop, the impulse of my desperation.   As my situation is the result of errors reaching through years, hasty action should be avoided.   I have learned by experience the necessity of reflection.   As I wish neither to injure you nor the Church, I give the pledge you ask, although I imperfectly understand your motive in desiring it."   Having spoken these words the Cardinal bowed, and left the room.   Returning to his own, he flung himself on his bed in a tumult of fear, remorse, mortification, and despair.

CHAPTER XXXII.

"Girls, before I explore Europe, I wish to understand Rome," said Edward Ellingwood to Mary and Anna as they sat together in the drawing-room of their palace expecting two gentlemen they had invited to spend the evening.

"Understand Rome!" cried Mary with her old bright laugh. "That I fear proclaims the neophyte. I presume Pio Nono is scarcely yet familiar with his own Capital. Do you mean Rome ancient, modern, political, or ecclesiastical?"

"Ah! sister, you are just as incorrigible in Europe as America," replied Ellingwood. "You have no more respect for the General than you had for Ned."

"Now Edward, I shall fly to your support, and save you from Mary's shafts," said Anna. "And here comes Mrs. Cleveland! Beneath our banner rest secure! If we fail, the Judge and my uncle approach, and together, we can defend ourselves."

While Anna was speaking, those two venerable gentlemen entered the room, one on either side of Mrs. Cleveland, and discussing, as usual, American unity and Papal usurpation. But before the party had time to pursue the conversation, there was a rattle of wheels before the door, and Mr. Fortescue and Mr. Percivale, were announced. Soon all the persons present were standing together in a group, and the buzz of busy talkers was heard in every part of the room, whose old splendors assumed youthful brilliance in the light of a superb chandelier.

Judge Ellingwood attracted to himself all eyes and ears, as he remarked: "Nothing has more impressed me in Rome, than the fact, that it is so absolutely a growth from the past, and yet so entirely itself in the present. The Italian springs from the Latin, and is another language. The ancient and modern people are the same and different. The Carnival has succeeded the Saturnalia with vast modifications. The worship of gods gives place to the worship of saints. How contrasted the Coliseum and St. Peter's! Yet the one represents the domination of old Rome by the soldier, and the other the sway of new Rome by the Priest."

General Brompton perceiving the Judge pause, began at once, with his usual tact, by saying: "And I am constantly reminded of the antagonisms between Latin and Saxon. Rome and England are significant types of modern ideas. The former represents mediævalism and imperialism; the latter, progress and liberty. Our Teuton ancestors first conquered Rome, and their children will over-master these Italians. Hence, I derive hope that the Pope will never sway America."

While the General was speaking, Dr. Elton had joined the circle, and his son came immediately after with Ada Cleveland glowing on his arm, in all the freshness of American youth and beauty. They had arrived a few days before, and as this was their first appearance in company, all eyes turned admiringly on the blooming girl.

The old Clergyman had caught the tenor of General Brompton's remarks, and to prevent interruption in the conversation, said gaily, "Pardon the garrulousness of my age, and office! These young people recall our visit, with

Jumbo as our guide, to the Catacombs, and my subsequent exploration of the Lapidarian Gallery. I have been enabled to contrast the Church of the Martyrs with the Church of the Priests. Not a figure, or inscription in tomb or chapel indicates one peculiarity of the Papacy. Every monument below is a protest against every innovation above. Spiritually, yet literally, **Day is Night, and Night is Day.**"

"Yet," continued Mr. Fortescue, "in despite of their darkness, while taxed by Priests in every imaginable way, to support the magnificence of St. Peter's, and the luxuriousness of the Vatican, and all the expensive splendors of Bishop, Cardinal, and Pope, the Italians are a joyous people. Brilliant skies, gay temperaments, and Church festivals promote a cheerfulness exaction, and superstition cannot suppress. Even labor is a species of carnival. Toil beneath the sun is forgotten in song and dance under the moon. The gleaming costumes, the jangling tambourines, the lively motions make an indescribable picture. Contrast our grave American harvesters with the gay companies in the Piazza Montanara! Carts in bright colors! Garlands of laurel, and box! Necks, yokes, and horns of oxen in ribbons and flowers! Song, pipe, laughter through the gates, and over the campagna to the very field! There Judge, and General is a social problem hard to solve."

"Yes, and the more we see of Rome the more difficult to understand Rome," interposed Mr. Percivale, a celebrated American artist.

Here Anna and Mary cast mischievous glances at Edward, who smiled in return, as they recalled his rather large undertaking recorded in the first sentences of this chapter. But the amused girls, and Ellingwood himself, were soon fixed in their attention to Mr. Percivale, as he proceeded to remark, "I have resided in this city ten years, and am more and **more struck** every **day with** the similarities and contrarieties suggested by the Judge. They especially pervade **Art.** Corresponding **to the** Pantheon of old Rome we have St. Peter's of the new. There is the **grace of the Venus,** and here is the beauty of the Madonna. **The** majesty **of the** Apollo is answered by the **grandeur of** the Moses. The dying agonies in the Gladiator and the Laocoon are supplanted by the tortures of a thousand martyrs. For the Last Judgment I can find neither contrast, nor similitude. But I beg pardon, **ladies.** We have forfeited forever our American title to gallantry, by compelling you into silence. Mrs. Cleveland, what has most struck you in Rome?"

That lady, remarkable for her intellect, and her culture, instantly answered, with a glow of sweet and modest enthusiasm, "The Campagna! the marvellous Campagna! I saw it this morning from a tower of the Capitol. All I had seen, and all I then saw, at once came before me—the distant line of the flashing sea, the sweep of the far hills, the gleaming villages, the feathery grasses, the numerous pines, the silent undulating plain resembling stiffened sea waves, and covered with green grass and golden grain, and brilliant **flowers; the** picturesque views of villa, and acqueduct, and tomb, suggesting in their decay, that former busy, buried, beautiful life—and then the whole encircled by azure mountains, and roofed by an Italian sky! But **I am ashamed of my tediousness and my** boldness. Mary! **Anna! hasten to** my relief."

Mr. Fortescue, bowing with a touch of the old and forgotten gallantry, and somewhat too of its antiquated stiffness, exclaimed, "Cannot Miss Ellingwood find something *within* Rome which exceeds its environs? Surely the city can equal the Campagna over which there has just been shed so beautiful a glow."

"Oh, the fountains! the fountains!" cried Mary, passionately. "Everywhere, by day and night, this murmur of lapsing water—now piling its columns in the sun, now waving its veil of silver spray beneath the moon, now roaring in cascades into carved basins, now rolling through grass and flowers into lakes where quivers the blue of heaven. Especially how wonderful the Triton of Bernini blowing pearls into the sky, or the Quirinal basin whose watery pillars crumble below the colossal forms of Phidias and Praxiteles!"

"Bravo! bravo!" exclaimed Mr. Percivale, interrupting Mary's apologies, and then making his obeisance to Miss Anna Austin. She, before he made a request, to her own momentary surprise and confusion, found herself kindled by the animation of Mrs. Cleveland and Miss Ellingwood.

"Excuse my rusticity," she began, with a fascinating sweetness of manner, "if I most admire the flowers of Rome! Nothing has ever so enchanted me as the laurustinus, the wild pea, the clustering eglantine, the splendid rose, the scented sweet-briar, the bright bloom of the orange, the odorous tassel of the locust, the purple of the vine, and all the mingling colors bursting and blazing over the Campagna when the lark sings from his cloud, or the nightingale in his thicket."

Anna was saved from the embarrassment which would have followed her boldness by the appearance of some refreshments beautifully served in glass and silver and gold by Jim and Jumbo.

After ices, and cake, and wine had regaled the company, General Ellingwood remarked playfully that he had been quite neglected amid the eloquence of the evening. "I propose," he said, "to vindicate my title to attention by a song, or," he added, "rather by two songs."

Several persons intimated their approval by exclaiming, "songs! songs."

"I must, however, premise," resumed Ellingwood, "that neither words nor music are my own, and to introduce the performer I must make an explanation. After the Ave Maria, I was enjoying the evening sports of the Carnival. Bonbons, comfits, and bouquets were still flying and pelting. Limepellets showered from window and balcony. Doctors and buffoons stalked and grimaced. Guitars were thrumming, and carriages clattering, and shouts ringing. Then came a cannon-boom. Dragoons clattered down the Corso, and clattered back again, and a rope was drawn across. Horses soon appeared, plunging and rearing, maddened by their noisy tinsel and pricking balls. When the signal was given and the rope removed, imagine my dismay when I saw Jim leap on a horse, and standing on his back, rush along the Corso and win the race, amid the wild shouts of the populace. He then had the effrontery to sing a song, which made those Italians scream with delight. Here comes the impudent fellow to answer for himself."

Evidently by a preconcerted arrangement with General Ellingwood, Jim bowing, and scraping, and grinning, began:

> Does ye'se know whar de orange bloom
>   And whar de suga grow?
> Dar's de gal in dat cabin-room—
>   Dis nigga lub her so,
>   Oho! oho!
>   Dis nigga lub her so.
>
> Her cheek am black as am de night;
>   Her eyes like staus dey glow;

Her lips am red, her teeth am white—
  Dis nigga lub her so,
    Oho! oho!
  Dis nigga lub her so.

De sunny Souf! dar Cactus flush;
  Dar 'nolia blossoms blow,
And dar my big-eyed Ginny blush—
  Dis nigga lub her so;
    Oho! oho!
  Dis nigga lub her so.

As Jim retired amid the evident surprise and pleasure of the company, General Ellingwood, said "My design was not wholly to amuse. After discussing the art of Rome I wanted to show you the genius of Africa. In the tone and sentiment and style of the negro there is something at once amusing, plaintive and picturesque. You are all more familiar than myself with the Piazza del Popolo where radiate the Babuino, the Ripetta, and the Corso. I could become enthusiastic as these ladies should I describe the terraced Pincio, the Dacian captives, the Egyptian obelisk with its couchant spouting lions, whose graceful shaft, no longer towering over the Pharaohs, now moves around its shadow in the moon amid the laughing crowds of modern Rome. Ah! you begin to smile. I proceed to my story. Last August I went to see the Gatta Sieca. Six persons were blindfolded, and whirled around before starting. The first fell sprawling into a fountain. The second came straight back to the obelisk. The third marched towards the Pincio. The fourth almost gained the prize when he stumbled, and was unable to rise. The fifth after circling about struck his head on the lion where he started. The sixth, with occasional pauses, and hesitations, went directly towards the Corso, where Jim stood shouting in genuine negro style.

When the bandage was removed, and I saw Jumbo beside his jubilant son, I perceived that the African had outwitted the Italian. Then succeeded such a song as old Rome never heard, and new Rome will never hear again.

The people did not understand a single word, and yet the plaintive music of the negro in a moment changed the yells of the crowd into tears."

Jumbo here entered, dressed as a respectable house-servant, and well instructed in the part he was to perform. The inevitable grin had disappeared from the face of the old man, and he bowed with a solemn gravity. His whole manner was inimitably sad, when putting forward his right foot, throwing back his person, resting his hands on his hips, and rolling his eyes heavenward, he sang as follows:

> Hab ye been wha de cypress-vine
>   Hang down de leabs?
> Dar wha de branches bend, and twine,
>   Dar Jumbo griebs.
>   Why, why, why,
>   He so cry?
> Cause in de groun' his ole Nell lie.
>
> Nell he lub, when a gal wa Nell;
>   Now Nell am dead;
> Hear de toll ob de berryin' bell!
>   Joy, joy, am fled.
>   Why, why, why,
>   He so cry?
> Cause in de groun' his ole Nell lie.
>
> But in Hebben de ole Nell smile
>   On dat bright shore;

> Dar Jumbo go after awhile!
>   He die no more.
>   Why, why, why,
>   He no cry!
> Cause to do Laud his ole Nell fly.

The company were melted into tears. It was acknowledged that the vivacity of Jim, and the pathos of Jumbo, produced effects unattainable by the most polished culture, where there was no native genius.

Not long after the scenes of this singular evening, the same persons assembled in the Protestant chapel, which was most charmingly decorated with the choicest Italian flowers. Dr. Elton was on the chancel in his surplice, holding his Prayer Book. · Before him stood Edward Ellingwood and Anna Austin, whose marriage excited peculiar interest, as indicating the heart-union of North and South, under the same old stars of beauty and glory. The service was said with an affectionate solemnity, made impressive by the gathering shadows of an exquisite Italian evening. That star which had looked so auspiciously on the vow, now smiled brightly on its consummation. No congratulations could have been more joyous. Judge Ellingwood and General Brompton were specially radiant, and read in the event hope for their common country. After the party dispersed from the chapel, they assembled at a later hour in a grand Roman palace. The edifice was in the noblest style of old Italian art. Pictures and statues from the masters were on its walls, and along its halls. The tapestried drawing-room blazed with lamps, and flashed with mirrors. Jewels worn in the days of Cæsars and Constantines sparkled on the fingers, and breasts, and brows of Italian ladies. The high position of Judge Ellingwood, and General Bromp-

23*

ton, attracted a brilliant company. Even the scarlet of a Cardinal, and the coronet of a Duke were not wanting to the scene. Nothing could exceed the excellence of the music and the exhilaration of the dance.

After a pause in the Tarantella, young Elton and Miss Cleveland, dressed as peasants, the latter tambourine in hand, entered for the Saltarello. Ada was superb in her beauty, and her gay attire gave the brightest charm to her face, and her person. The young gentleman did not sink the dignity of the clergyman in the gaiety of the dancer. He and Ada wheeled around each other in rapid circles, balancing their hands, and imitating every attitude and motion of peasants as if they had been born amid the vineyards of Italy. The lady flung her tambourine gracefully around her head, and Mr. Elton knelt before her with an expression of love too natural not to be real. The happy company separated at a late hour. General Brompton, Edward, and Anna Ellingwood, Dr. Elton, his son, and Miss Ada Cleveland, attended by Jim, left immediately in the train on their way to Athens and Constantinople. They visited Egypt and Palestine, and then Calcutta and Jeddo, returning through California to New York, and Willow-Shade.

CHAPTER XXXIII.

It was his advancing age which prevented Judge Ellingwood from accompanying the wedding party. Mrs. Cleveland and Miss Mary remained with him, and Jumbo was kindly left by General Brompton, not only on account of his qualifications as a servant, but his marvellous aquaintance with Rome. Although quite old, he had an instinctive sympathy with Italian ways, and seemed born for the eternal city. After the carnival frolics, with the Lenten season, an unusual solemnity settled over our Roman household. A shadow was evidently on Mrs. Cleveland. Mary found her one day pacing the library in an agony.

"What, what, my friend," she cried, "has thus disturbed your peace? Surely you can confide to my ear any grief."

Mrs. Cleveland paused. An angelic serenity suddenly overspread her face. She exclaimed: "Oh, Mary, the struggle has been severe, but I trust I have conquered. I will tell you my secret. I have seen Mr. Cleveland."

"Mr. Cleveland!" Since you left the Russia? In Rome? When? where? or do you dream?" inquired Mary, holding up her hands, and expressing in her countenance the utmost surprise and curiosity.

"No! no!" she answered. "It is true! sadly, fearfully, terribly true!" Here her struggles were returning, and she seated herself on the sofa, making every possible effort to preserve her tranquility. Having recovered her composure, Mrs. Cleveland looked through her tears, and said: "Be seated, and I will tell you all that has happened." Mary took her place on the sofa beside her friend, and Mrs. Cleveland resumed: "I was at a window above the Corso, to witness the carnival. In the height of the frolic a mask appeared, representing an ancient knight, and to the confusion of the wearer suddenly fell from his face. It was instantly replaced. A single glance, however, was sufficient to show Mr. Cleveland. You may imagine my agitation, especially after our proximity on the America."

"Have you ascertained," asked Mary, "where he lives? What can be his errand at Rome!"

"I have learned, through the American Minister, that he is in the Vatican, and has a Cardinal's hat."

"Marvellous! marvellous!" burst forth Mary. "Heaven has some deep design in your history."

"Nor is this all," continued Mrs. Cleveland. "I have seen this morning, in the *Civilta*, an advertisement for a servant, signed by his initials, and stating where further information will be given."

"How strangely your paths touch, and separate!" exclaimed Miss Ellingwood. "You resemble two vessels on an ocean, each crossing and recrossing the track of the other, now nearing, now parting. Possibly you may yet voyage together towards the eternal sea."

"He will be saved, Mary," answered the heroic wife. "*How* I leave to the wisdom of our great Father. Do you think me liable to whims?"

Mary smiled and replied: "Whims! The last thing conceivable! If your sympathies are easily moved like the branches of the tree, your principles resemble the sturdy trunk." Then rising, and standing before her friend with a countenance of glowing admiration, she added: "Your faith is sublime! Your purpose is sublime! Your heroism is sublime!"

Mrs. Cleveland, deeply affected, said: "Mary, your friendship is my greatest comfort, and what buds on earth will, I trust, bloom in glory. I am now encouraged to make a request I feared you might deem both selfish and singular. A strong desire pursues me that Jumbo should apply for this situation. It is so constant, and so intense, that I must believe it from above."

"Certainly," returned Miss Ellingwood, "certainly. I can answer both for papa, and myself. Such an arrangement appears most desirable." Then with a beam on her face from her joyous heart, she added: "How funny to have a living link of connection between the house of a Congregational Elder and the palace of Pio Nino!"

Judge Ellingwood was immediately consulted, and cordially consented to the plan. Soon after, Jumbo made application to the Cardinal, who was delighted to see once more, the honest face of the noble old negro. He perceived at a glance, how important he might be to the consummation of schemes, rapidly assuming a definite shape. Jumbo had a small room prepared for him adjoining the splendid apartment of the Cardinal, and communicating with it by a door at the end of a narrow passage.

One day his eminence was sitting at his window looking from the Vatican, towards St. Peter's, when he said to his servant: "I little thought, Jumbo, when you waited on me at Sea-Side, you would ever be with me in Rome."

"De Laud," replied the negro, turning toward him, rolling his eyes, and a solemn countenance, "hab quar ways. He reserb for you de robe and de tippet, and de hat, and de gold, and de scarlet, and dis room in de Pope-palas."

"But you, Jumbo, are much the same in Italy, as in America."

"De same, your eminens, and not 'zactly de same."

"What do you mean?" inquired the Cardinal.

"I'se de same in de flesh; de same wool grow on de smoove head; de same skin am on de ole face; de same limp knee Tiga kick lame; de same outside, massa; but not de same in de heart." And Jumbo significantly striking his heart with his right hand, closed his eyes in pious gratitude.

"And how and when did this all occur?" asked the Cardinal.

"'Fore my Nell shut her eyes, and go unda de cypress, she send up prars to de hebben like de incense ob de Preese swung in de sweet clouds ober de alta, and dey come down from de trone just afore we left Sea-Side, in convartin' power, when our Mcfdist Parson, Joe, he preach, and all de niggas shout and jump, and sing, wid dar faces shinin' in de light, streamin' from de udder wuld."

"And may I ask," said the Cardinal, more interested by the simple recital, than he chose to admit, even to himself, "what is the difference between what you were and what you are?"

"Berry great! answered Jumbo, reverently, "Berry great! Wuns dis nigga swar and cuss, and lie and git mad, and steal massa's tings and tink no harm. Now he pray; he read de Bibul; he trust de Laud's death on de cross, and lub de Laud, and sarv de Laud, and hope see de Laud on His trone, and be like de Laud, and be wid de angels, and de saints, bright and shinin', and glitterin' as de sun, and to fly on de wings ob light, and wabe de palm, and sing de song, and hab de harp, and see ole Nell, and talk wid her, and lub her foreva in dat glory ob de hebbenly wuld."

While Jumbo talked, his face glowed with a preternatural lustre. His voice became musically soft, and melting, a tear gathered in his eye, and a celestial meekness shed over his black, wrinkled face, an unearthly charm. Cleveland's reddened lids showed his sympathetic interest. After a moment's pause, the Cardinal inquired:

"And how do you like Rome, Jumbo, and all the splendid ceremonies of its churches?"

"Gran'! 'nif'cent! gloryus!—de lights, de incens', de music, de colas, de pillas, de windas, de pictas, de auches! Dat Saint Peta's standin' like de dome ob Hebben! but, but," hesitated Jumbo.

"Do not be afraid," interposed the Cardinal, "tell me just what is in your mind."

Thus encouraged the veteran negro proceeded. "Dey 'semble, 'cordin' to my idees, de 'Merican woods in de Autum—den dey be all cubbered wid glory—red, green, yaller on de hills like de robes ob angels! But" he continued shaking his head mournfully, and significantly, " dose same leabs dazzlin in de sun hab de chill ob death, and so to dis nigga's heart dese big churchas—bright to de eye ob de flesh, Massa Card'nal, but to de eye ob de sperit radder, when de leabs fall, like de snow glitterin', but freezin on de mountains ob ole Virginny." The conversation was here interrupted, but the simple old African had unconsciously expressed the exact experiences of his disappointed master.

Perhaps we should not conclude this chapter without for one moment explaining a circumstance described by

Mrs. Cleveland near its beginning. After his interview with Bishop Frances the Cardinal felt a resistless impulse to forget his sorrows in the frantic fun of the Carnival. The genius of these Christian Saturnalia completely possessed his mind. Under the cover of a mask he had mingled in all the frolics of the Corso, and was seen by his wife as we have already related. The recognition was mutual. A pale, sad, lovely face was never again absent from his thoughts. But another image also entered his soul. Ada stood laughing beside her mother radiant with a splendid beauty.

The Cardinal returned to his lonely chamber in the Vatican oppressed with gloom. Before him rose his home. He saw the house, the lawn, the piazza, the library, the trees, the walks—nay, every shrub and flower, and leaf seemed photographed on his memory. In his sleep he would cry and reach out his arms, and embrace his wife, and kiss his daughter in his old study with its old furniture amid the old books. Once he shrieked as he found himself clasping shadows which vanished from his breast. Then his house was changed into a palace. He dreamed that it was lifted by angels into the air, and transported to the radiancy of a celestial light.

CHAPTER XXXIV.

LENT drew around Mrs. Cleveland a deepening gloom. The lights which flashed, and waved on the Corso had been extinguished. From window, and balcony there was no more streaming brilliance over a rushing, laughing, shouting crowd. The frolic has ended. The masks have vanished. The theatres are closed. Solemn Priests are making their annual visits. Tinkling bells, and shrill chants from boys in shabby church-robes, are heard along the streets, as the youthful devotees march behind the black cross calling the children to catechism. Processions of ecclesiastics have begun, preceded by music, and followed by lanterns, and soldiers, and the gonfalon of the Virgin, and the great wooden cross with its garlands of ivy shaking, and gleaming in the torches.

Shut away from these strange scenes without, Mrs Cleveland and Mary Ellingwood are conversing in the parlor, while the Judge, overcome with fatigue, lies dozing on the sofa. Old tapestries with faded figures, and dimmed splendors, are looking from the walls, and the lamp hangs low, and burns uncertainly.

"Mary, I have another secret for you," began Mrs. Cleveland.

"And have you not always a friendly ear for your sorrows?" asked Miss Ellingwood, with an attempted smile.

"Always! always! I thank Heaven for your sympa-

thy, and the Judge's protection. Without you, how helpless and how desolate would I be in this city of Priests!"

"The reason of my feeling is entirely unknown," replied Mary, "and yet I am strangely comforted when I
think that Jumbo is in the Vatican."

"All will soon be plain," said Mrs. Cleveland.

"Do you know I have been attending the service of the
Sistine Chapel?"

"I have missed you again, and again," answered Mary,
"and could not conjecture the cause of your unusual absence. But I approve your choice. The histories on those
walls, the marvels of the music, the Last Judgment, with
the grandeur of its forms, and the sublimity of its scenery,
may excuse the presence even of so staunch a Protestant
as yourself."

"But these have not charmed me to the place," said
Mrs. Cleveland—with the old sorrow heaving in her breast,
and struggling up to her face—"Mr. Cleveland officiates
there."

"Marvel added to marvel!" exclaimed Mary in astonishment. "Where will terminate a series of events so
wonderful?"

"Yes! I have seen him," returned Mrs. Cleveland, "repeatedly there, so pale, so melancholy, so spiritual, so lofty!
His person clad in his robes has an almost seraphic dignity, and in the midst of such striking pageantries, I sometimes seem looking on a celestial being whose form is on
earth, and whose soul is in heaven. Can you be surprised
that my poor heart impels me to the place by a spell I
cannot resist? The woman conquers the Christian. I
condemn myself, and yet yield to the fascination. I gaze,
and gaze, and gaze, until my heart seems bursting from
my eyes." Placing her hands over her breast, and turn-

ing her face upward, she added: "Surely our Father will not blast the lonely, thirsty, scorched oasis for looking on the heavens."

Mary Ellingwood was overcome both by the sentiment and the manner of her friend, and could only relieve her own emotion by sympathetic tears.

"Your life is ever becoming more strange and more intense," she exclaimed. "Yet I believe from the tangled skein is weaving a future to be bright, and beautiful forever. Do you think you were recognized by your husband?"

"I am certain in one instance he gave a start of surprise. His check became red as the scarlet on his robe, which appeared rustling with his agitation. Ever since I have felt a strange consciousness of mutual communion casting over both of us its magnetic spell."

Leaving the ladies to pursue their conversation we return to the Cardinal himself. The design of Bishop Frances in the extorted promise was to concentrate on him the personal influence of his Holiness, and recover him by the æsthetic effects of the Lenten and Easter services. Nor was he insensible to their charms. The Miserere of the Sistine Chapel in its wild wailings of grief transported him in tears to the Cross, and all the surrounding miracles of art often elevated him to a rapturous fervor. The mild face and noble person of the Pope, with whom he was now so constantly associated, deeply and favorably impressed his sensitive nature. But he had learned to analyze and suspect mere emotion. He studied in his chamber his Bible, his old Prayer-Book, and the Apostolic Fathers. Often with Jumbo he descended from the Chapel of St. Agnes to explore the Catacombs, and he examined the remains of Primitive Christianity in the

Lapidarian **Gallery.** His faith **was not now** the result of impulse **but of reason.** He found himself a Primitive Catholic, **and a** Protestant Catholic, **but no longer a** Roman **Catholic.** Magnificent ceremonies **were changed into gilded mockeries.** In an interview with **his Holiness even Papal argument** produced **no effect.** An inherited **Saxon** nature **had forever overmastered that Roman adhesion which was an exotic implantation.** He looked **forward to** Easter as **a man** confined **in a** splendid **palace awaits the hour** when **the door will** open, **and he will step forth from his** gilded **imprisonment** free beneath **the roof of heaven. Thundering** cannon, exploding mortars, **ringing** bells, **pealing trumpets announced** not only the **resurrection, but his own approaching liberty.** Yet **he was strangely** affected by **the appearance of the Pope pronouncing his annual blessing. Protestant as he now was, it is not** surprising **that he should be** impressed **with the** spectacle **of** the swaying **crowd, the worn pilgrims, the** hooded sisters, the glittering soldiers, **as below the dome** of St. Peter's, **Pio Nono,** rising from **his golden chair,** clothed in white, and between peacock plumes, with **his** musical, penetrating voice, pronounced **his** benediction over the vast kneeling multitude. **But the emotion of the Cardinal** reached its climax **as he** gazed on the illumination of St. Peter's terminating his promise. **His soul was concentrated on that** vast **pile. His eye gleamed. The blaze** of the sun has disappeared. **Twilight is veiling the sky.** A glow trembles over the distant basilica. **The** splendor increases until the edifice outlined against the heavens stands a structure of fire. Bells clang **away the silver illumination.** A flame bursts from the **Cross. There is a** flash whirling down the dome, and a rainfire **over the** cupolas, and St. Peter's is a blaze of golden light. As it waves and shakes and vanishes Cleveland feels that the succeeding gloom is not to him darkness, but rather like an illumination of Truth and Liberty.

24*

CHAPTER XXXV.

WHEN the Cardinal returned to his chamber in the Vatican he found the lamps unlighted, and his apartment contrasted strangely with the brilliance he had witnessed. He had no time, however, for reflections. He had scarcely taken his seat and ordered the lights, when Bishop Frances was announced, and entered.

He said immediately, "You perceive I am punctual, your Eminence."

"I am in all respects ready for our interview," he replied, with a look and tone of resolution which surprised the Bishop, who at once proceeded.

"I hope the services in which you have participated, your interview with his Holiness, and your own reflections have banished doubt from the mind of your Eminence and restored you to the·Church."

"I must not disguise," replied Cleveland, with entire calmness, "my true feelings and opinions. The effect has been different from what you intended. I am now forever separated in head and heart from Rome. A near survey has dissipated the colors with which she was invested by distance. Familiarity has scattered fancies. My Saxon nature recoils from your Latin rule. I have returned to the faith from which I was led by impulse and deluded by ambition."

Frances arose, a terrible spectacle of hatred and scorn. Glancing down on Cleveland, and shaking toward him his

282

long, bony finger, he seemed for a moment a tiger preparing to spring on his victim.

"For this," he cried, "I have guided you to our holy mother, that you may wound the bosom which sheltered you! For this, my prayers, my counsels, my labors, that you may betray the man by whom you were converted! For this, my influence at the Vatican to procure you a mitre and a hat, that as Bishop and Cardinal, your apostacy may intensify our disgrace! For this I obtained your entrance to our Order, that your oath might blast forever your body and your soul! Boy! Woman! Traitor, you shall never leave this palace, to proclaim your infamy and our disgrace!"

Cleveland sat meekly under an explosion he deserved and expected. With a beautiful mildness, he replied:

"Bishop Frances, I only blame myself. Vexation and ambition led me astray. I am sorry for myself. I am sorry for you. I am sorry for the Church."

"I suppose," returned the Bishop, with a bitter sneer, and in a tone of cutting taunt, "your thoughts of Mrs. Cleveland have not at all influenced your conclusions. Doubtless, they have not been unpleasant, or unfrequent. I am told, that even in the Sistine chapel, from its very altar, you returned her glances. A Priest before Heaven defiling himself with adultery! And your beautiful daughter! What an argument in her image! I presume your Eminence, before all the world, will return to the embraces of connubial love and the delights of your family!"

Satan could not have been more provoking. A few weeks since, such words, and such a manner, would have stung Cleveland to madness. He now felt his selfishness and vacillation deserved infinitely more.

"No words can express how I deplore the injury I inflict," said Cleveland, mildly. "I do not mean to mitigate my faults, and yet your words suggest one wrong in the Church. She severed what God united. Her unlawful power came between me and my wife, alienating her from my protection, and thrusting my daughter from my care, and making my home a ruin. Where began the sin, must commence the cure. Whatever the consequence, I cannot, I will not, I dare not conceal my purpose to return to my family."

Frances lifted himself on his feet to his greatest height, then bending down his flashing eye, and placing a hand on each shoulder of Cleveland, he cried:

"Never! your Eminence, never! We cannot compel your opinions, or constrain your heart, but we can control your person. While you live, until the Papal throne is a ruin, you shall never pass beyond the Papal dominion, or even the Papal palace."

Cleveland had sometimes feared that the disgrace of his apostacy would be concealed by the restriction of his liberty. He had, however, thrust from his mind, the hateful thought. Now his worst anticipations were to be realized. Controlling the tempest in his breast, he said, with a persuasive gentleness of manner, and in a voice plaintively musical:

"Will you not remember our old friendship? Will you not pity my misfortunes? Will you not ask your Order to release me from my oath? Will you not seek a dispensation from his Holiness? I beg your kind interposition."

"Dispensation!" sneered Frances, savagely. "*One* should, I think, suffice for us both." But he was, after all, softened by Cleveland's tone and suffering. Musing a moment he answered gently, almost tenderly, "Our **Order** is now sitting in the **Vatican, and I** have an interview appointed with his Holiness. I will **comply with your** request, and meet you here at midnight."

He then withdrew, leaving Cleveland in the calmness of either resignation **or** despair. **Frances** passed along the **hall of the Vatican,** entered a gallery, descended a stair-**way,** reached a **low, narrow,** dark, subterraneous passage, and walking rapidly **in the** sepulchral light of a solitary lamp, reached a massive iron door. Three peculiar raps caused **the ponderous barrier to swing back** on its hinges, and **revealed an apartment piled with** the tokens of death. **On every side, leaving** a narrow passage next the wall, **hung rows of skeletons.** A hideous pyramid of skulls **towered in the centre.** Around were bones—ghastly, **grotesque,** hideous. Seated beneath **the** low ceiling, like **spectres in** the gloom, were **solemn men in black.** One, evidently their President, **occupied a chair at once fantas-tic and** frightful, **yet precisely corresponding to his gaunt form and implacable face. When Frances** entered, after **the** salutation **of his Order, he, too,** assumed a sombre **costume like** that of his associates. He was immediately **required to state his errand.** Everything indicated **busi-ness, not ceremony.**

The Bishop rose, using **the most** concise language pos-**sible. Without preface, or** apology, he said: "Cardinal **Cleveland is more** than ever opposed to the Papacy. He wishes **openly to** renounce our Church and Order. Shall **he be** released from his vow, and return to **his** family? **I wish** an instant answer."

A Satanic grimness followed this statement. The Fathers consulted in a low under tone. But the case was **too** plain for **discussion, or even vote.** The Superior soon replied : "The request is unprecedented, and compliance impossible. Apostacy is a forbidden crime. Until the Pope, our supreme and infallible master, directs, Cardinal Cleveland must never leave the Vatican."

Frances removed his robe, made a reverential obeisance, and withdrew backward to the door. The transition was great from such a solemn gloom to the apartment of the Vatican, beaming and flashing with splendors, where Pio Nono stood in his pontifical magnificence, encircled by a brilliant company. Bishop Frances having obtained permission, awaited his opportunity, approached his Holiness, and first prostrating himself to the floor, kissed the outstretched finger of the Pope. Being a known Infallibilist, he was received with the blandest and brightest smiles of welcome. Having hastily stated the contemplated defection of Cleveland, he received from Pius an opinion exactly confirming the judgment of the Order, and retired with the formalities which marked his introduction. Returning quickly to the room of the suffering man, and obtaining admission, he said, without ceremony, "May it please your Eminence, the Order and his Holiness have decided, as I deemed inevitable. Your apostacy cannot be tolerated. No violence is intended, but you cannot leave the Vatican."

Frances, with a cold bow, withdrew, and left Cleveland alone. To his surprise his heart was tranquil. His day of caprice and sentiment was gone. He had now a developed manhood. Wealth and rank had given him a position for which he had not been qualified, and his untried bark on the perilous sea of life had shifted with the winds, and tossed with the waves. A mere breath had blown the painted, graceful, gilded craft from its moorings, where the strong ship would have smiled in the conscious security of a safe anchorage. Cleveland was no longer the pretty yacht, but the tried vessel. He felt a new resolve, a new spirit, a new power. He was face to face with a tyranny he defied, and from which he was calmly planning his escape. Manhood is above contingencies. It yields alone to Heaven.

CHAPTER XXXVI.

ON the morning after the events of the last chapter, Judge Ellingwood was sitting thoughtfully in his study. Without was the murmur of a fountain, lifting its column in the sun to fall back in plashing pearls, and glide from its basin between flowery banks. In every direction towered Roman palaces. Away in the mist of the distance stood against the sky the dome of St. Peter's. In another direction was seen the stately Vatican, where the Judge was now concentrating his thoughts.

While he was musing, Mary burst into his study with a sunny, "Good morning, papa," followed by such a kiss on the paternal cheek as bright, loving daughters only know how to give.

Judge Ellingwood returned the joyous salute with a corresponding affectionateness, and said, "I am quite glad you have come. Some important events have transpired, and I must join your young wit to my old brain. Are you ready for the alliance, Mary?"

"Ah! Papa," she replied, "I have brought you to terms, and you are now willing to treat. Yesterday I felt quite banished. Mrs. Cleveland closeted in your study made me fearfully jealous. Messengers passed to and fro! Mr. Percivale was announced! the American Minister was whirled to our door, and whirled away again, and your daughter ignorant of the excitement. But your proposition makes her forgiving, and she receives you into her favor."

"Mary, I am too grave to return your banter," replied the Judge sadly. "I know Mrs. Cleveland has told you everything. Two ladies in the same apartment always click like telegraphic machines in a thunder-storm. Besides, the requisition of his Eminence, the Governor of Police, took us by surprise."

"Can it be possible we are peremptorily commanded to leave Rome?" inquired Mary.

"Of that there can be no doubt. There on my table lies the order. Mr. Fortescue remonstrated in vain. Nothing but his removal to our house, and the American flag over our heads saved us from expulsion. See there," said the Judge rising, and pointing to its shadow dancing over the lawn, "the pledge of our safety! What music in the flutter of those folds! Our stars awe even the Vatican."

"And what can be the explanation of this strange movement?" asked Mary.

"The Cardinal has renounced Romanism, and we suspect is a prisoner in the Vatican," replied the Judge. "The presence of his wife in this city of Celibate Priests is of course a perplexity, and an offence."

"I know Mrs. Cleveland," said Mary. "An Italian Pope will yet find himself defeated by an American woman."

At this juncture the eulogized lady knocked at the door, and was admitted. She was terribly excited, but evidently in command of her spirit. Slightly flushed, there was a fascinating sweetness and dignity in her matronly beauty. "My dear friends," she began mournfully, "I fear I am ever to be the disturber of your peace.

25

Here is a note, directed to Judge Ellingwood, in the writing of Mr. Cleveland, and brought by Jumbo. It will doubtless prove the key to our future history." She gave it to the Judge with a trembling hand, and sank down upon the sofa. Hastily removing the envelope, and darting over the page his quick, practiced eye, he returned the note to Mrs. Cleveland. As she caught its contents at a glance, exclamations of gratitude burst from her lips, and again she fell back fainting, and nearly lifeless. It was a communication from Cleveland to his old friend, declaring his renunciation of Romanism, his detention in the Vatican, and his resolution to escape. It concluded with an earnest request for an interview with his wife. Such a joy could scarcely fail to overcome her, who for years had lived solely for the rescue of her husband. She lay pale, with her lips moving, and her face turned towards Heaven, while over her features seemed to play a celestial radiance. Still reclining on the sofa, she said, in whispers, "Jumbo waits in the hall; let him be called at once." A servant was sent, and the venerable negro immediately made his appearance. Mrs. Cleveland, animated with sudden strength, inquired: "Where is he? How is he? Tell me! Tell me quickly!"

Jumbo, with a solemn look of mystery, replied: "Missus, de Ca'dnal he anudder man. Hes'e no more walks his room, and cry, and strike his breast, and trow himself on de bed. He look at peace. De Laud hab cum to his heart. He seem like de Virginny pine afta de staum, and de lightnin', when de limbs be cubber'd agin wid de leabs, and standin' on de mountin, it say to de Hebbens to flash and rore. He look noble, Missus." These simple words brought tears to every eye. Mrs. Cleveland wept convulsively.

When she had sufficiently recovered, Judge Ellingwood asked: "Has he told you his plans, Jumbo?"

"O yes, Massa Judge. He say de Pope want to keep him in de Vatican, and he'se want to 'scape; and he will, Missus. He got new sperit. Dey can't keep him dar. His soul bust dat palas, and send de Pope a kitin' trough de air."

The company smiled at this figure. A consultation followed. It was feared the guard would be more strict, owing to the action of the American Minister, and that Jumbo's connection with the Judge's household could not long be concealed. After weighing every circumstance, it was concluded the interview should be attempted that night, and the final escape arranged at the earliest possible moment. A rope ladder was procured, separated into parts, and conveyed at several different times to Cleveland's apartment by Jumbo, in a satchel he had frequently carried to the laundress. A chapel in the Catacombs was designated for a midnight meeting. The entrance was from a garden, where Dr. Elton and Jumbo had repeatedly descended.

When Cleveland learned these plans, he made corresponding preparations. While a church-clock was striking eleven, all the doors of his apartment were locked within. A window was raised. The ladder was tied to an antique massive bedstead, itself fastened to the floor. A fortunate projection of the palace on the side most exposed, formed a screen for the descent. Jumbo first let himself down, and held the ladder below. Cleveland stood a moment in the window. Uttering a prayer, he climbed over the sill. Step by step he lowered himself towards the earth. He was speedily on the last rung. Leaping thankfully to the ground, a cloudy, moonless, starless night, offered a friendly gloom. Through solitary and obscure streets, Jumbo led their way to the appointed garden.

Judge Ellingwood and Mrs. Cleveland, closely muffled, had already arrived. All emotion, and even recognition, were suppressed. One after another of the party passed down through the entrance, and silently descended a rude stone stairway. Jumbo preceded with a lamp, and proved a faithful guide through familiar passages and galleries. At last a Chapel, brilliantly illuminated, was reached. Arthur Cleveland and his wife alone entered, while Judge Ellingwood and Jumbo withdrew to a contiguous tomb. A scene ensued language cannot paint. The fires of love, suppressed for years, burst into instant flame. Separation only increased the intensity of the blaze. Mrs. Cleveland flung herself into the arms of her husband, and, folded to his breast, kissed his lips with a passionate eagerness, while his tall manly form shook as he pressed to his heart his recovered wife.

Every association of the spot lent sacredness to the interview. Around were the graves of martyrs, whose bodies had been carried from the crowded arena, torn by beasts, and gashed with swords, to sleep in gloom until the light of their last triumph. Here were the ashes of women and children who had perished in the flames. Here was the dust of noble ecclesiastics, who, after being hunted over the world, had crept down to die. Here had been the home of the Church, and here still were the simple monuments of her immortal faith. This very Chapel had heard the voice of Primitive Preachers, and possibly seen Apostles celebrate the holy mysteries of the Gospel. Aisle, and gallery, and roof, had echoed the songs of saints wafted from their gloom to Heaven.

Arthur and Emily, after the first violence of their emotions, sat long gazing at each other in a silence interrupted by fervent kisses and warm embraces. The former at last gave a sudden start. He gently extricated himself from the arms of his wife, and falling on his knees at her feet, exclaimed, passionately: "My first error was against Heaven, in my formalism, my infidelity, my rebellion, my apostacy. For these I trust I have found forgiveness. My next sin, Emily, was against you. I permitted a blasphemous tyranny to come between myself and my wife. I deserted your bosom. I abandoned our Ada. I desolated our home. I have wrung your heart with long years of agony. Oh, Emily, can you pardon the wretch at your feet?"

Mrs. Cleveland, weeping, bent over her husband, and kissed his forehead, saying: "Rise, Arthur, we are one forever. Let us bow before that altar, and beg the smile of Heaven."

Cleveland arose, took the hand of his wife with an eager clasp, and they long knelt in silence before the venerable stone. Returning to their former seat, he broke forth: "My Ada! where, where is my forsaken Ada?"

"A few days since she left Rome in perfect health with Edward and Anna Ellingwood, General Brompton, Dr. Elton, and his son. In a few months I trust we will see her in America."

"I need not ask how she looks," he proceeded. "I saw her radiant beauty as she stood in her bloom beside you on the Corso. Does she remember me? What are her prospects for the future?"

"In culture, manners, disposition, she is all we could desire. She is engaged to young Elton, who is in every

25*

respect worthy of our daughter.   On her breast she has always worn her father's image."

"Thank Heaven!" exclaimed Cleveland.   "Thank Heaven! But, Emily, I must reserve further inquiries. Arrangements must be made for my escape. I long doubted whether I was not bound by my vow as a Priest and my oath to my Order. Finally I saw my obligation to you was paramount, and now my only desire is to repair my error by beginning at its root."

"This is doubtless the will and work of that Infinite Love, which, having given us a needed discipline, has at last restored us to each other. How grateful I feel for my persistent faith!" Pointing to the walls of the Chapel, covered with sculptured forms, her eye and face glowed and kindled in the light while she continued:

"See that ark floating amid storm and billow! See Abraham delivered from Isaac's sacrifice! See Moses kneeling move Heaven! See those youth walk singing in the furnace! See Daniel sit among lions protected by an angel! See our Lord ascend triumphant to His glory! Such are the images which express the victories of my own faith."

Cleveland gazed at his wife with amazement and rapture. She stood like a martyr risen from an adjoining tomb, and clothed in light, to inspire him with courage for the future. While he still looked, the step of Judge Ellingwood was heard, and he was requested to enter. The joy of the party was complete, and was shared by Jumbo grinning at the door. Conversation was now directed to the best methods of effecting the escape of Cleveland. It was decided that on the third night after, he, attended by Jumbo, should meet Mrs. Cleveland in the Piazza Montanara, all being disguised as peasants.

Mingling with the laborers they were to pass with them through the city-gates. Beyond, Judge Ellingwood would provide a carriage, to convey them to the valley of Lucerne, in Piedmont. He and Mary were to remain at Rome, and join them at some other place when advised of their safety.

When the consultation was over, the party knelt in the Chapel, and Cleveland poured forth words of petition whose earnestness recalled the supplications of a former age in the same place and for a similar deliverance. When all had arisen, after affectionate farewells, they silently followed Jumbo back to the stairway. The Judge and Mrs. Cleveland reached the palace safely, and relieved the anxious fears of Mary by their appearance. Cleveland and Jumbo, obscured in a dense darkness, arrived at the Vatican, and drew down their ladder by a string which had raised it back within the window. Both arose without difficulty, and found their apartment undisturbed. Cleveland slept with a tranquility he had not known for years. Once he dreamed of a bright home and above it the glory of Heaven.

CHAPTER XXXVII.

ON the third night after the meeting in the Catacombs
two seeming peasants walked along a street near the Vatican. On the elder and stouter was a mask. Both passed
a group of three persons, and were joined by one of them,
a female, in the dress of an Italian harvester. As the
party stopped in apparent doubt as to their direction, they
heard an American voice, deep and mellow, accompanied
by a guitar, singing the following words.

> Sleep, Love! and bright thy dreams!
>   Ah! o'er thy bed
>   What rosy head!
> Light-wing'd the boy-god gleams!
>   Sleep, Love!
>
> Sleep till his arrow flies !
>   Twang, twang the dart
>   Goes to thy heart!
> He smiles, and mounts the skies—
>   Sleep, Love!
>
> Wake, Love, and see the moon!
>   Hear my guitar,
>   And watch yon star!
> Thy bright face show soon! soon!
>   Wake, Love!
>
> Wake, Love, and from thy lip
>   Fling, fling one kiss.
>   Far drops the bliss,
> When near the bloom I'd sip,
>   Sip, sip!

Instantly, borne on the morning breeze, in evident response, was heard a beautiful song in Italian, wafting its melody from a distant street. This latter strain was accompanied by the tinkle of the tambourine, and indicated the direction of the Piazza Montanara. Guided by the sound, our party no longer hesitated, but proceeded rapidly and directly to the place. A gay scene burst on their eyes. Decorated carts! Garlanded Oxen! Gay groups chatting, laughing, dancing to the music of the pipe and tambourine! As the glad sounds rang far and near, the setting moon revealed here and there in lifted windows the white night-cap of some Roman disturbed by the early revelry.

Soon the company organizes, forms into procession, passes through the gates, scatters over the Campagna to scenes of daily toil. The three persons we first observed found no difficulty in mingling unnoticed with the noisy crowd and reaching without the walls a carriage apparently in waiting. Mr. and Mrs. Cleveland at once enter and occupy the back seat, while Jumbo, having closed the door, climbs heavily to a place with the coachman, and removing his mask thrusts it down in the box.

The moon hangs above the dark peaks of a distant hill, and through a rosy morning trembles a brilliant star. The lark is already singing in his cloud. On every side is a blaze of flowers. Vast acqueducts on lofty arches, festooned with ivy, and brilliant with bloom, stretch in silent grandeur over the plain, whose ruined tombs and villas stand sad monuments of a buried world. Circling mountains now shine in the rising sun, and white villas gleam along their sides. Flocks of sheep, and goats, and the pipes of shepherds indicate that the carriage is leaving the city far behind.

Hitherto the hearts of Arthur and Emily Cleveland have been too intense for words.

At last the husband broke forth, "Thank Heaven, Emily, we are free! And amid what scenes of marvellous beauty!"

"Never, Arthur," she exclaimed with rapture, "will we forget this hour. How fresh this air! How bright yon plain! How brilliant yon sky! This morning is an emblem of our bliss, and liberty."

"Oh, Italy, Italy, how has superstition darkened thy glory, and turned this matchless plain from a garden to a tomb! See, Emily, the dome of St. Peter's sublime on yon gorgeous heavens! How different my emotions from those first excited by its incomparable grandeur! Alas! Alas! I know it the emblem of a spiritual tyranny which would enslave a world."

"Perhaps, Arthur, Heaven intends you to testify against Rome. The witness of the eye and ear has a peculiar power."

"I know not," he answered, "what is designed in our future. Our furnace has been severe, but the flames were necessary. Whether we have been refined for action, or for suffering, is not ours to determine."

"Fire alone brings from the incense its fragrance," said Mrs. Cleveland.

While the carriage is whirling over the Campagna amid clouds of dust, and the husband and wife are conversing, we may pause to notice their appearance. From the face and form of Cleveland all feebleness has vanished. The lips are compressed, and firm. The jaw denotes power. The forehead is full, noble, commanding. Every feature indicates strong, invincible, manly determination.

Mrs. Cleveland, on the other hand, has become more
gentle and tender in her expression. On her face is a
sweet composure, refining and spiritualizing her beauty,
and indicating that the heart of the woman has found
rest in a nature formed by struggle into a mould stronger
than her own, and capable of affording the guidance and
protection she desires and expects. She and her husband
sit together in the calm, joyous consciousness of a perfect
sympathy. Years have been necessary for this process.
Its consummation constitutes the bliss, the strength, the
glory of the married state. How many mistake this discipline intended to harmonize discordant lives! Fretted
and wretched, they seek remedy in divorces permitted by
human, forbidden by Divine Law. Thus families are
brought to shame and ruin; the State to demoralization
and disgrace.

CHAPTER XXXVIII

"QUICK, Jumbo, quick! call your mistress!" said Arthur Cleveland as he stood on the piazza of a cottage situated amid the mountains of Piedmont. The negro instantly withdrew his black visage, and entered the door. Mrs. Cleveland very soon was at the side of her husband. "My dear," he exclaimed, "here! take my field glass! You can now see the city."

"How glorious," cried the lady, while she stood gazing for a moment with the instrument in her hand. "See, Arthur, that gigantic cloud lifted from the vale into the heavens! It seems like a snow-mountain in air! How white, how vast, how majestic!"

"Now Emily direct your glass to the old city no longer concealed by the morning mists."

Obeying the direction, and continuing her gaze for some moments, she cried, "Beautiful! beautiful! Most beautiful! I can distinctly see in the sun the palaces, and churches, and spires of Turin. One gigantic cross stands on the sky like flashing fire."

"And there," said Cleveland, pointing to a huge cliff towering sublimely behind them, "you can behold at once two of nature's grandest objects! A breath only seems necessary to hurl that avalanche thundering into the gorge! Yon glacier in the sun gleams and glitters like a gate of Heaven."

"Oh, Arthur, how grand this entire scene!" exclaimed

Mrs. Cleveland, glowing with beauty and joy. "See that valley melting away into the blue of distant Italy! Mulberry groves! Clumps of silver chestnuts! Fields of gold! Climbing vineyards! Alp towering over Alp! The brilliance of valley and mountain varied by passing cloud-shadows!"

"Grand, indeed," replied Cleveland, with a kindling and kindred enthusiasm. "This air is an inspiration! Every breath, fire and freedom! How boundless seems the soul encircled by such sublimity! These mountains are God's emblems of His Tranquility, His Eternity, His Omnipotence."

These sentiments were interrupted by a certain bell-tinkle, humiliating mortals, by a not unwelcome reminder, that they have bodies as well as souls. We are compelled to confess, that in their place coffee, omelettes and beefsteaks are quite as necessary as clouds, and glaciers, and avalanches. After a substantial breakfast, Mr. Cleveland said to his wife, "Emily, we have been here four weeks, and I have spent ten days of the time alone in exploring these marvellous mountains, everywhere interesting with their associations. Having become familiar with both scenes and histories, I propose to be no longer solitary."

"Thank you, Arthur, thank you!" she answered. "I will instantly make preparations for an exploration in your company."

Mrs. Cleveland retired, and speedily made her appearance in a dress of white, fitting beautifully around her elegant person. Her mountain-hat was singularly becoming, and it is not wonderful, that the eye of the husband sparkled as it rested affectionately on the form and face of his wife. He himself appeared greatly invigorated by pure air and healthful exercise. His clerical habit was discarded, and he wore the attire of an ordinary gentleman, which he found in a trunk, provided by the thoughtful care of Judge Ellingwood. All the love and pride of the wife appeared in the countenance of Emily Cleveland, as she gazed on the splendid figure of her noble husband. As we trace them up a steep, winding path, followed by Jumbo, with a luncheon basket, we will confess an increased interest in their destiny. With hearts and tastes united, they were now revelling in a world of beauty, and sublimity, where every spot was hallowed by the blood of martyrs. Pausing a moment on their ascent, Cleveland said: "Emily, let me point out two venerable objects. See that cliff above! A Roman soldier hurled from its height into that fearful abyss a woman and her child! Her husband was to follow! Rushing from his guard he clasped the executioner, and leaping, they fell together into the dizzy depth. Now behold that crag far beneath, from which grows a single laurel! The spray of the cataract just touches its edge! Below are quivering rainbows! There is the entrance of the cave where three hundred Vaudois are supposed to have perished! Down yon valley were driven the shattered forces of the Count of Trinity!"

"What a contrast, Arthur, between your Vatican prison, and these free mountains," cried Mrs. Cleveland, raising her eyes to Heaven in gratitude. "Yet I am more thankful for the emancipation of your spirit than the liberty of your body."

"Yes! Emily, eternity will not suffice to express our joy. Papal Infallibility was my snare, and my deliverance. Fortunately, I saw that it was the Alpha and the Omega of the Roman System, and when I found, after years of effort, that it grew into a palpable absurdity, I was virtually free. My Bible, my Prayer-Book, the Primitive Fathers, with your prayers, and old Jumbo's experience, confirmed me in my ancestral faith. I see you smile when I make an old negro a link in the chain of causes. But, remember, even that stone beneath your foot is a mountain-step towards Heaven."

"And do you not think that, both in England and America, many are similarly misled?" asked Mrs. Cleveland.

"The claim of Rome to authority, unity and perpetuity, has for some minds a resistless fascination," he replied.

"The phantom of union, before Reformation, with the Greek and Latin Churches, has misled multitudes, by weakening that Protest of our Catholicity against corruption, and idolatry and usurpation, which must be lasting as the errors it opposes. Still, standing on our Apostolic Order as an historic fact, my sympathies are intense with all Christians who agree with me in Faith. If Catholicity resembles the universal air which gives life to our world, Protestantism is as necessary for its defence as once were these mountains to that of martyrs."

While Cleveland uttered these words, he stood on a lofty crag. Above him was a towering pine, which had for ages defied the thunderbolt. Beneath him roared a torrent dashing over rocks. He seemed inspired by the scene. A glow was diffused over his countenance. Light beamed from his eye. A noble dignity appeared in his person. Mrs. Cleveland gazed on him as if he were a Prophet. Resuming their journey, he said, as they walked, "Before ten years the Jesuits will call a Vatican Council to declare Papal Infallibility. Everywhere through the Greek and Latin Churches I have found illuminated men anxious for Reform. I shall seek to combine these heroic spirits with noble representative Protestants, and accomplish the union of Christendom. **We will return to America,** and, in our own home, **pass our** declining years."

They had now attained the altitude of **the mountain,** and about them was a sublimity, we will not attempt to describe. As they stood together, arm-in-arm, enraptured by the scene, Mrs. Cleveland turned towards her husband eyes tender and beautiful with love. "May Heaven prosper your **plans,** Arthur!" she exclaimed. "How pleasing such a consummation, after so many wanderings and sufferings!"

Here Cleveland caught a new inspiration. Before him was passing the future of the nations, and his soul kindled with the grandeur piled everywhere around.

"Further, Emily, further," he broke forth, "I am no longer an aristocrat. Emancipated from class I sympathize with humanity. These restless European nationalities are struggling towards those rights embodied in our own matchless Declaration and Constitution. Whatever its form, government should be *from* the people, and *by* the people, and *for* the people. If Primogenitures or Establishments, or Aristocracies, or Thrones, stand in the way, let them be scattered like the clouds from yon cliff, that Humanity may brighten with eternal liberty!" Mrs. Cleveland followed the direction of her husband's finger. The dark mists were rolling from the summit of the mountain, now dazzling in the sun. "See that rock," continued Cleveland, pointing aloft. "Every crag is stained with sacred blood. Rome has made these hills the monuments of martyrs. What a sublime Protestant is yon Balsille! From its cliffs, Henry Arnaud hurled death on his foes. What a victory he achieved in a solitary fortress of nature! Balanced on dizzy precipices, he

26*

conquered that Glorious Return which shall live in all future history." As Cleveland spoke, an eagle soared through a cloud into the lofty light. Gazing on the silent bird, he cried: "Behold a type of our humanity, emancipated from all social, and political, and religious slaveries!"

We may smile, when we read these speeches, delivered before a single woman. But Emily Cleveland, to a feminine softness, united a masculine strength of intellect. She comprehended the utterances of her husband, and regarded them with sensitive sympathy, and passionate admiration. Moreover, after a painful imprisonment, he was inspired by the breath of liberty, and the sublimity of mountains. Possibly his glow was kindled by a beam from heaven, and prophetic of his future.

After the excitements of such scenes, Mr. and Mrs. Cleveland climbed in silence down the cliffs. Even the rainbows dancing in the mists of a tumbling waterfall, excited no remark. When the beauties of a lower region were softening in the evening, they still walked absorbed in reflection. Before they reached the piazza, night had drawn around her curtains, and hung out her stars. After a refreshing supper they assembled the family for the usual devotions, when they were startled by the clatter of hoofs and the sound of wheels. Speedily a large vehicle dashed before the piazza, and six masked men, armed with swords and pistols, burst into the room. Mrs. Cleveland screamed, and fell fainting into the arms of her husband. Regardless of her situation, and his entreaties, both, with Jumbo, were hurriedly blind-folded, and thrust into the carriage. The air and the motion restored Mrs. Cleveland, and she sat speechless with her hand in that of her husband, who, bending down in the darkness, silently kissed his wife, with an infinite melancholy only equaled by her own. For hours they were whirled down hills, and along valleys, and over bridges, pausing only for relays of horses. At last, they felt themselves flying across the smooth Campagna, and heard the rattle of their wheels on the pavements of Rome. Mrs. Cleveland was driven to the palace of Judge Ellingwood, and there deposited. The carriage then rushed furiously to the Vatican. In a few minutes Mr. Cleveland and Jumbo, having been freed from their bandages, stood together in their former apartment, and heard behind them the clank of an added bolt. Bars of iron also had been placed in their windows.

CHAPTER XXXIX.

THE contrast between Arthur Cleveland in Piedmont and Arthur Cleveland in the Vatican can be easily conceived. Amid sublime mountains, and beneath the grand heavens, with his wife at his side, he had reached the perfection and dignity of his manhood. His cup overflowed with sparkling joys. But he was now no longer on the Alps. The Alps were rather on him. His chamber seemed continually contracting, and he would thrust about his hands as if to push up the ceiling, and to push out its walls. The atmosphere, dead and heavy, stifled his lungs. Yet, Cleveland, to his surprise, experienced neither anguish nor despair. Nature had exhausted her possibilities of spiritual suffering. His soul, having attained its ideal, contemplated trials from an altitude, as we regard storms below us on mountains. He saw that confinement was his doom, and he accepted as a child, not as a slave, the mysterious will of Heaven. The purpose of his destiny was accomplished. He had no thought of escape. Yet the very vigor of his spirit had consumed the strength of his body, and he rapidly sank away. His meekness and his feebleness touched every heart. The Pope treated him with the most tender consideration. Bishop Frances was melted into sympathy. The Chief of the Jesuits showed every possible attention to the dying man. His American friends were forbidden to visit him, but Jumbo was kindly allowed to nurse his master. The faithful fellow was indefatigable.

"Massa,"—as he now delicately styled the Cardinal,—
he one day began, "De Laud hab quar ways. Fust he'se
make you happy on de big mountins, free like de soarin'
eagul—den he'se shut you in dis Pope-prisin."

"Since he has confined me here," mildly replied Cleveland, "I must now imitate the nightingale, which often
pours from its cage its sweetest notes."

"And didn't you say, Massa, dat de song in de prare-
book cum from de chilren in de flames, wha dey call on
de clouds, and de hills, and de staums, and de dews, and
de wells, and de whales, and de fire, and de snow, and de
hail, and de saints and de angels, and eberyting in de uni-
vars, to prais de Laud?"

"Certainly, those strains of victory burst from the fire
into the sky."

"And in dis Pope-funas, Massa, we'se lib a singin', and
a shoutin', and a 'joicin', and show dese Rome-fellers dat
de Prot'stent sperit be strong as dem rocks wha dey burn
de martas, who had no long way from sich mountins
into hebben."

While the old negro was discoursing Cleveland smiled
amid his exhaustions, and the hectic of his cheek was suf-
fused with the light of the inner glory.

"Did you know, Massa," resumed Jumbo, "Missus
pray for you? She'se look like de angul ob peace smilin'
ober de chile and de mudder in de stable. Once I'se
chance into her room. I tot her dat woman in de picter
lyin' on de groun', and claspin' de feet ob de Laud, and
'seechin' for her dautta. De Pres'terian Missus ask dis
Mef'dist nigga pray, and de blessin' cum down like de
light streamin' from de big white cloud ober de oshun at
Sea-Side."

"Thank you, Jumbo! Thanks to my Emily! Thanks

to Heaven for such assistances!" exclaimed Cleveland, in a faint, tremulous whisper.

"And Massa," he resumed, "may dis ole, bald, stammerin' nigga tell what he'se dream ebery night for tree nights."

Cleveland by a nod of his head signified his desire to hear.

"Well! allers jist as de big clock was a strikin twelf, and a soundin' like de trump ob de Judg ober dis city, Is'e fall into doze, twixt a wakin' and a sleepin'. Den Is'e see ober Rome a cloud glitterin' like de snow on de Alps. In de middle was a hole a lookin' 'trough into de blue sky. From dat cum an angul big as de dome on St. Peta's. His wings white as de swan on de lake. His face bright as de sun. He cum a floatin' down like wun in de winda ob de Sistin' chapl. Den he'se sail a smilin to de Vat'can, and he tuk Massa in his aums, and fly wid him 'trough de air, and de cloud scatta way, and he'se pass de moon, and he'se pass de sun, and he'se pass de staus, and de gates ob pearl opun, and he'se carry Massa to de foot ob de Trone, and de Laud smile like de maunin' light a breakin' on de tops ob doze Alps, when de fogs roll 'way, and de un'vars git bright. Den he'se cum and tuk Missus. Den he'se cum and tuk Jumbo. We'se all tree be gwine' to Hebben soon. We'se be gwine, Massa; we'se be gwine! Glory to de Laud."

The Vatican never heard a nobler strain of triumph than burst from those African lips, and the very room seemed filled with light and peace.

Cleveland continued to fail gradually. The physician of his Holiness advised the open air; and a chair, and a carriage were always at the disposal of the patient. Once he stopped before the colonnade of St. Peter's and gazed long at the sublime dome. In the Sistine Chapel he lay for hours absorbed in contemplating the grand figures of the Last Judgment. He loved in the Vatican Gallery to linger around the Laocoon, and the Apollo, and even ventured a more distant visit to the Dying Gladiator. But the Transfiguration of Raphael was most in harmony with his soul, next to the simple inscriptions, and emblems of the Lapidarian Collections. It seemed as if he wished to take with him from earth to heaven every image of beauty, and of glory.

When he could no longer leave his apartment Jumbo carried his attenuated form from his bed to his window tenderly as a nurse bears a dying infant. The end was approaching. Angels doubtless were hovering over the palace to convey Cleveland home. That day arrived recorded for his death in the Book of Eternity. A subduing influence pervaded every room, and heart in the Vatican. Partly from policy, partly from sympathy, and partly from curiosity, the Pope, with several Bishops and Cardinals visited the chamber of the expiring man. While the imposing group, brilliant in their gold, and scarlet, stand around his bed we will return to Mrs. Cleveland.

When that lady came back to the palace of Judge Ellingwood she received in silence his surprised welcome, and with an agony of tears flung herself into the arms of Mary. The transition from so much joy to so much misery made her inconsolable. Soon, however, her passionate grief was succeeded by a deep tranquility. Suffering had evidently exhausted her vital energies. Pale, sad, speechless she moved about the house like a Bride of Heaven.

As the sun was pouring his last glory over the cross on

St. Peter's, she was observed to go forth alone in the calm evening. Every beholder was impressed with her countenance and mien. She united the meekness of the Roman martyr, and the dignity of the Roman matron. By some strange instinct, she proceeded to the door of the Vatican, and passed unchallenged. She ascended to the apartment of Cleveland, and entered with a preternatural majesty. A phantom could not have been more unwelcome or alarming than a WOMAN in that chamber. There was an instant impulse to arrest her progress. She paused with the look of an angel. Bishop, and Cardinal, and Pope, shrank from her gaze. Darting towards her dying husband, she flung herself on his body. He reached forth his arms, and embraced his wife. Long she lay on his bosom. The sanctity of love in the presence of death could not be violated. There was a long waiting for the woman to arise. Jumbo wept, kneeling at her side. The hush of the chamber became intense. Moments passed like hours. Dignitaries, before such a spectacle, were awed into impotence.

Finally, the embarrassment was no more endurable. Bishop Frances approached the bed. He lifted the woman's arm. It fell back cold on the bosom which had long been its pillow. He placed his hand on the forehead of her husband. It was ice. Arthur and Emily Cleveland had expired together in the embrace of connubial love. Heaven laughed at the earthly Pontiff who dared dissolve a marriage ordained by the Eternal God.

CHAPTER XL.

Judge Ellingwood and Mary waited hour after hour
for the return of Mrs. Cleveland. Their alarm and suspense became painful. Messengers had been dispatched
in all directions. No intelligence was obtained, and the
search was abandoned for the night. While the father
and the daughter sat watching in the study, Jumbo was
announced, and bidden to enter. He staggered into the
apartment. His black cheeks were sunken. His bald,
shining head was bowed between his shoulders. Yet he
brought with his presence a species of sanctity. Judge
Ellingwood perceiving his exhaustion seated him in a
chair.

"Oh," he exclaimed, clasping his great hands and rolling up his old eyes, "Massa Judge, Missus Mary, me hab
cum from Hebben, from Hebben, jist right from Hebben."

"Explain yourself, Jumbo," said Judge Ellingwood,
"that is a long way with a narrow road."

He replied, "De angel, dis evenin' wid de set ob de sun,
cum for Massa Cleveland. De Bishop, and de Ca'dnals,
and de Pope stan' roun' in dere red and dere yaller, and
den Missus wauk into de room like de queen ob dis wuld.
Dey dar not stop her. She had a look dat make de Pope
nobuddy. Dey all stan' 'side, and shes'e trow herself on
Massa, and he'se put his arms 'bout her, and dey stay dat
way long, long, long time 'till wes'e hear de Pope's heart
a thumpin', and den a Bishop raise her arm. It fall back

312

cold. He touch Massa's for'ed. Bofe dead, dead, dead, and dey all star and look quar, and go out wid dere heads down, and I'se war lef' 'lone wid Massa and Missus, and Hebben cum down to dat room, Hebben, Hebben!" and the poor fellow wept, and shook the very floor with his agitation.

Before the Judge could reply, there was a startling ring, and as the hour was late, he answered the bell. He found before his door an immense carriage. Soon six sturdy men brought within the body of Mrs. Cleveland, which was gently laid on the sofa. Mary Ellingwood kissed, with tears, the cold brow, and the Judge wept in silence, while Jumbo renewed his grief. Perhaps no circumstance could have been more embarrassing to the Pope and his College than the corpse of a Cardinal's wife in the Vatican. There, however, was the humiliating fact. Nothing remained but to send the body to the house of Judge Ellingwood, now occupied by the American Minister. He was immediately called for consultation, and the funeral was arranged for the next evening.

During the excitement of the last hour, Jumbo had been overlooked. The Judge now happened to turn towards the chair where he had himself seated the venerable negro. His head hung drooping on his bosom. His limbs were relaxed. His body had fallen to one side, and was supported by an arm of the chair. The Judge lifting up his face saw there the peace of death. His strength had been expended in nursing his master. His work was over. The angel had come through the cloud to bear him up into the "hebbenly" light.

On the next day a quiet funeral procession wound through the Protestant Cemetery just without Rome. The Cestian pyramid lifted itself in silent grandeur. The

27

daily circle of the cypress-shadows had been traced over those graves of strangers. Slanting sun-beams gilded the tombs and lay upon the grass. Birds warbled on the branches. Between the tree-tops was seen the blue sky, with its Italian glory. Soft breezes swayed the limbs. Violets and daisies mingled their hues, and the stately rose lifted its blushing beauty.

The stillness is now broken by the tread of horses, and the noise of wheels. A procession stops before a fresh grave on a secluded slope. A coffin is lifted from the hearse. Judge Ellingwood, with Mary on his arm, followed by Mr. Fortescue, Mr. Percivale, and a few friends, now gathered round. The service was said by the American Chaplain. While the benediction was pronouncing over the grave of Mrs. Cleveland, another hearse halted at the gate of the Cemetery, whither the company proceeded on foot, and then reverently followed the body of Jumbo, and with the same ceremony, gave it to the earth.

Arthur Cleveland was laid in state in a magnificent apartment of the Vatican. Perhaps to counteract the report of his apostacy his funeral was celebrated with unusual pomp. A massive coffin, richly ornamented, contained the body, attired in the scarlet of a Cardinal. On the breast flashed a diamond crucifix. Over all was a red coverlet brocaded with gold. When the night of interment arrived the corpse was transferred to a gorgeous catafalque, and conveyed in a hearse plumed and draped with black. The liveries were dazzling. Grenadiers preceded with arms glittering in the bright torches. Nobles, Princes, Bishops, Cardinals, in splendid carriages, followed amid the dismal chants of the Frati. Before a venerable Church the procession stopped. The catafalque was placed beneath a blazing altar. Mass was said after a magnificent ceremonial. The body was solemnly deposited under the aisle, and on the Roman stone was traced the name of a Protestant Cardinal.

Above the spot some years after stood a group of strangers. Edward and Anna Ellingwood in mourning for their father and uncle, are accompanied by Mary, also in black, who is leading her beautiful little nephew and niece. They were soon joined by Albert and Ada Elton. Jim may be discerned at the door of the Church. As the party gaze on the tablet, the colored light streaming through a painted window illuminates the inscription. Leaving the place they proceed to the Protestant Cemetery. Now we see them gathering around a graceful shaft of white marble, on which they read

TO EMILY CLEVELAND AND ANOTHER.

IN LIFE, DIVIDED: IN DEATH, UNITED:

IN HEAVEN, ONE.

Flowers were scattered over the grave, and on it was planted a rose. The company then wound their way to a modest monument of Sienna marble bearing the inscription:

TO JUMBO,

THE FAITHFUL.

www.ingramcontent.com/pod-product-compliance
Lightning Source LLC
Chambersburg PA
CBHW031043120726
47905CB00007B/2293